KISSING GAMES

EVIE ALEXANDER

ISBN (eBook) 978-1-914473-04-3

ISBN (Print) 978-1-914473-05-0

ISBN (Audiobook) 978-1-914473-53-1

A CIP catalogue record for this book is available from the British Library.

www.emlinpress.com

By Evie Alexander and Kelly Kay

EVIE & KELLY'S HOLIDAY DISASTERS SERIES

Cupid Calamity

Cookout Carnage

Christmas Chaos

Get Evie's books in all formats as well as special offers, early releases, and exclusive deals direct from her website:

www.eviealexanderbooks.com

EMLIN
PRESS

Charlie scanned the area. They were almost home free. This was what he'd trained for: protect lives, save lives, take lives. He was on high alert, muscles primed.

He pushed through the crowds, his body shielding hers. Through the glass front doors, the car waited, engine running.

Nearly there.

He shouldered the door open and hurried her outside.

She stopped, holding the package out for him. He ignored her, pulling the back door of the car wide. 'Get in, ma'am.'

'Take it.'

'No, ma'am,' he said, eyes fixed on the street, the people, the danger. His asset was another's target. 'Get in the car, ma'am.'

The woman pursed her lips. 'Do your job,' she hissed.

The pressure was rising. The longer they were out here, the greater the risk. 'I *am* doing my job. Now get in the fucking car. *Ma'am.'*

She dropped the package at his feet, got in and slammed

the door. He heard her shouting at the driver, then the car screeched away. He was stranded.

He bent and picked up what she'd dropped.

'Hey, sexy!' A group of teenage girls giggled at him. One took out her phone. He moved and they ran off through the crowds. A passing van driver wolf-whistled. He looked at what he was holding: an oversized, pink, fluffy, heart-shaped pillow, the words *'Hey, Sexy'* emblazoned on it—a present from Olga Petrova for her oligarch husband, Igor.

Charlie sighed and strode away from the front door of Harrods. It was a fifteen-minute walk to their Belgravia mansion. Fifteen minutes to prepare himself.

Once again, he was in the shit.

Igor Petrov sat behind his desk, elbows resting on the expanse of white Carrara marble, pudgy fingers playing idly with a razor-sharp letter opener.

He stared Charlie down.

Charlie stared back.

Igor looked like a secret military experiment: part bull, part bear, and all berserker. The sleeves of his tailor-made silk shirt were rolled up, revealing thick forearms covered with coarse black hair. A Rolex glinted on his wrist. The folds of his giant neck mirrored the grooves in his forehead. His eyes were cold points of darkness.

'Mr Hamilton,' he began, his voice low and guttural. 'What am I to do with you? When you disrespect my wife, you disrespect me.'

Charlie bristled. He wasn't the fucking problem here. He remained silent. Whatever he said would be wrong.

'I am a businessman,' Igor continued, opening his hands wide, the letter opener gleaming with intent. 'I choose the best and expect them to perform. You,' he gestured to Charlie, 'are one of the best. But...' He sighed theatrically. 'You came with a certain...'

Here we go.

'... reputation. Very popular with the ladies.'

A muscle twitched in Charlie's jaw and the side of Igor's mouth turned up. *Fuck.* Charlie relaxed his stance. He'd been up against bigger bastards than this. He wouldn't rise to the bait.

Igor leaned forward, the letter opener now tight in his fist. 'I see the way you look at Tatiana. She is my pearl. If—'

'I have a girlfriend,' Charlie spat, clamping his mouth shut before putting Igor straight about the coke-snorting, vapid little pearl of a daughter who kept trying to get into his bedroom at night.

Igor turned his attention to the tip of the letter opener, using the point to clean his fingernails. 'Ah yes, Caroline...'

What the fuck?

Igor's dark eyes flicked up to meet his. 'Caroline Eleanor Baskerville. A *married* woman.'

Charlie clenched his fists.

'Enough!' barked Igor, slapping the letter opener on the desk. He sighed again and sat back in the leather chair, hands behind his head. 'Charlie, synochik. You can't be a playboy all your life. When are you going to settle down?' He reached a fat digit towards the intercom on the desk. 'Because if you can't'— he shrugged—'the only job left for you will be policing copper mines in the Congo.'

He pressed a button. 'Bring the car.'

Igor lifted his hips to free a phone from his trouser pocket and opened it up. He flicked his fingers in a dismissive motion at Charlie as he put the phone to his hairy ear. 'Mischka! Kak dela?'

. . .

BY THE TIME CHARLIE REACHED HIS ROOM IN THEIR mansion, his rage was volcanic. He slammed the door and kicked off his shoes. He needed a shower to wash off the filth of the Petrov family.

He knows about Caroline... Charlie shook his head at his own naivety. *Of course he does.*

Petrov would know everything about him. *And* her. He tugged off his clothes, throwing them to the floor. He wanted to burn them—scour everything in his life touched by the Petrovs.

He stalked into the shower and turned it on, letting the full force of the cold water batter his face. Icy needles pointing out his stupidity, over and over. Resting his forehead on the wall tiles, he let the water flow down his back.

Is this my life? Always judged by my looks and what happened with Caroline? By what happened before that?

He turned off the shower and got out, staring at his reflection dispassionately. He filled the mirror. Six foot four inches of battle-hardened, gym-sculpted muscle, decorated with tattoos. His thick chestnut hair was cropped short, his green eyes hard, his jaw set tight with frustration.

Water dripped down the inked planes of his body, following the contours of his chest. Pulling a folded towel from the rail, he rubbed himself dry, watching the movement of the muscles under his skin.

In the army, he'd always wanted to be the best—the fittest, the fastest, the strongest. But his killer body also came with killer looks. 'Pretty boy', 'player'. People decided who they thought he was before he'd even opened his mouth.

Then he'd met Caroline, his commanding officer's daughter...

His bedroom door opened and closed with a click.

Tatiana. *Again.*

Fuck's sake! Would she ever leave him alone? *That's what happens when you don't lock your door, dickhead.* He wrapped the towel tightly around his hips and sighed. He'd made the same mistake twice before and wasn't doing it again. Even if he could see past Tatiana's façade, any physical attraction he might have felt was rendered void by her personality: entitled, arrogant, stupid. Her mother's beauty lay under the contoured layers of make-up, but she had all the charm of her father.

'Char-lie?' A soft, sing-song voice drifted in from his bedroom. 'Are you in there?'

He tensed, icy fingers of fear scraping up the back of his neck. *No fucking way. It couldn't be.* He glanced around the sparse bathroom. No robe. *Fuck!*

'Charlie, darling.' The voice was coming closer. 'I wanted to say sorry...'

He wrenched open the door.

There, standing in a thin silk robe, her nipples pointing straight through at him, and holding an oversized, pink, fluffy, heart-shaped pillow, stood Olga Petrova, his boss's wife.

'Hey, sexy,' she purred.

FIVE MINUTES LATER, CHARLIE WAS STRIDING UP SLOANE Street, phone clamped to his ear.

'Mack, I need a new gig. I can't do this anymore.'

'What's happened now?' Mack replied. 'Tatiana jump you again?'

'Mrs P just tried it on as I was getting out of the shower,' he replied tersely, rubbing at his forehead with his free hand as if to erase the memory.

There was a pause, then Mack started laughing.

'It's not fucking funny,' Charlie huffed as his friend made wheezy whooping sounds like an owl having an asthma attack. 'This is my life. You've got to reassign me.'

He could hear Mack trying to control himself, and imagined him passing a hand over his face, like a mime artist rearranging his features.

They'd known each other for years. As Charlie was entering the SAS, Mack was leaving to set up a private security business. He'd done well for himself and always tried to find jobs for people like Charlie—those who found the adjustment to life on Civvy Street hard.

'Okay, mate, here's the situation,' Mack began. 'The Arabs won't touch you after that sheikha and her sister took a shine. Male celebs think you cockblock them, and you won't handle females after that incident with the girl band. There's a limit to how many Russkies need new security and the Chinese use their own. You're burning bridges with every job—'

'What about diplomats? CEOs?'

Mack sighed. 'We've been through this. You're too tall. Too good-looking. They don't want someone drawing attention. They want someone unobtrusive, not a fucking supermodel.'

'I'm just an ordinary bloke!'

'Mate, I'm as straight as they come and even *I* know you're hot. Fuck, we all thought you'd turned Rory after he grew his hair long in Afghan.'

'I'm not a player, Mack. Come on, you know me. I've been with the same woman for ten years.' He rubbed his forehead again. A headache was coming on.

His friend was silent. He'd never approved of Caroline. No one in Charlie's life did—but he didn't care.

Eventually Mack sighed again. 'I know you're not a player, Charlie. But you've got that rep and it's hard to shake. There are already rumours in the media about some hot bodyguard who likes getting in trouble. You can't have that shit made public.'

Charlie's stomach rolled and his step faltered. If that happened, he'd lose Caroline forever.

'Look, mate, there's always new opportunities coming up. I'll keep my ear to the ground. In the meantime, try and be cool with the Petrovs.'

He gave a non-committal '*hmm*' in response, a ball of lead sitting in his belly.

'Oh, and one more thing,' added Mack. 'Do us all a favour and use the fucking deadbolt on your door. Okay?'

Half an hour later, Charlie sat in a chic coffee house on Kensington High Street, waiting for the love of his life to arrive. He took a corner seat, back to the wall, and surveyed the scene.

Well-dressed upper-class women with sleek brown locks brayed at each other and cooed over poodle crossbreeds. Men with floppy hair, Gucci leather bracelets, and skinny red chinos fist-bumped and called each other 'homie'. This was the world he was born into but never felt a part of.

Charlie's happy place was in the field: camo paint on, weapon to hand, surrounded by men you could trust with your life. Men who would die for you.

He reflexively touched his shoulder, feeling a thin ridge of scar tissue under the shirt, then dropped it back to cradle Caroline's latte, keeping it warm.

Where is she?

His leg bounced impatiently. She was always late, but any later and her drink would be cold.

His phone lit up and he grabbed it. *Tabbie.* His older sister.

She only ever rang to give him a bollocking. He rejected the call.

In his peripheral vision he saw a flash of gold. He stood, heart thumping. *Caro.* She was finally here.

Caroline Baskerville, née Fitzroy, was tall, slim, and stunningly beautiful, with straight blonde hair, pale-blue eyes, and high cheekbones. She was dressed in a long fawn cashmere coat, a matching scarf hanging down her front.

Charlie's chest expanded. He'd fallen for her the first time they'd met, at a formal dinner. He had the honour of sitting at his commanding officer's table thanks to a favour his father, another officer, had called in. Charlie rewarded both men by sweeping his CO's daughter off her feet and straight into bed. It could have been perfect: the joining of two upper-class military families. But it had gone tits-up from day one.

'Caro.' He reached for her, but she turned her head to the side and his kiss grazed her cheek.

She pulled back and sat, putting her phone on the table. Charlie looked instinctively at her left hand, but she was wearing gloves. She made no movement to take off her coat. Not a good sign.

He pushed the latte towards her. 'I've got your favourite.' Liquid sloshed over the sides. 'Fuck, hang on, let me get a napkin.'

He stood, banging into the table, sending more coffee spilling out. He grabbed the mug before it tipped over completely.

Fuck's sake! Hold it together, dickhead.

He forced a smile. 'Let me get you a fresh one.'

'No, it's fine. This is fine.' Caroline took the mug, sipped, then frowned. 'Has this got milk in it?'

'Tall, skinny chai latte. Right?' Unease uncoiled like a snake in his stomach.

She put the mug down. 'No, I'm lactose intolerant.'

'Since when?'

'Over a year. Remember when my tummy was bad on that weekend in the Lake District?'

The snake inside started to bite. 'We've never been to the Lake District.'

Caroline's cheeks reddened and she dropped her head.

He held his breath, willing his emotions to crawl back under their rock.

'Caro,' he began quietly. 'You said if I left the army you'd leave him. I've been out for over a year now.'

'I...' she began. 'It's complicated.' She looked wretched, the fingers of her right hand twisting what he guessed were the rings under the glove of her left.

'Is it? We love each other. You only married him because I wouldn't leave the army. You don't love him. You've *never* loved him.' He rubbed his forehead in frustration. 'Fuck's sake, we were in bed again two weeks after you got back off honeymoon.'

Her head darted around. 'Charlie!' she hissed. 'Shh!'

He lifted his hands. 'Why? I'm not ashamed.'

'You know I never wanted to be an army wife.'

'And I left.'

'It's just more of the same, Charlie.'

'No, Caro. It's not. I'm babysitting rich people. I choose my hours and where I work. I'm in London for you. I've done everything you asked me to do. What have I missed?'

The background hum of chatter and laughter filled the silence between them. Caroline's phone lit up. Charlie read "ICE Gareth Baskerville" before she rejected the call. *In Case of Emergency. That prick was her emergency contact?*

'Caro, I left my career for you, I—'

'I'm pregnant.'

Yes, yes, yes. Oh god, yes. He didn't question how it could have happened. *Finally.* Light filled his chest and tears pricked his eyes. He blinked the blurriness away.

Caroline crossed her arms over her stomach protectively. 'She's not yours.'

She? 'What?'

'She's not yours,' Caroline repeated.

'But, but...' Charlie stammered. 'You weren't sleeping with him.'

She stared at her hands, then tugged off her gloves impatiently and touched her wedding and engagement rings as if for reassurance.

'*It has to be mine, Caro,*' he whispered.

She shook her head. 'I conceived in the Maldives. We had the twenty-week scan yesterday. She's Gareth's.'

Invisible hands closed around his neck, choking him.

She pocketed her phone and sighed. 'I didn't know how to tell you, but I think it's for the best. This ...' She gestured between them. 'Was never going to work.'

He was being squeezed into nothingness.

'Caro—'

'I'm sorry, Charlie. I am,' she replied, her voice wobbling. 'I know we've had our ups and downs, but we don't really know each other. We've always wanted different things.'

'I wanted a baby,' he managed, his voice hoarse. 'I wanted this with you.'

She didn't reply, but her eyes filled with tears.

How could he fix this? His heart was breaking into a million pieces, but he still believed their love could glue them back together.

Caroline dabbed carefully at the corners of her eyes with a napkin, then stood. 'I've got to go.'

He got to his feet, reaching for her again. She shook her head and stepped back, her gaze everywhere but on him.

'I'm sorry,' she repeated before walking away.

CHARLIE COULDN'T REMEMBER LEAVING THE CAFÉ. HE walked on autopilot whilst his mind shut down. Even when Caroline dumped him and got married it hadn't hurt in the same way. He knew the marriage was meaningless. This was so different he didn't know how to process it.

The sound of his phone cut into the emptiness and he pulled it out.

Rory. The Earl of Kinloch and his best mate.

They'd met in the army and joined the SAS at the same time. Rory had left the forces a year before Charlie, to take on a dilapidated castle in Scotland and an estate on a financial precipice.

Since then, his new girlfriend, Zoe, was helping him turn it around. As Charlie hadn't spoken to Rory in a couple of months, he had no idea what was going on.

'Mate, you there?' Rory rumbled down the line.

He grunted in response. The fact that neither of them was a great conversationalist was perfect for a time like this. Charlie didn't want to talk to anyone right now.

'I need your help,' Rory continued. 'Brad fucking Bauer is shooting a film at the castle, and I need you to keep an eye on him.'

At the words 'Brad Bauer', Charlie was jolted enough out of his fug to respond. 'What?'

Brad was the Hollywood superstar who'd made *Death Party,* a film about the Afghan conflict. Charlie and Rory's unit found it so offensive they'd put Brad's picture in the centre of their regiment dartboard.

'Yeah, he's making *Braveheart 2*. It's a load of bollocks, but we need the money. The problem is, I'm out of my depth and don't trust him farther than I could kick him. He's got this weird thing for Zoe, and I can't be everywhere at once. I need a second pair of eyes. Someone I can trust. Can you come up?'

Charlie sighed. 'I don't know, man, I'm really stacked right now.'

'If it's about the money, don't worry—I've got it covered. You'll get paid.'

'I'll think about it. When do you need me?'

'Soon as poss, mate. He's already here, swanning about like he owns the fucking place.'

Charlie let out a short, hollow laugh. 'Have you punched him yet?'

'Not yet, but my fist is itching all the time. Will you think about it? It'll only be for a few weeks.'

'Will do. I'll let you know.'

Charlie ended the call and looked where his feet had brought him.

Dave.

It had been nearly two weeks since his last visit. He stared at the austere Victorian building: the bars on the lower windows, the layers of peeling paint. He rang the buzzer to gain entry.

Inside was warmer, but still bleak. Judy met him at reception, her polyester uniform stretched over her large frame, a ring with hundreds of keys clanking at her hip.

'Charlie! Long time no see.' She smiled, taking his hand. Static shot up his arm as they touched. 'Bloody bastard uniform. Sorry, love. I'd like to think it's the animal attraction between us, but unfortunately, it's man-made fibres and safety shoes.'

He smiled, concentrating on the moment so nothing from

Caroline could spill in. 'There's always an animal attraction,' he replied, wiggling his eyebrows.

Judy shrieked with laughter and slapped his arm. 'Stop it! I know who you're here for, and it ain't me. Let's get you signed in and I'll take you to him.'

THEY WALKED TOGETHER DOWN THE WIDE CORRIDOR, THEIR voices bouncing off the metal and concrete. Charlie had started visiting as soon as he got to London. Being a volunteer gave him a sense of purpose. He was always drawn to the underdogs, the ones who would never fit into society.

'How's he been?' he asked.

'Same old, same old. Mad as a box of frogs and a bit smelly. Misses you, of course.'

'Do you think he'll ever...?' Charlie let the question hang in the air.

Judy shook her head. 'He'll die in here. No chance of parole or escape when you're Dave. You're the only one who's ever given him the time of day.'

'You know if I could, I—'

'I know, love.' Judy squeezed his arm and stopped in front of a metal door, sorting through her keys. 'Here we are. Dave! Look who's come to see you!'

Dave had been in more fights than Charlie had. He was missing an eye and ear on one side and walked with a perpetual limp. Created from the sludge at the bottom of the gene pool, there was ugly, then there was Dave. He had looks even a mother would struggle to love.

But Charlie didn't see any of that. People never saw past his exterior, so he'd be buggered if he treated Dave the same way.

'Alright, Dave?' he asked, smiling broadly.

Judy unlocked the door and Dave lunged at him—drooling,

barking, his stumpy tail a blur of excitement. Charlie sank to his knees as Dave launched himself into his arms, licking all over his face. Finally, someone was pleased to see him.

Judy laughed. 'I'll leave you with him. Come and get me when you're ready to take him for a *you know what*.'

Charlie pulled his head out of tongue range. 'What was that, Dave? Do you think Judy means a *walk?*' At that word, Dave completely lost his shit, running in circles and bouncing off the walls, his bark getting more frenetic. The other dogs in the building joined in.

Judy threw back her head and gave her own howl of frustration. 'Now look what you've done!' She turned on her heel and strode off, shushing the other dogs.

Dave hurled himself back at Charlie, toppling him to the floor. He held Dave's head in his hands and looked into his working eye. 'Good to see you too, mate.'

CHARLIE STROLLED AROUND THE PARK AS DAVE investigated everything around him, returning to Charlie's side every couple of minutes to check he was still there.

Walking helped him think. In the army he'd marched for days. Yomping up and down mountains, a pack almost as heavy as a man on his shoulders. The constant, repetitive movement helped to focus and free his mind.

What now? Was it really over with Caro? Could he get her back? Or was it finally time to listen to what people had been telling him for years about their on-off relationship?

His phone rang. *Mack*. He picked it up. 'Any news?'

'Yep. I've got you a new job. But it's not in London.'

'How far away? Commutable?'

'Angola.'

'Fuck's sake! Okay, I'll stick it out at the Petrovs.'

'Sorry, mate, no can do. You're out. You pissed off Mrs P good and proper when you turned her down. I've just had the main man himself spitting blood down the phone. What a charmer.'

'Did you tell him his wife tried it on?'

'You soft in the head? I'm quite attached to my testicles, thank you very much.'

Charlie's phone beeped with another call coming through. *Tabbie.* 'Mate, can I call you back? I've got Tab on the other line.'

'Yeah, no worries. Say hi from me.'

He switched calls and took a big breath, trying to think what he'd fucked up this time. He was always on the naughty step when it came to his big sister.

'Hey, Tab, how's it going?' he asked, his voice artificially light.

'I'm not even going to go through the rigmarole of getting you to guess what you've forgotten, so here it is on a plate: Mum's birthday. It was yesterday. You forgot. Again.'

He bent over as if punched in the stomach.

'How difficult is it to put a reminder on your phone?' Tabbie continued. 'She's so upset.'

'Really?' Charlie retreated from his shame behind a wall of belligerence. His family weren't the most emotionally open. He was taught to have a stiff upper lip before he could walk.

'You're such an arsehole. Yes! Of course she's upset. I don't know why you keep trying to paint Mum as some kind of soulless ice queen.'

'I'll order her some flowers, get a card.'

'No, Charlie. Ring her. Go and visit. Be fucking present with them.'

He shook his head. He couldn't start to unpick the last

thirty-two years. Not now. Not after Caroline. 'I can't. I'm working.'

'Being a personal shopper to the stars? Come on, you can get time off.'

'I can't. I'm flying tomorrow.'

'Where?' His sister sounded suspicious.

'Angola,' he lied.

❧   3   ❧

eathrow airport was buzzing.

Charlie went through security and stood on the edge of the central atrium, watching the crowds. He was used to airports, but they always made him feel lonely. There were too many families and too many kids.

He ignored the odd flirtatious glance tossed his way. His exterior may have appeared strong and confident, but it was a cracked shell. Inside he was hollow.

He'd spent years believing his love for Caroline was enough to fill the aching hole in his chest. That her love for him could mask his deep self-loathing. But now she was gone for good and what was he left with? The gut-wrenching realisation that their part-time relationship had always been one-sided and built on constantly shifting sand.

A flash of white teeth and a throaty laugh caught his attention as a woman walked past on her phone. She stopped a couple of feet away, her entire focus on who she was talking to. Her smile and the personality behind it was a spark to his heart, reminding it to keep beating.

One day he wanted someone to be that pleased to speak to him.

The woman was small, maybe five foot four, and wearing well-worn black boots and a big dark-green parka over leggings. A plain baseball cap was pulled low on her head, and gloriously thick, glossy black hair spilled down her back. He couldn't see the top half of her face but her smile was dazzling.

He stood rooted to the spot, mesmerised by her lips as she chattered away. Over her shoulder was an old khaki canvas rucksack. A Colombian flag had been stitched on and was starting to come off. Was she a student?

He watched her stroll to a coffee concession in front of him and queue, her small frame hemmed in by people and their luggage, her free hand gesticulating as if the person on the other end of the phone could see her.

Despite how miserable he'd been, the corners of his mouth turned up. The woman had more life in her little finger than he had in his entire body. Everything about her made him want to be alive.

A little boy was standing with his father behind her, and reached for a side pocket on her rucksack.

What's he up to?

Charlie shifted position to get a better view. The boy was pulling at a loose thread at the bottom of the pocket. His father was on his phone, facing away, and hadn't noticed what his son was doing.

The woman dropped her purse in the pocket, still chatting animatedly. Half of it poked through the hole the boy was making.

Seeming captivated by the unravelling thread, the boy continued to pull.

The woman's order arrived. She finished her call, took her drink and weaved out of the concession. Striding towards the toilets and lounges, she didn't notice her purse dropping through the hole in the pocket to the ground.

Charlie dashed over, scooping it up and jogging after her. 'Excuse me?'

She didn't stop.

'Excuse me, Miss?'

No response.

He tapped her on the shoulder and she spun around.

'¿Cómo?'

She was beautiful. Deep dark eyes framed by long lashes. Soft brown skin and full, luscious lips.

He thrust the purse towards her. She looked between it and him, her eyes narrowing. She snatched it, shoved it back in the pocket, and pushed past him. It took six stompy steps for the purse to work its way back through the hole and out. Charlie caught it before it hit the floor, and tapped her again on the shoulder. She whirled around, and he held it out.

'How did you do that?' she asked, grabbing the purse.

Her voice, low and accented, sent a jolt of heat down to his dick. *Woah there, boy*.

'The side pocket on your bag has come apart.'

She took the rucksack from her shoulder and turned it around. 'No!' She pulled at the separated edges, her lower lip trembling.

'It's okay, we can fix it.'

She looked at him, her eyes liquid. 'How? How can I fix it?'

Don't cry. For fuck's sake, don't cry on me. His heart was cracked enough right now. He didn't need a pretty girl breaking it open any further.

'I'll sew it.'

'Sew it? *You?*'

Charlie clutched his chest in mock offence. 'I'll have you know I've got a black belt in embroidery.'

She laughed, and Charlie felt his cock swell. *Fuck's sake!* He needed to hurry up and get his kit out, then repeatedly stab himself in the groin with the needle. He opened his bag and pulled out a smaller one, lifting from it a tiny sewing kit.

'See? I told you *sew*.'

She rolled her eyes and giggled.

'It appears I already have you in *stitches*,' he continued, on a roll.

She shook her head at him, but her eyes were dancing. 'My patience is hanging by a *thread*, strange man.'

Charlie grinned and gestured towards a row of seats.

She sat and handed him her rucksack. 'Be careful now, Mr Sew-and-Sew... this is very precious to me.'

'I'll treat it as the holy relic it is,' he replied solemnly. 'Does it predate the Turin Shroud?'

The woman laughed again, showing off her perfect white teeth. His stomach flipped. Who knew he was such a comedy genius?

'I admit it is from the last century,' she said with a smile. 'Now fix it please—I have a plane to catch.'

He threaded the thickest needle in his kit, took the bag and carefully began stitching the bottom of the pocket back in place. She watched his hands, seemingly fascinated.

'You really *can* sew. If my abuela could see this, she would propose marriage.'

'Abuela?'

'My gran. I have a gran and a granny, Abuela and Abuelita.'

'Well, I'm open to offers,' he replied with a grin. 'You're from Colombia?'

'You don't get any points for knowing that.'

'Not everyone knows the Colombian flag.'

She frowned.

'The flag,' he continued. 'It's on the outside of your bag.'

She narrowed her eyes and nodded.

This was taking a weird turn. 'Colombia is a beautiful country.'

'Have you ever been?'

'A few times, yes.'

'Uh-huh, and what were you doing there?'

There was a nanosecond before he responded, 'Management consulting. In an office. With paper.' *Stop talking!*

'No, you weren't,' she said. 'You're lying.'

Charlie glanced up from the bag. Her eyes were huge and fathomless.

'I have very few skills in life, but one is to know if someone is telling the truth.'

He swallowed.

The corners of her mouth lifted. 'You're good, but you're not *that* good.'

'I have that skill, too,' he countered. If she could bluff, he could bluff right back. 'Cats or dogs?'

'What?'

'Which do you prefer, cats or dogs?'

'Cats.'

'No, you don't. Ice cream. Chocolate or vanilla?'

'Vanilla.'

Charlie shook his head. 'You're a chocolate fudge sundae girl all the way. With extra sprinkles.' He watched her with a smile. 'Your pupils just dilated. I know I'm right.'

He finished the final stitch and bit off the end of the thread.

'You had a fifty-fifty chance of being right,' she said.

'Do you want me to fix the flag?'

'What?'

'The stitching is coming loose. I might as well as fix it now.'

She looked at her watch. It was small and unremarkable. 'Yes, thank you. I still have time.'

He threaded a smaller needle and set to work. 'Where are you flying to?'

'Colombia.'

'No, you're not.'

She harrumphed in response and looked closer at his tiny stitches. 'Who taught you to sew?'

'A bloke called Shawn.'

'What was his job?'

Charlie cleared his throat. 'He was a doctor.' He dropped the needle, his hand moving to his shoulder without thinking.

'Did he stitch your shoulder after you hurt it?' she asked softly.

He stared at her. *How the fuck?*

She smiled, but with understanding, not victory. 'I told you I have a skill. But you're also quite easy to read.'

He raised an eyebrow. If she could only read his mind now.

She blushed and glanced down. 'You've finished.'

He nodded, finished the stitch and handed her bag back. He didn't want the conversation to end. He needed to see her again.

He put his sewing kit away. How could he ask for her number? *Fuck!* He was supposed to be a player, but it had been ten years since he'd been single. He didn't have a clue.

He swallowed. 'I wondered, could I please get your—'

Something changed in her expression. 'Yes, of course. Do you have a pen?'

Fuck me, that was easy!

'Er, yes, somewhere I think.' He thrust his hands into his bag, scrabbling around. *Where the fuck is it?* 'You could put it into my phone?' he suggested, giving up the search and taking his phone from his pocket.

'Your phone?' She was holding a black Sharpie and frowning.

'Yeah.' He unlocked it and handed it over. She shrugged, scrawled something on the back, then handed it to him and got up.

'Thank you for fixing my bag. I have to go now.'

Charlie stood, his bag sliding off his knees to the floor with a thump. He stared at the phone in confusion. 'What's this?'

'My autograph.'

'What? Why?'

'You wanted my autograph,' she replied, beginning to back away.

Huh? 'I wanted your number.'

Her eyes widened. 'Oh no. That's not going to happen.'

'Do you have a boyfriend?'

'I don't hand my number out to fans.'

'Fans?'

She lifted her chin. 'You're claiming you don't know who I am?'

He shook his head. 'I thought you were a student.'

'Student?' Her arms crossed.

'Yeah. Knackered rucksack, phone with a cracked screen, cheap watch...' he trailed off. *Oh fuck.*

'Have you been stalking me?' she squeaked. 'Did you rip my bag?'

'No, no, god no. I just notice things. I swear I don't know who you are,' he babbled. 'You say you know if someone's lying? Read me now.'

He saw confusion cloud her face. 'Do not follow me.' She strode into the first-class lounge, flashing her boarding pass, and was ushered out of sight.

Well, that went well.

Charlie turned his phone over and gazed at the scrawl.

Valentina.

She was too small to be a model. An actress maybe?

He opened his browser and searched *Valentina actress*. Less than a second later, he found her: Valentina Valverde, the most famous actress Colombia had ever produced.

Way to go, player...

At least he'd never see her again.

❄ 4 ❄

Charlie sat in the small seat, his long legs sticking out into the aisle, his heart racing.

Back in the terminal, he'd promised himself he would stop googling Valentina after five minutes. But time became elastic when he was looking at pictures of her. He'd been snapped back into reality with his name echoing through the Tannoy for his flight.

He'd then had to sprint to the gate for the walk of shame down the centre of the plane as passengers tutted and looked obviously at their watches.

Now his breath quietened and he closed his eyes, letting images of Valentina spin through his mind—her smile, her glossy hair, her luscious curves poured into designer dresses. Strutting her stuff on the red carpet, lounging in low-slung yoga pants at her beachfront Malibu mansion. She was luminous.

Charlie couldn't remember watching any of her films. He'd read online that she'd been working since she was a child, starting on a Colombian soap and graduating to films in her late teens. She'd had top billing in Spanish language films, but her Hollywood roles had been small.

He'd also googled 'Valentina Valverde boyfriend', but couldn't find anything that looked serious.

He shook his head. As if he would ever see her again, let alone have a chance to make amends...

A humming unease lurked at the outer edges of his consciousness, a warning of thoughts and feelings left unprocessed.

Now his relationship with Caroline was finally over, he'd taken his memories of her, boxed them up, and buried them behind a ten-foot wall topped with razor wire. But they and other darker memories were fighting to get out, sending tremors through his mind, pushing for his attention.

He couldn't go there. He just *couldn't*. So, he kept his thoughts on Rory, the job he was going to do, and his brief encounter with Valentina.

'Excuse me, sir?'

His eyes snapped open.

An air hostess smiled benignly at him and gestured to his outstretched legs. 'Could you move a little so we can get past?'

Charlie pulled them in, his knees now wedged into the back of the seat in front as the air hostess continued on, followed by someone carrying a rucksack.

A very familiar rucksack.

Glancing up, he caught Valentina's eye as she stopped and stared at him.

He opened his mouth to speak, but she flicked her hair and walked on. Going to follow, he forgot his seat belt was fastened, and was pulled back down. Flipping it open, he stood, bashing his head on the overhead lockers.

'Fuck!'

He strode down the aisle towards the small first-class

section at the front. He needed to see her, to apologise. The plane was now taxiing down the runway and the fasten seat belt signs were on. He ignored them.

Ahead, Valentina was stowing her rucksack. She gazed at him as the curtain separating first class was whisked across the aisle, blocking his view.

The air hostess faced him down. 'Please can you return to your seat and fasten your belt for take-off, Sir?'

Charlie mumbled an apology. Maybe he could catch her at the end of the flight. It was a short hop north to Scotland. It wouldn't be long to wait.

THE PLANE DISEMBARKED FROM THE FRONT, VALENTINA getting off first. Charlie was left at the back, waiting for everyone to sort their shit out.

He kept his hands by his sides, resisting the urge to pull down bags and bark orders at people who had no sense of fore-thought or urgency. He internally berated himself.

She was gone and that was that.

He had to put thoughts of Valentina into storage and focus on the job. Soon he'd be back with his best mate and reunited with Bandit, the unit dog who'd saved both their lives.

Reaching baggage reclaim, he glanced skyward to offer a prayer of thanks. Valentina was still there, on her phone, tapping her foot impatiently.

His bag appeared next to a large, battered suitcase with a scratched sticker of the Colombian flag. He strode towards the carousel next to Valentina, her voluble Spanish rattling out.

'Mi maleta está aquí. Te llamaré en un momento. Te amo.'

She finished the call and reached for her suitcase as Charlie lifted off his bag.

'¡Mierda!' she yelled.

The wheels of her suitcase had been ripped off. She looked up at him as if it were his fault.

He dropped his bag and held up his hands. 'Nothing to do with me. I swear!'

She turned her head away, but he could see her jaw trembling.

It's only a suitcase! He bit his lip to stop the words tumbling out and knelt to look at the damage. He'd been to some poor places in the world, but had never seen such a sad-looking piece of luggage.

The side handle was missing, the zip held together in one place with a cable tie. The fabric was stained and scuffed and now the wheels were gone. This was not the suitcase of a movie star.

When he glanced up, her face was still turned away. He cleared his throat and she gazed at him, her smoky eyes liquid, her lips pressed tightly shut.

'I can't fix this here, but I do have a solution,' he said.

She blinked, and a small tear ran down her cheek. She swiped it away as if angry with herself.

'Option one,' he continued. 'We swap the contents of our bags. You take my bag, I take yours, and we walk away and never see each other again.'

Her eyes widened.

'Option two: we swap contents, you take my bag and I try to fix yours over the next few days, then drop it back to wherever you're staying.'

'Unpack my bag here? In front of you?' Her voice was soft and husky. 'Is there an option three?'

'I won't look, if that's what you're worried about,' he said.

She blushed.

'I suppose with option three, I help you carry your bag to wherever you're going and then we call it quits? It's not my preferred option. To be fair, it should really be option five or six.'

The corners of her mouth lifted in a hesitant smile. 'If you could help me get it outside, I have a car waiting and the driver can take it from there.'

Charlie stood, threw his bag over his shoulder, and picked up her suitcase with the other hand. Her gaze flicked to his muscled arms, then away. He swallowed his grin. This was exactly what all the hours in the gym were for.

He did slow bicep curls with her suitcase.

'Are you sure you've even got anything in here?' he asked sceptically.

Her smile spread. 'Are you trying to show off?'

'Yes. Is it working?'

She laughed. 'Come on then, Mr Muscle. Let's get out of here.'

He walked beside her, still bicep-curling her suitcase.

'Oh my god, will you stop! There are no more women left to impress.'

He shrugged. 'I'm only trying to impress one.'

The doors to arrivals slid open. They were the last to exit and there were only two people waiting: the first, a man in a chauffeur's uniform and cap, holding a small sign which read: '*V Valverde*'.

The second, a man with a beetroot-red face holding up a giant sign that read: '*Charlie Hamilton! Congratulations on being two weeks syphilis-free!*'.

Charlie dropped his bag and let out a groan.

Rory.

Valentina glanced between the sign and him, then started laughing. The sound was so joyous, so infectious, he couldn't help but grin back. He handed her suitcase to the chauffeur.

'That is *not* true,' he told her. 'My mate just thinks he's a comedian.'

She giggled. 'It worked for me.'

There was a pause as they stared at each other. His stomach did another flip, but he stayed quiet, not wanting to ruin the moment by speaking. Her pupils dilated and her cheeks flushed.

She looked away. 'I have to go. Thank you for fixing my rucksack.'

He stepped back, shrugged, and smiled. Everything was okay. He may never see her again, but at least they would part like this.

He gave her a little bow and went to the man holding Rory's homemade sign.

'You Charlie?'

'Yep, that's me.'

The man thrust the sign at him. 'Take this and I'll get your bags—I'm not holding that a second longer.'

Charlie took the sign and turned to look back at Valentina. He pointed at his name, then at himself. She grinned and gave him a thumbs-up.

They stared at each other for a moment, then Valentina turned and walked away.

As the taxi wound its way through the Scottish Highlands, Charlie stared out the window. The rain pelted down and the world was full of greys, browns, and greens. Compared to London everything seemed so big, so empty.

He wound down the window an inch and breathed in the cool, damp, peaty air. It took him back to army training when he and Rory had been dumped in the middle of nowhere and left to find their way back.

This is the right place to be.

He needed distance from the rest of his life. The only thoughts of home he allowed were of his family.

His stomach knotted, thinking of his mum. He'd sent flowers, chocolates, and an apology for missing her birthday. But Tab was right—it wasn't enough. Still, having them think he was in Angola bought some time. Time to work out if he could ever have a different relationship with them.

Rory knew him better than his mum and dad did; he understood what it was like to grow up with distant, upper-class parents who still worked from Victorian parenting manuals.

Charlie's elder sister had turned out fine—confident, assured, happy to fit into the family mould. She was now a colonel, running a base with charmingly cold-hearted efficiency. He'd never wanted to rise through the ranks. He wanted action, not admin.

The road narrowed as it wound its way down the glen towards the small village of Kinloch. At the highest point stood Kinloch Castle, Rory's ancestral home. Dominating its surroundings, it was large, and largely falling down.

Charlie had only ever visited once, and remembered it as cold and musty. Every other visit to Scotland had been to Rory's parents' townhouse in Edinburgh. But the townhouse had been sold to pay off estate debts, and Rory's mum, Barbara, was now a widow.

The taxi pulled off the road into the vast front courtyard, jiggling across the cobblestones. Charlie could see Rory and a tall redhead he knew was Zoe greeting—

No fucking way!

His heart sped up. How was this possible?

A Hollywood film. A Hollywood film star. Do the maths, dickhead.

He had to be cool.

The car stopped and he got out, drawn into a bear hug by

Rory. 'Syphilis?' he grunted in his best friend's ear. 'You fucker.'

'I couldn't spell gonorrhoea,' Rory replied, disengaging with a grin. He stepped back. 'Charlie, this is Zoe, my fia—*girlfriend*. Zoe, this is Charlie. He holds rich people's shopping for a living.'

Zoe shook his hand. 'Lovely to meet you, Charlie, and I know you do much more than that.'

She had a smattering of freckles across her nose, wild red curly hair, and a warm and open smile. Charlie smiled back.

Rory punched him hard on the arm. 'Back off. And this is Valentina, one of the stars of the film.'

This was it. He was no longer a random stalker with syphilis—he was the Earl of Kinloch's best mate, and meant to be here.

He took Valentina's small hand, feeling electricity crackle between them. He didn't want to let go.

'You were on my plane,' he said, watching her lips part.

'I thought you were on *my* plane...' She disengaged her hand and ran it through her hair. 'And what are you doing here? Are you the muscle?'

His heart leapt. 'I'm the brains *and* the muscle.'

There was a pause as they gazed at each other.

Rory broke the moment by punching him on the arm again. '*I'm* the brains and the muscle, arsehole. You're just the house sitter.'

Charlie laughed. 'Too slow with your comeback, mate. I think you've just proved my point.'

Zoe strode forward and pushed them apart. 'Right,' she said firmly. 'That's enough testosterone for one morning.' She took Valentina's suitcase off Rory. 'You show Charlie where he's staying and try not to fight or have sex with each other. I'm removing the brains *and* the beauty from this situation. Come on, Valentina. I'll show you to your room.'

Following Rory through the castle, Charlie turned his head back and forth as he took in the changes. Gone was the dusty relic, in its place a palace. People wearing headsets walked briskly past them, and voices filled the space.

He glanced at Rory. 'I don't remember it looking like this. Did Brad's company pay for all of it?'

'Yep. And you should see the bedrooms.'

Charlie followed him up the main staircase. 'Do I get a four-poster bed?'

Rory snorted. 'You're lucky you've got a room at all. Everyone wanted to play lord of the manor.' They reached the first landing and turned right. 'I'm putting you at the end by the stairs to the attic rooms. It might be noisy, but I want you at the centre of everything.'

The room was small, with dark wood panelling and a double bed. New radiators lined a wall, and the fireplace was clean and stocked with fresh wood. A small shower room lay off the main bedroom. Charlie dropped his bag on the bed and whistled.

'Mate, Brad Bauer must be your new best friend. If this is a shit room, I'd love to see a good one.'

'The phrase "don't bite the hand that feeds you" keeps running through my head every time I see him,' Rory huffed. 'It's my new mantra.'

Charlie grinned. 'You're a crap hippy. Is that why I'm here? To stop you thumping him?'

'Pretty much. You're the only person I trust around here apart from Zoe. Let's go to the office and I'll fill you in.'

CHARLIE REMEMBERED THE ESTATE OFFICE AS A TOTAL DUMP with papers stacked floor to ceiling. Like the rest of the castle, it had undergone a makeover; now it was tidy, warm, clean, and the parquet floor gleamed.

They sat either side of a massive wooden desk and Rory handed him a sheaf of papers. 'Ever been on a film set?'

He shook his head.

'Well, the good news is they're organised. The bad news is they're a bunch of luvvies. The top brass are all staying at the castle and most of the rooms have open fires.'

'Seriously?'

'Yeah, I know—you don't need to say anything. In that pack, there's a complete layout of the castle with who or what is in each room. Each day, they produce a call sheet with more details about the day, which you'll also be given. And...' Rory pulled a ring of keys out of a drawer and passed them across the desk. 'These will get you into any room.'

Charlie looked at the plan. A big room in the basement was marked *B Bauer Personal*. 'What's this for?'

Rory glanced over. 'It's a gym for Brad and his co-stars. He had it custom built.'

'Can I use it?'

He shrugged. 'As long as you avoid the times he might be there, I don't have an issue. But why don't you build muscle doing proper work?'

'Chopping down trees and lifting cows? No ta. Looking this good requires sculpting. I'll go for a yomp over the hills if I want some cardio.'

Rory shook his head. 'Pretty boy.'

'Caveman. So, if there isn't anything to do now, can I be reunited with the real reason I'm here?'

Rory stood. 'Yep, but remember he's mine and not going anywhere.'

THE BACK COURTYARD WAS SMALL AND UTILITARIAN. A LONG, low building ran down one side. Previously stables, it was now Rory's workshop. At the back, an old German shepherd lay in a bed.

'Hey, Bandit,' Charlie called softly.

Bandit's ears pricked up, followed by his head. He saw Charlie and leapt to his feet, running towards him, barking furiously, tail thrashing wildly.

He knelt and rubbed Bandit's head as he was licked to death. 'Who's a good boy, then? Who loves Charlie more than Rory?' Bandit barked loudly, and Charlie turned his head. 'See? I'm his favourite.'

Rory rolled his eyes. '*My* dog, dipshit. You've got visiting rights only.' He glanced at his watch. 'I've got to meet and greet Kirsten Bjorkstrom and her "spiritual advisor".'

'Spiritual advisor?'

Rory ran his large hands through his hair and tugged on the

roots. 'Yep. Some kind of holy man called Vlad. I don't know if we're getting the Dalai Lama or Rasputin. Apparently, he had a vision that Brad was the earl in a past life and Zoe was his wife.'

Charlie snorted. 'You're joking, right?'

'Wish I was. Can you give the fire safety briefing to Valentina, Kirsten, and Vlad this afternoon? If Bandit doesn't want to stay here, take him to the flat and Mum can keep him company. You should go anyway—she'll want to see you.'

Charlie tried to hide his excitement about seeing Valentina. 'How is your mum?'

Rory let out a puff of air. 'We need more time to go down that rabbit hole. It's been bad, but it's getting better. She'll be pleased to see you. She's not keen on the Yanks.'

Charlie strode from the bottom to the top of Kinloch Castle, Bandit at his heel. He wanted to get the lay of the land, check out every nook and cranny, every entry and exit.

To one side of the castle, in the old kitchen gardens, trailers were parked cheek by jowl. The place was buzzing.

Brad's personal gym was locked, but Charlie let himself in. It was every musclehead's dream, filled with machines, free weights, benches, and giant racks. Mirrors lined the walls and the room had air con and a sound system. He stretched his arms over his head, feeling the need to burn off some serious energy.

But the gym could wait. He wanted to see Valentina.

He kept Bandit with him as he went back upstairs, fingers tangled in his fur. Bandit had worked with their unit in Afghan and saved them more than once. They may have left with their lives, but none of them truly emerged from the conflict unscathed. An IED had put Rory in hospital and Charlie still had shrapnel scars on his back and shoulder.

The mental scars often ran deeper. Rory dealt with his by getting out into nature. Charlie punished himself in the gym, put more boxes in the far corners of his mind, and spent time with Dave.

Reaching the top of the stairs, he glanced around. No one. He sat on the top step and put his face level with Bandit's.

'One day, my fine fellow, I want you to meet Dave. He's not as handsome or as clever as you, but his heart is just as big.'

Bandit nodded in return and licked Charlie's nose.

'Now, listen up. I need your help. I'm going to talk to a really nice girl. But I'm nervous and don't want to act like a muppet.' Bandit whined and put his paw on Charlie's knee. 'So, you'll do all the talking?' Bandit wagged his tail and gave a short bark. 'Excellent. Glad we got that sorted. Come along, this way.'

Outside Valentina's room he paused, wiping his palms on the sides of his jeans. He could hear people talking loudly in Spanish inside. Did she have visitors?

He knocked. There was a brief silence, then the voices started up, even louder. He was about to knock again when Valentina opened the door an inch, her eyes widening a fraction as she saw him.

She whipped her head away and yelled, '¡Espera un segundo!', then turned back to Charlie. 'One moment please.' She shut the door and he heard more Spanish before it abruptly cut off.

When the door re-opened wider than before, his heart stuttered. Valentina's baseball cap and coat were off and there was nothing left to hide her beauty.

Her hair was deeper than night, framing her face and falling to below her shoulders. Her chestnut brown eyes held his.

'Mr Hamilton,' she said, her eyes alight with mischief. 'Mr *Charlie* Hamilton.'

Fuck! Her voice was aural Viagra, sending blood surging to his cock.

She smiled. 'I know why you're here.'

He swallowed. 'You do?' His voice cracked like a teenager.

'Yes.' Valentina lowered her long, dark lashes and peeked up at him through them. 'You're here to light my fire.'

If Charlie's blood was hot before, now it was thermonuclear. His brain melted, frying any cognitive function beyond imagining her in his arms, his lips on hers, the gasping sounds of her pleasure as he buried himself inside her. His mouth fell open, but no sound came out.

A bark broke the silence and Valentina glanced down.

'Oh! And who are you?' She dropped to her knees to pet Bandit, her face inches from Charlie's straining cock. 'What a big boy. You're so gorgeous! What a gorgeous big boy you are.'

Fuck's sake! He turned away, willing his body to behave. Valentina laughed as Bandit said hello.

'And what is your name?' she asked him.

'Bandit,' Charlie managed through gritted teeth.

'Woah! Down boy,' she said before he heard a thump. His head snapped around to see her sitting on the floor, Bandit still licking her face.

'Bandit! Heel!' The dog immediately fell back. Charlie helped Valentina up. 'I'm sorry. He's a bit overexcited to meet you and lost control. He's usually much better behaved.'

She brushed her trousers with her hands, then combed her fingers through her hair. 'It's fine. It reminds me of wrestling with my brothers when I was growing up. You here for the fire safety thing?'

He nodded, once again robbed of the power of speech.

'Okay, come in, Charlie and Bandit.'

He followed her into the large and spacious room with bay windows looking out onto the front courtyard. An enormous four-poster bed was set back against a panelled wall opposite an open fire surrounded by ornate tiles.

In the window alcove was a desk, and on it sat a scuffed tablet and the same filming schedule Rory had given him. Through a door he could see into the bathroom, with a roll-top bath and Valentina's toiletries lined up neatly by the sink.

She looked around the room with him. 'Isn't it beautiful?'

He nodded, his eyes filled with her. Bandit barked and he started, as if waking from a dream only to find he was in a fantasy.

'The fire... okay, yes. Er, I'm here to show you how to use it safely.'

He crouched and cleared his throat. Valentina knelt beside him, her hands resting on the front of her thighs. He stared at them, the back of his neck heating up.

'Um, so, er, you've—'

'The fire guard is here and must be used whenever the fire is lit. I should only use wood provided. To make a fire, start by twisting whorls of paper, then put tinder on top, making sure to create a tepee to keep air flowing in from the bottom, then add the larger logs. It is always preferable to use the wall heaters instead of the fire, and there is a fire extinguisher in case of a conflagration,' she rattled off.

He glanced up, his brain refusing to work properly. 'Conflagration?'

'A large, destructive fire.' She smiled sympathetically, as if dealing with a confused child. 'I learned to make a fire when I was a kid. I read the information pack left on the bed. And I know long words because I went through an English dictionary with Abuela for all the years I was on *La Vida Familiar*.'

'Is that who you were talking to?'

Valentina glanced behind her at the tablet on the desk. 'Yes, and Abuelita. I speak to them every day.'

'Every day? Both of them?' She probably spoke to them more in a week than he did with his entire family in a year.

She smiled, but he could see a tightness about it. 'Yes, they live together. With mi abuelito, my granddad.'

'Er, the three of them? Live together? Like, er...'

Her eyes widened. 'Oh no!' She slapped him on the arm. 'How can you think such a thing? They are best friends from being little girls. Abuela is my papá's mother and Abuelita is the mother of my mamá. When Abuelo, my grandfather, died, Abuela moved in with Abuelita and Abuelito, my granny and grandad.' She got up. 'I have to go for a costume fitting.'

He stood, his cheeks burning. She ushered him out the door, following him into the corridor.

'See you later, Charlie Hamilton,' she said with a wink before striding off, her hair swishing with every step.

Charlie gazed down at Bandit. The dog tipped his head to the side quizzically, as if asking how he could have been so uncool.

'Yeah, I know, dude,' he said, shaking his head. 'Not my best work...'

He flicked through the sheaf of papers Rory had given him. He needed to figure out when Valentina might be free so he could speak to her again. But first, he needed to deal with another film star and a holy man.

❈ 6 ❈

Hollywood megastar Kirsten Bjorkstrom had an entourage of two: His Holiness Vladyka Mirov and personal assistant Shauna Merritt. They'd been relegated to the attic rooms, and his Holiness had snagged the biggest, which had a working fire.

Charlie decided to start with him, figuring a harmless holy nutcase would be an easier job than someone who'd won their first Oscar aged eight.

Starting up the stairs, Bandit's ears pricked up and he barked. Memories from Afghan came tumbling and crashing through Charlie's mind.

'What is it, boy? You got something?'

Bandit trotted up the rest of the stairs, down the corridor, and sat beside a door. By the time Charlie reached him, even *he* could smell smoke. He knocked sharply. No answer. He tried the handle. Locked. He selected the skeleton key from the bunch Rory had given him and entered.

Pungent smoke filled the room. Sitting cross-legged on the bed, eyes closed, was the man he presumed was His Holiness.

A long black cassock had ridden up above his knees as he sat, revealing pale, spindly legs covered in black hair and large feet with yellowing toenails.

His face was thin with dark circles under his eyes. A straggly black beard, constrained by silver rings, reached the middle of his chest. What hair he had left was pulled into a frizzy ponytail.

This was the harmless holy man? It seemed they'd got Rasputin after all.

Charlie cast his eyes around the room. A bundle of leaves was smouldering in the grate. The smoke alarm had been dismantled and the battery lay on the nightstand.

'Leave,' the figure intoned.

Charlie ignored him. He picked the bunch of leaves from the grate, opened the nearest window, bashed the smouldering edge against the roof tiles, then threw it to the cobbles below.

'I said *leave*,' the man repeated, his eyes still closed. 'I am meditating.'

Charlie opened the rest of the windows. Bandit barked.

His Holiness opened his eyes. 'Get it out of my room! I'm allergic!'

Bandit was sitting by a large bag. Charlie knelt beside him. 'What have you found, boy?'

Bandit barked again and pawed the bag. The man was now off the bed, extending a scarecrow arm.

'I said get out! Don't you know who I am?' he spluttered, his fingers vibrating with rage.

Charlie stood and made a show of looking at his notes.

'Ah yes, here we have you: His Holiness Vlad-why-car... Hang on, His Holiness Vlad-ee-ka... Fuck it.' He glanced up. 'Let's stick with Vlad, shall we? Yep, that'll do. You're Vlad. I'm Charlie. I'm here to make sure everyone's safe and the castle doesn't burn down.'

He picked up the battery on the nightstand and inserted it into the smoke alarm.

'If you touch that again, or put anything in the fireplace that isn't the wood you've been given, you'll be staying in the Travelodge off the Inverness ring road. Clear?'

Vlad snatched his phone and stabbed at the screen. 'In five minutes, you won't have a job,' he spat. 'I know the earl.'

Charlie leaned back against the wall. 'Really?'

Vlad turned his back as the call connected. 'It's His Holiness,' he said into the phone. 'One of your staff has broken into my room and destroyed personal property. His employment will need to be terminated.' There was a pause and Vlad turned his head with a reptilian smile. 'What's your name?'

'Charlie.'

'Your *full* name.'

'Charlie Hamilton.'

'His name is— What did he destroy? Er, spiritual supplies.'

Vlad looked away and Charlie grinned. He couldn't hear exactly what Rory was saying, but he recognised the tone.

'But, I—'

Rory's voice got louder, then cut off. Vlad stared at the phone in silence.

'So,' Charlie began conversationally, 'it seems we both know the earl.'

'Get out of my room,' he hissed.

Charlie called Bandit to heel. 'I'll get someone else to give you the safety briefing.'

Bandit whined at him as they strode away down the corridor. 'I know, buddy. He's got some dodgy shit in there, but let's bide our time, eh? We've just got Kirsten to deal with now. She'll be child's play compared to that.'

Outside Kirsten's room, he heard a high-pitched voice calling someone a 'useless bitch' before the door opened and a high-heeled shoe flew through the air towards him. He dodged just in time, and it bounced off the opposite wall with a clatter. He picked it up.

'This belong to anyone?'

Standing before him in the opulent room were two women: one he recognised, and one he didn't.

Kirsten Bjorkstrom, star of stage and screen, was wearing a long black puffa coat that reached the floor. She was small, with an elfin face, bright blue eyes, and blonde hair. She would have been pretty had she not been mid-scowl when Charlie entered.

The other woman, who he presumed was her assistant, Shauna, looked like she'd been crying. Dressed in drab clothes with her brown hair tied back, she was clutching a notebook to her chest as if for protection. She took the shoe from him.

'Yes, it's mine, thank you,' Shauna said in a soft voice.

He flicked his gaze to her worn trainers, and she blushed.

'Good afternoon, ladies. My name is Charlie Hamilton and I'm in charge of security at the castle for the duration of the shoot. I'm here to give a fire safety briefing to...' he glanced at his papers, 'Kirsten Bjorkstrom.' He turned to Shauna. 'Are you she?'

Out of the corner of his eye, he saw Kirsten's mouth drop open. Shauna's blush deepened, and she shook her head.

Kirsten snatched the shoe from her, tossed it on the bed, and stood in front of him, allowing her puffa coat to fall open. Putting her hands on her hips, she thrust her chest forward.

'*I'm* Kirsten.'

Charlie kept his eyes glued to hers, even though his peripheral vision had alerted him to the fact that every detail of her gravity-defying breasts was showing through her top.

He wasn't impressed by celebrities—he'd worked with far

too many. Most were pleasant, but a lot were just like Kirsten and set his teeth on edge.

'Marvellous,' he said blandly. 'Let's begin.'

She turned away and climbed onto the bed. 'Shauna can do it,' she said, picking up a pile of paper. 'I've got lines to learn.'

Charlie clenched his jaw. Was this really going to be the hill he chose to die on?

'Of course,' he replied smoothly. He gazed at Shauna. She looked bloody miserable. He gave her the best smile he could muster. 'Okay, let's light a fire. Do you have any marshmallows?'

BY THE TIME HE'D FINISHED WITH SHAUNA, CHARLIE needed to burn off steam. He changed into shorts and a running top and took Bandit into the hills around Kinloch.

When he ran in London, he always listened to music. Anything to take his mind away from his surroundings. Here, there was no need. He wanted to immerse himself in the wildness, feel the uneven ground beneath his feet and breathe in the damp earthiness of the glen. He wanted to feel part of the landscape, not separate from it.

After an hour, they circled back around the village and ran to the shores of the loch. Daylight was fading and the air was still. Bandit sniffed the edge of the water and Charlie leant down to splash his face.

He smiled with the shock of the cold. 'Fancy a swim?'

Bandit turned away and trotted up the bank towards the village.

He laughed. 'Maybe another day, then.'

They jogged up the hill through the village and entered the front door of the castle.

Valentina was a few yards away, her back to them. Dressed

in trainers, black leggings, and a tight red crop top, she was looking at a map of the castle, presumably trying to figure out where Brad's gym was.

Charlie's mouth ran dry as he drank in her curves. She set off in the wrong direction before he could move his feet towards her. Bandit brushed up against him, and he glanced down.

'Are you thinking what I'm thinking?'

Bandit put his head to the side.

'Exactly! Come on.'

He ran the other way down to the gym, opened the door and turned on the lights. He threw his top off and stared at himself critically in the mirrors. He'd lost weight over the last month and was more shredded than usual.

Untying the strings on the top of his shorts, he tugged them down an inch. Time to pull out all the stops. A dragon tattoo snaked down his lower abdomen, over his V lines, before disappearing under his shorts. He pulled them lower.

'Bandit, lie down.'

One of the gym racks was opposite the door, facing away. Charlie reached up and gripped the pull-up bars. As soon as he heard footsteps coming towards the door, he started lifting himself up and down, counting out loud.

'Sixty-seven, sixty-eight, sixty-nine, seventy...'

He kept his eyes fixed forward, pretending to strain with the effort as he clocked Valentina in the mirrors, hesitating in the doorway.

'Seventy-four, seventy-five, seventy-six, seventy-seven...'

Was she going to come in? How many more would he have to do before she made her decision?

'Seventy-eight, seventy-nine, eighty...'

He heard Bandit's tail thumping in excitement and dropped down off the rack, bending forwards, his hands resting on his thighs, breathing heavily. Valentina cleared her throat and he turned slowly, straightening and breathing into his upper chest, puffing out his pecs.

She looked away, chewing on her bottom lip.

'Hey, how did the costume fitting go?' he asked casually.

'Um, yes, as expected.' She brought her gaze back to him, then away again.

He followed her eyes as they found his body in a mirror. He changed his stance slightly and flexed, giving her the best angle to ogle the guns.

'Do you want to train together?' he asked.

A flush spread across her cheeks and her lips parted. She splayed her fingers against the outside of her thighs.

'I, I can't right now, I...' She hesitated, her eyes flicking across his body.

He saw how large her pupils were and his heart quickened.

'You have a lot of tattoos,' she said in a rush.

Charlie bent his head to look at them, trying to control his desire whilst ramping up hers. 'Yeah, each one tells a story, most of them involving alcohol.'

She laughed nervously.

He ran his fingers over his hard torso, tracing each image, moving slower the lower he went. Valentina's breathing quickened. He lingered on the dragon as it curved across the side of his abs, then hooked his thumbs underneath the top of his shorts as if to pull them down even further.

Her eyes were glued to his crotch, her lower lip trembling. Charlie's head went light as all the blood rushed south. Valentina swallowed and his cock gave an involuntary twitch. She squeaked.

'Hey guys, how's it going?'

Charlie's gaze snapped to the door.

Brad Bauer.

It was really him. Smaller than expected, of course, but still wearing the handsome face he and Rory had skewered with thousands of darts.

Brad strode forward and took his hand. 'Hey, you must be Charlie, right? Awesome to meet you, man. Rory told me all about you.'

The Hollywood superstar circled him. Valentina had turned away and was smoothing her palms down the outside of her leggings.

'Sick physique,' said Brad. 'How much you bench?'

Charlie shrugged. He hated these kinds of conversations.

'Come on, don't be shy,' Brad exclaimed, feeling his bicep. 'Cool tats. How far does the dragon go?'

Charlie's cheeks warmed.

'Hey, you wanna work out with us?'

He shook his head. 'I'm done—I'll let you crack on.'

Charlie turned to retrieve his top. Valentina was still facing away from them both, but he caught her eyes in the mirror and held her gaze whilst he called for Bandit.

'If you've got some spare time, we should train together,' said Brad. 'It'd be dope.'

He cleared his throat. 'Yeah, sure, anytime.'

Brad clapped him on the shoulder. 'Awesome, man. Can't wait.' He turned to Valentina, who was stroking Bandit. 'Hey, babe, ready to go?'

Charlie walked to the door and whistled. Bandit didn't move.

'Bandit, heel!'

The dog's head snapped away from Valentina and he followed Charlie out of the gym, looking back at her over his shoulder.

'I know how you feel, mate,' he muttered under his breath as they went up the stairs together. 'I know how you feel.'

❀   7   ❀

After showering, Charlie met Rory in his workshop. Bandit ate his dinner as they talked, Rory absent-mindedly whittling a small piece of wood, Charlie leaning back against one of the workbenches.

Rory's girlfriend, Zoe, lived in a small wooden cabin a few miles out of Kinloch and that was where Rory wanted to spend all his time.

'Mate, it's right on the loch and there's no one for miles. No phone signal, no internet. As long as Zoe's with me, it's perfect.'

Charlie nodded, digging his fingernails into the bench. 'You really love her, then? Does she "complete you"?' he asked, his voice sounding hollow.

Rory nodded. 'In every way. She's the other half of me.'

He looked into his friend's pale-blue eyes, seeing the truth shining out. His heart stretched apart like dough.

Rory cleared his throat. 'What's the latest with—?'

He shook his head vehemently and Rory fell silent. Charlie

stared at the floor, scuffing his feet through the piles of sawdust, the soft sounds filling the silence.

'She dumped me for the final time...' He paused, then bit the bullet. 'She's pregnant with his baby. She said it was never going to work and we didn't really know each other.'

'Oh, mate...'

Rory took a breath to say more, but Charlie shook his head again. He was empty. A wasteland.

'So, what are you going to do?' Rory finally asked.

He shrugged, still eyeballing the floor. 'Shag around, be a player. Do what I should have been doing for the last ten years, rather than waiting around for her like a sad sack.'

'Player? You?' scoffed Rory, attempting to lighten the mood. '*Bridge* player, more like. The only place you could score is down the Women's Institute once they'd copped a load of your macramé.'

'It's embroidery, dickwad.'

Rory shrugged. 'I just don't get how you could even thread a needle with your ham hands.'

'Says the Neanderthal who carves things small enough for fairies.'

Rory glanced at the tiny piece of wood in his hands. 'Fair enough, but I'm usually holding an axe.' He put the piece of wood to one side. 'Have you seen Mum yet?'

Charlie shook his head.

'Can you go tonight? I'm not around that much, and I need to know she's okay.'

'Your mum's always okay. She's tougher than mine and that's saying something.'

'It's different now. She doesn't like Zoe, and her home is filled with people she likes even less. Zoe says if we don't keep Brad on side, he'll screw us over and shoot the exterior stuff for the film at another castle. You're a familiar face to Mum. You can keep her calm.'

'Yeah, no worries. I'll go up later.'

'Thanks, mate. What did you think of our new spiritual advisor?'

'Vlad? Fuck me, he's a bad 'un. Bandit got wind of something in his bags, so I'm going to take a look when he's out.'

'Cheers. I hate him almost as much as Brad.' Rory ran his hands through his hair. 'The sooner this is over and they all fuck off, the better. Then life can get back to normal.'

He cast his eyes around the room.

'Right. I'm off. They've got a catering van in the side garden you probably saw. You can eat from there or use one of the kitchens in the castle. Help yourself to any of my steaks. Keep Bandit out here at night so he can keep an ear out for anyone in the back courtyard. You need anything else?'

'Nah, I'm all good. I'll see you in the morning.'

Rory smiled. He looked relieved. 'Thanks, mate. I'm glad you're here.'

Joining the end of the queue for the catering truck, Charlie saw Valentina up ahead getting her food. As soon as he filled his plate, he went through to the dining room. Valentina wasn't there. He noticed Shauna sitting by herself, shovelling food into her mouth like she was in an eating competition.

'Do you mind if I sit here?' he asked.

She looked up, surprised, and quickly swallowed her mouthful. 'Oh no, of course not. Please, be my guest.'

He sat. 'Are you in a hurry?'

She nodded as she chewed, then gulped from a glass of water. 'I have a very small window while Kirsten and His Holiness eat, then I have to get back.' She glanced at her phone, as if the very act of talking was a crime against her employer.

'You're Kirsten's personal assistant?'

Shauna nodded, chewing faster.

'What do you do for her?'

She swallowed. 'Everything. Answering emails, shopping, liaising with her agent, giving orders to the rest of her staff, booking travel, doing laundry. Anything she needs.'

'Have you been working for her a long time?'

'Nearly six months. I've lasted the longest,' she said proudly.

Charlie didn't know how to reply. 'So, where are Kirsten and Vlad eating, then?'

Shauna dropped her fork with a crash and looked around guiltily. '*Shh!*' she whispered. 'You've got to refer to him as "His Holiness".'

He leaned in. '*That's never going to happen,*' he whispered back. He grinned at her shocked face.

She glanced furtively around again. 'Brad's chef cooks food for them separately. They eat an organic, raw, whole foods, plant-based diet and His Holiness blesses everything.' She scraped the last of her food into her mouth.

'No cookies in the middle of the night when they get hungry, then?'

Shauna bit her lip as if stopping herself from talking further. She put her cutlery together on the plate and stood. 'I'm sorry to appear rude, but I have to go.' She blushed. 'Thank you for earlier—you were very kind.'

He shook his head. 'It was nothing.' He took her plate from her. 'Leave it. I'll take it back when I'm done. You do what you have to do.'

She mouthed a '*thank you*' at him and scuttled off.

Charlie finished eating quickly. The shepherd's pie was

good, but unless he was sharing it with someone, it was merely fuel. He took the plates back to the catering truck, then went to find Barbara, Rory's mum.

BARBARA LIVED IN A MODERN FLAT IN THE WEST WING OF the castle, built for her when she got married. As Charlie strolled down one of the long corridors towards the entrance to the flat, a small woman in chef's whites was ahead of him, pushing a trolley. She reached the door to the flat just before him and rang the bell.

Barbara opened the door with a smile, then glanced at Charlie, her face falling. She recovered quickly and turned to the woman.

'Just go on through and set up—he's waiting inside.' She let the woman pass, then pulled the door so she was standing in the corridor. 'Charles, what a pleasant surprise, I was looking forward to seeing you,' she said, coming in for an air-kiss.

'I can come back tomorrow if it's not convenient?'

Barbara lowered her voice. 'If you wouldn't mind, that would be most appreciated. Mr Bauer insisted I dine with him, and experience the talents of his personal chef. I didn't want to appear rude by declining.'

'No problem, I'll leave you to it.'

She placed her hand on his arm. 'Charles, I don't want to put you in an awkward position, but this is something Rory really doesn't need to know about. My son is awfully touchy about Bra—*Mr Bauer*, and we could all do without any more unnecessary scenes. Do you understand?'

He nodded. 'I know how he can be. I'll see you tomorrow.'

Barbara squeezed his arm. 'Thank you, dear.' She slipped back inside the flat.

· · ·

ON THE WAY TO HIS ROOM, CHARLIE PASSED VALENTINA'S door and slowed to a stop. He could hear her inside, chatting and laughing in Spanish, presumably on another call with her family.

A yearning pain filled his chest. Valentina's life was filled with love. In comparison, his was filled with empty failure.

In his room, he flopped on the bed and glanced at his phone. Should he ring his mum? Even though there were no new notifications, he opened his message app—the way he and Caroline communicated—and stared blankly at the screen. The ball of lead was back in his stomach, making him feel sick.

He turned the phone over, looking at Valentina's name scrawled on the back, and felt a little lighter remembering how he'd made her laugh in the airport. Had he ever made silly jokes with Caroline? Made her laugh like that? Felt comfortable enough to be truly himself?

He put the phone down. *Just go to sleep.*

THE NEXT MORNING CHARLIE ATE BREAKFAST IN THE DINING room, taking his time with the food, hoping Valentina would appear.

As he waited, he went through the filming schedule. She wasn't in many scenes, so, on paper at least, had a lot of free time.

He thought about her suitcase. Could he fix it? Maybe make some new wheels in Rory's workshop? He rubbed his face. Why was all her stuff so knackered? Most toddlers in London were better kitted out. She was a rich movie star, for fuck's sake. It wasn't like she couldn't afford it.

As Shauna rushed through the dining room, he gave her a wave. She swerved and ran to him, out of breath.

He sprang up. 'What's happened?'

'It's Kirsten. She needs guava.'

'Guava?'

'Yes, and I can't find any. She can't work without it. Do you have some?' Her voice was tinged with desperation.

He held his hands wide. 'Sorry, I'm all out.'

Shauna bit her lower lip and nodded. She looked like she was about to cry. 'Okay. I'm going to try in the village now. See you later.'

She ran off, and Charlie sat. Who knew guava was so vital to the acting process? He picked up the schedule again. In an hour, there was a photoshoot for the main actors.

His stomach flipped. He would soon see Valentina again.

THE GREAT HALL HAD A DOUBLE HEIGHT, VAULTED CEILING and ancient family portraits lining the walls. At one end was a raised dais, on which sat two ornate wooden thrones. Huge lights were trained on them in preparation for shooting publicity shots of Brad, Kirsten, and Valentina in their costumes.

Brad had not only written *Braveheart 2*, he was producing and directing it, and was also the star. The story was a bonkers fantasy, with Brad playing Robert the Bruce. Rory had read the script and told Charlie it included Brad's character discovering America and bringing an army of Native American ninjas back to help him liberate Scotland.

Valentina was playing one of the ninjas—Brad's second love interest after Kirsten's character. Charlie thought the story proved people would pay to watch just about anything, no matter how historically inaccurate or culturally inappropriate.

He stood against the wall watching crowds of people buzzing around their brightly coloured queen bee. Brad was dressed like a mediaeval king who'd put his nation's wealth into his clothing.

Charlie imagined him showing the costume designer a portrait of Henry VIII and telling them Henry's outfit was a one out of ten, and his needed to be an eleven. So many fake jewels were stitched on that under the lights he'd morphed into a human glitter ball.

Blinking, Charlie looked for Valentina, his heart sparking when he saw her. She was on the other side of the room talking to Zoe, wearing an outfit that could only have been designed by a man.

She was meant to be the daughter of a Native American chief but looked like a stripper. Her beaded leather dress barely covered her bottom and was cinched so tight around her chest that her breasts had almost completely spilled out the top. The only sign she was apparently meant to be a ninja warrior was shuriken throwing stars hanging off the bottom of her dress, a long knife at her hip and a bow and arrow over her shoulder.

The costume was terrible, but Charlie was more concerned about the weapons. Had they made the blade edges safe? There was more likelihood of her causing injury to herself than someone else.

He shook his head, then noticed her staring back at him, a look of hurt on her face.

Oh fuck.

She turned away, striding towards Brad, who greeted her with open arms.

Charlie ground his teeth. *Idiot. Stupid fucking idiot.*

Inside him, caveman Charlie was in a fight with his higher self, whilst his internal logic threw rocks at them both. That Valentina looked hot enough to melt diamonds was beyond question, but the warrior accoutrements were cringe-worthy lip service to an idea of female empowerment when she was dressed like someone attending a Halloween frat party.

He dug his fingernails into his palms. *She can wear whatever the fuck she likes*, he yelled inwardly, before another part reminded him smugly that Brad Bauer chose the clothing, not her.

Brad was sitting on a throne, manspreading, his XXL codpiece reflecting light out into space and putting satellites off course. He beckoned Valentina over and she sat on his knee.

By now, Charlie's inner caveman had ripped the head off his higher self and torn logic and common sense limb from limb. He wanted to punch Brad into the middle of next year and sweep Valentina away.

As she got up and Brad adjusted his codpiece, Charlie moved towards them. Valentina stared at him coldly and it stopped him in his tracks. This was her life and her job—he had no right to interfere.

He turned and left the hall as fast as he could without breaking into a run. In the corridor, he bumped into Rory.

'Hang about,' Rory said. 'What's up, mate?'

'Brad,' Charlie spat. 'It's like he's making a fucking porno or something.'

'With Zoe?' demanded Rory, his face turning white. Charlie put his hands on his upper arms, feeling the muscles primed for action.

'No, fuck no. He's just all over Valentina like a rash. I don't know how she does it. It makes me sick.'

Rory relaxed. 'Mate, if it makes you sick watching it, think about how Valentina feels *doing* it.'

Charlie shook his head. 'I'm such a dickhead.'

'We all know that. How did you finally figure it out?'

'I'm pretty sure I've pissed off Valentina.'

'Already? You've surpassed yourself.'

'Fuck off.'

'Will do. I'm off to make sure Brad's nowhere near the love of my life.' Rory slapped him on the shoulder and strode past him into the great hall.

Charlie sighed and rubbed his face. How could he explain the disgusted look he'd given Valentina without making it all worse?

He glanced at his watch. He had plenty of time to kill whilst he worked out what to say to her. Right now, he owed Rory's mum a visit.

※ 8 ※

Barbara opened the door to her flat and ushered Charlie through to the living room. 'Take a seat, dear, whilst I make tea. You can cast your eye over my latest project.'

Charlie sat on one of the sofas and picked up Barbara's needlepoint from a side table.

He'd always been fascinated by the skill of the surgeons who'd patched him and his friends up. Shawn, the doctor who'd operated on him, had shown him the various techniques, and Charlie had practised on pigskin.

Rory had been more seriously injured, and when Charlie visited him in hospital, Barbara had been there, passing the time doing embroidery whilst her son slept. She'd left a piece behind, and Charlie finished it, then sent it back to her.

Only Rory and Barbara knew about his secret sewing hobby, and he wanted to keep it that way.

Her latest work was a landscape showing the glen sweeping up from the loch with the castle in the distance. It was perfect, neat, immaculate.

Barbara brought a tray through with a teapot and china cups. She set it down and poured for both of them.

'It's so nice to be able to use the china with someone other than myself. You know Rory only drinks water.'

He nodded.

'And he insists on drinking it,' she shuddered, 'from a *pint* glass.'

Charlie smiled. Barbara oozed posh. Beautiful, with short blonde hair and cornflower blue eyes, she was in her early fifties, yet looked twenty years younger. She'd never hidden her dismay that her son grew his hair long and looked more like the wild man of the woods than the Earl of Kinloch.

He lifted her needlepoint. 'This is looking good.'

Her pert nose wrinkled. 'I don't know. It's not inspiring me anymore.' She lifted three more frames out of a drawer and handed them to him. 'Take a look at these. I just can't seem to finish anything at the moment. I get bored and start again with a new one.'

He glanced through them. The bottom one was of an English cottage garden at the height of summer, filled with flowers.

'This is lovely. These are the flowers Mum grows.'

Barbara smiled. 'I did think of her when I was doing it. How are your parents? Is your father enjoying his retirement?'

Charlie shifted in his seat and put the embroidery to one side. He took a sip of tea and looked down into the cup.

'They're fine. They both seem busier than when Dad was serving. They're on so many boards and committees I've lost count.'

'And Tabitha?'

He puffed out his cheeks. 'Colonel now, running the signals regiment down in Blandford. I expect her to outrank Dad by the time she retires.'

'Hmm. Unless she has children, of course.'

'Tabbie? Kids? She got about as much mothering instinct as a cuckoo. I think the only reason she married Miles was for show.'

'Charles, really now,' Barbara scolded.

'Sorry, I'm not in Tab's good books at the moment.'

'Have you tried picking up the telephone?'

He gave her a cheeky grin. 'I can pick it up, but do I actually have to use it?'

CHARLIE LEFT THE FLAT AN HOUR LATER, THE UNFINISHED cottage garden piece in a bag with spare embroidery silks. Barbara had insisted he take it, telling him she was never going to finish it, so he might as well have it.

Rounding a corner, he saw Valentina facing away from him, her phone held in the air. She'd changed, now dressed in leggings and an oversized sweater that had ridden up over her perfect backside as she waved the phone around.

Charlie forced his eyes to stay on the back of her head. She stomped down the main staircase, pausing at the half landing to hold the phone up again.

'Can I help at all?'

Her head whipped around. 'No, thank you, you cannot.' She continued down the stairs.

'Do you need to borrow a phone?'

She shook her head. 'I just need Wi-Fi. It's stopped working.'

He pulled out his phone to confirm the lack of signal. 'Could you use data?'

Valentina didn't stop. 'The signal is too bad.'

'I can sort it.'

'How?'

'The router probably needs a reset or the boosters might be down. Come on, I'll show you.' He started towards the production offices. 'When did it stop working?'

'About five minutes ago.'

They reached an intersection, and Charlie opened a cupboard in the wall. The router had gone. *Huh?* He knew there were boosters throughout the castle, so went to the first one. Gone. He started walking quicker, Valentina jogging to catch up.

'What is it?'

'The router and downstairs booster have gone. I'm going to check if the rest are still in place,' he replied, taking the stairs two at a time.

He searched the whole first floor with Valentina but didn't find a single one, so moved upwards. As they reached the first attic corridor, he saw a familiar figure crouching down and unplugging a booster from the wall.

'What the fuck are you doing?' Charlie exploded.

Vlad sprang up like an enormous, startled spider and kicked the booster behind him.

Charlie turned to Valentina. 'Why don't you go back to your room? I'll come and find you when everything's back up and running.'

Her eyes sparkled. 'Are things about to get ugly?'

His heart flickered into life. 'I hope so.'

'Then I'm staying. Seeing someone take down Vlad the Impale-her is one of my fantasies,' she whispered with a grin.

His heart beat faster.

Vlad slammed his door and locked it. Charlie got out his keys, hearing the sound of something large and heavy scraping across the floor inside the room. He unlocked the door and barged in.

A pile of boosters and the castle's Wi-Fi router lay on the

bed. A large wardrobe was pulled away from the wall. Vlad peeked his head around the side of it.

'Let me repeat myself,' Charlie said slowly. 'What the *fuck* are you doing?'

Vlad stepped out from behind the wardrobe. 'Wi-Fi is non-native EMF and interferes with the ancestral energies of the castle.'

'And *you* are interfering with the present-day functioning of the castle,' he replied. 'How do you think anyone can work around here without it?'

'They can use Ethernet cables and radios.'

'How is that going to work with a phone? How am I meant to speak to my family?' Valentina interjected.

Vlad ignored her. 'I cannot work in electromagnetic pollution. The spirits concur.'

Charlie took two steps forward and Vlad ducked back behind the wardrobe.

'Listen up, sunshine. There's a queue forming of people who can't wait to kick your sanctimonious arse out of here and, unlucky for you, I've just pushed my way to the front. Now, I'm going to take these and put them all back. And if the Wi-Fi signal so much as loses one bar, you and I are going to have a major falling out. Understand?'

Vlad looked coolly back at him, his thin lips pressed shut.

Charlie pulled the edges of the counterpane together, creating a makeshift bag for the router and boosters, and left the room following Valentina.

'Do you have a key that unlocks every room?' she whispered as he knelt to plug the first booster back into the corridor wall.

'Yep, for emergency use.'

'Is this an emergency?'

He used the excuse of whispering to lean closer to her. 'If you aren't happy, then I class that as an emergency.'

She blushed and moved away towards the stairs.

Charlie followed her, pausing outside her room. 'I'll sort this and let you know when we're back online. It might take a while to get going again.'

FIFTEEN MINUTES LATER, EVERYTHING WAS BACK IN PLACE and the router was flashing as it got up to speed. Charlie knocked hesitantly on Valentina's door.

She opened it and beckoned him in. 'It still isn't working.' She pointed at her tablet. 'Can you do anything?'

He picked it up as there was a knock on the door. Valentina had a hurried conversation with a young woman wearing a headset on the other side.

She turned to him. 'I have to go and sort something with Wardrobe. Are you okay to stay for five minutes and see if you can get it going?'

'Yeah, no worries.'

'Thanks.' She smiled at him and left.

Charlie sat down at the desk as the Wi-Fi icon appeared at the top of the screen. He put the password in, and everything came back online.

That was easy.

A call flashed on screen. He stared at it.

'Mis abuelas' were calling.

His finger dithered over the phone icon on the screen. It was bouncing up and down like an angry child demanding attention. He swiped to end the call but caught it mid-bounce. Suddenly he was looking at the faces of two old ladies.

'¿Dónde está mi chiquita?' the one on the left demanded.

Charlie stuttered. *Oh shit.* He was FaceTiming Valentina's grandmothers.

'Er, hola,' he began, wracking his memory for what Spanish he knew that didn't involve swearing or ordering a beer. 'Valentina es... Er, Valentina no está aquí. Er, lo siento.'

The woman on the left had dyed black hair scraped back in a bun, fierce black eyeliner, and bright-red lipstick. The woman on the right had white hair in a long braid that fell over one shoulder, and no make-up. Both had eyes that penetrated the screen and bored into his.

The woman on the right put on a pair of glasses. 'Are you Charlie?'

He nearly dropped the tablet in surprise. They knew who he was? The woman on the left put her glasses on and moved closer to inspect him. Charlie instinctively pulled back.

'Are you Charlie? Mr Charlie Hamilton?' she asked, talking slowly and articulating every word.

'Er, yes. Yes, I am,' he replied, starting to get flustered.

'Do you have a tattoo of a dragon on your stomach?'

His cheeks heated. 'Um, yes, I do.'

'Can we see it?'

His mouth dropped open. The woman on the right turned to the other and poked her. There was a brief argument in Spanish, then they turned back to face him. 'We do not need to see it.'

He sagged with relief.

'Do you have syphilis?'

What the fuck? The heat in his face spread down his neck.

'No! No, I do not!' What else had she told them about him? They both stared at him, then simultaneously sat back and nodded.

'Si,' pronounced the scarier looking one. 'We believe you.'

There was silence. He stared blankly at them. His mind

had decided the situation was too weird and temporarily suspended all operations.

'Thank you for mending Alejandro's bag,' said the white-haired lady.

'*Valentina's* bag,' corrected the dark-haired one.

His mouth opened, but no sounds came out.

'That was kind of you,' she continued.

'What did you do in Colombia when you were here?' asked the lady on the left. 'Were you—' she lifted a big pad of paper and flicked through it '—a management consultant? In an office? With paper?'

They had a file on him? A fucking *file*? And how good was Valentina's memory? He cringed at his words being flung back in his face by a little old lady on the other side of the world.

He cleared his throat. 'No, I was part of an army task force. We were seconded to the Colombian government to help fight the cartels.'

They nodded slowly.

Charlie forced a smile. 'Okay, so I should probably hang up now. Valentina will be back in a minute and she can call you herself,' he said, keen for the Colombian inquisition to be over as quickly as possible.

'No!' the ladies cried.

'We wanted to meet you,' said the white-haired lady. 'But mamita said no.'

'Si, we will be nice now,' said the dark-haired lady. 'I am Isabella and this is Ana, but you can call us Abuela y Abuelita.'

TEN MINUTES LATER, THE DOOR OPENED AND VALENTINA rushed in, out of breath. Charlie was sitting back in the chair, his feet up on the desk, the tablet on his lap, laughing at something Abuela had said.

'No! No, no, no, no, no!' Valentina gasped, snatching the tablet. 'What are you doing?'

'¡Mi muñeca, no hay problema!' cried Abuelita.

'Te llamaré luego,' replied Valentina, ending the call. She stared at Charlie, her chest heaving and fire in her eyes. 'You cannot do that. You broke my privacy.'

He held up his hands. 'They rang when I was sorting out the Wi-Fi and I accidentally answered. I told them you would be back, but they wanted to speak to me.'

Valentina hesitated. He saw her uncertainty.

She took a deep breath and squared her shoulders. 'Please leave.'

He went to the door. 'Is there anything you didn't tell them about me?'

'I don't know what you mean,' she said, tossing her hair.

'Management consultant, dragon tattoo, syphilis...'

She blushed and opened the door, pointing out into the corridor.

He paused in the doorway. 'Who's Alejandro?'

The colour drained from her face.

She pushed him into the corridor. 'Get out!' she yelled, slamming the door.

9

Charlie wasn't ready to process what had just happened, so he went to the gym. Pushing his body to its limits was familiar and therefore comfortable, despite the pain.

After an hour, when his muscles were screaming for mercy, he ran up into the hills. Rory had messaged him earlier to say he had Bandit, so Charlie was alone.

A few miles out, as the mountains rose out of the heather and the ground grew steep and rocky, he stopped. His breath puffed into the cold air and the sweat on his arms condensed into little wisps.

He thought about how he'd parted from Valentina. Who was Alejandro? A brother? A boyfriend?

Whoever he was, she was still using his rucksack, and the mention of his name was enough to trigger deep emotion. And then she'd told her grandmothers all she knew about Charlie. Did she do this with everyone she met? Was he different?

He passed a hand over his face. He still hadn't explained

himself from earlier when she'd caught him shaking his head in disgust at her costume.

Fuck!

Words were never his strong point, so he'd have to use honesty and hope she recognised it.

A breeze chilled his body and he glanced at the sky. A rolling band of clouds was coming in from the east, promising wind and rain. Time to get back.

Despite the extra exercise, by the time evening came, Charlie was fidgety and hyped. He took Bandit and patrolled the castle, checking the router and boosters were in place.

In the attic corridor, he stopped outside Vlad's room and knocked. No answer. He knocked again. Still nothing.

He gazed at Bandit. 'Shall we?'

Bandit gave a bark of approval, and Charlie opened the door with his skeleton key.

The curtains were drawn and the room was dark. It smelled like someone had eaten all the sprouts at Christmas dinner, then been locked in a room to sweat and fart it out till New Year. Bandit whined.

Charlie ruffled his fur. 'Yes, I know it's rank, but if we open a window, he'll know we've been here.'

He flicked on the light and glanced around. It was a tip. Clothes were discarded across the floor and an empty wine bottle poked out from under the bed. He began a systematic search. He'd been trained for it and knew every trick.

Ten minutes later, the room had only revealed that Vlad was an alcoholic slob who had red and black budgie smugglers for underwear, some adorned with the image of fire.

Charlie's stomach rolled. If there was any fire in Vlad's

crotch, it was most likely due to a combination of poor hygiene and venereal disease.

He moved to the bathroom and in less than a minute hit the jackpot. Taped to the inside of the cistern was a plastic bag. Bandit barked excitedly as Charlie pulled it out. Inside was another bag for extra waterproofing, containing pills and powders.

Charlie didn't bother attempting to confirm what it was. He stuffed them into the back pocket of his trousers, then dried the first bag.

Back in the bedroom, he gingerly pulled a pair of Vlad's used underwear out from under the bed. Bandit put his head to one side and whined.

'If we need to find him one day, we need a scent. Okay?'

Back in his own room, Charlie lit a fire in the grate, opened all the windows and burned Vlad's stash. It was highly likely Vlad had more drugs in the man-bag he carried with him, but he was confident the motherlode had now been destroyed.

CHARLIE HADN'T SEEN VALENTINA SINCE SHE'D THROWN HIM out of her room earlier. He lay on his bed, listening to the distant banging of doors, the whooshing of water through the old pipes as people turned in for the night. Then silence.

His body was tired, but his mind was awake, revisiting the conversation with Valentina's abuelas, imagining what their advice might be for making amends to their granddaughter.

What would they say?

He wished he could speak to them.

A NOISE WOKE HIM.

Charlie opened his eyes and checked the time: 2.00 a.m.

He listened intently. What had he heard? He sat up and swung his legs over the side of the bed. Still dressed, he put on his shoes and left, closing the door quietly behind him.

The first-floor corridors were clear, so he moved to the sprawling ground floor. At the back of the castle, he saw a sliver of light ahead, coming from the door to the kitchen of Brad's personal chef.

He knocked.

'Yes?'

Pushing the door open, he stopped in the entrance.

Valentina was standing at the stove, wearing a white towelling dressing gown, her long black hair tied in a loose braid. It dropped over one shoulder like a dark river cutting through snow. The only light came from above the hob, illuminating her softly in a room full of shadows.

Charlie knew he should make his excuses and leave, but the moment felt out of time, as if they were the only two people in existence.

'You okay?' he asked.

She shrugged. 'I couldn't sleep.'

'What are you making?'

She turned back to the stove. 'Chocolate caliente.'

Charlie rubbed his face. *Come on, use your words.*

'I want to apologise,' he began hesitantly.

She didn't respond, just continued stirring.

He cleared his throat. 'At the photoshoot. I was looking at you and shaking my head.'

'Yes, I saw. You were judging me.'

'No, no, I wasn't. I was pissed off about the costume and the knife and the throwing stars being right next to your skin. The whole set-up was dangerous. I didn't want you to get hurt.'

'Oh,' she replied softly, turning to look at him. 'They're

fine. They're made of plastic. I thought you were criticising me. For my costume. I am very sensitive about it.'

'Did you help design it?'

She snorted. 'You don't know much about Hollywood, do you?'

He shook his head.

'I have less power than the caterers. There is nothing I can do about my costume, no matter what I think about it.'

'I'm sorry.'

'So am I. But there are thousands of women who would kill for the chance to play this role. So, I wear what I'm given, no matter how much I hate it.'

'I'm sorry.'

She gave him a faint smile. 'You keep saying.'

'Sorry.'

Her smile broadened. 'You're very British.'

'Yes, and also a dickhead. So I've got a lot to be sorry for.'

She indicated the pan on the stove. 'Would you like some? I've made too much.'

'Yeah, sure, thanks.' He moved into the room, closing the door behind him. 'What is it again?'

Valentina raised an eyebrow. 'You'll drink it but you don't know what it is?'

'Story of my life...' She could have offered him a cocktail of bleach and arsenic and he'd still have drunk it.

'It's chocolate caliente, Colombian hot chocolate with cinnamon. Come see.'

He gazed over her shoulder at the swirling hot chocolate. He was so close that he could feel the heat from her, smell the scent of flowers from her hair as it mingled with the chocolate and spice. His mouth watered.

'Smells so good.'

'It's traditionally made with cheese.'

'Cheese?'

The corners of her mouth twitched. 'You put pieces of cheese in the bottom of the glass and pour the hot chocolate over. Some people love it like that, but I prefer it this way. My abuelita used to make it as a treat when I was a little girl. And Abuela made it for me all the years I was working on *La Vida Familiar.* It reminds me of home.'

His heart tugged towards her.

She stopped stirring. 'It's ready.'

He reluctantly moved away and let her pour it. She handed him a mug and they sat opposite each other at the prep table in the middle of the room.

Valentina cradled hers and brought it to her nose, a smile spreading across her face. Charlie stared, drinking her in. Her soft amber skin, her deep liquid eyes, the fluttering of her long lashes.

'Why couldn't you sleep?' he asked.

She took a sip, then put it down and looked away. 'I'm not used to having so much time on my hands. It's strange.'

'What do you mean?'

Her gaze came back to the mug. 'I'm always working. Filming, publicity, meetings, auditions. It's constant. But here, now?' She drummed her fingers on the metal surface of the table. 'I'm in so few scenes, it's crazy. They should have flown me in right at the end for two days.'

'So why don't you kick back and chill out? Have a holiday?'

She stared at him as if he'd suggested she start eating babies. 'I can't. I have too much to do. Too many emails. I can never keep up.'

'Don't you have a PA, like Shauna?'

She shook her head.

'What about your manager?'

'I don't have one.'

'But who organises your schedule, your staff?'

'I do. I don't have any staff.'

She sounded tired. He desperately wanted to cradle her in his arms, to ask why she didn't have anyone to help her, but knew it all must be for the same reason she dressed down and all her stuff was knackered.

She sipped the hot chocolate as if trying to find solace in it.

Charlie lowered his mug to the table. 'So, if you can almost do it all when you're busy, surely now you've got time to do it *and* have a break?'

She shrugged. 'I've been on this treadmill since I was a kid. I don't know how to get off.'

'But you didn't work all the time when you were growing up. You still had holidays?' he persisted.

Valentina stared off into the darkest corner of the room, her eyes unfocused. 'The show aired five times a week, fifty-two weeks a year, and my character was popular. When I finally left, I went straight to a film set. I had time off here and there, but I was also trying to do schoolwork, so it wasn't a normal childhood.' Her voice was lifeless.

Charlie tried to compare his teenage years to hers. 'So, you never got drunk with your mates and threw up over your dad while he was reading you the riot act? Never streaked through the centre of town on New Year's Eve for a bet? Never gave yourself a tattoo?'

Valentina shook her head, the corners of her mouth turning up.

He wanted to make her laugh. 'You never had wild monkey sex on top of a bus shelter and got arrested for public indecency?'

Her eyes widened and she shook her head again.

'You never made hash brownies and accidentally fed them to your mother?'

She clapped her hands over her mouth to stop a shocked laugh from escaping and shook her head vigorously.

Charlie leaned back in his chair and put his hands behind his head. 'Well then,' he said, puffing out his cheeks. 'You've never lived.'

'Did you really do all that? How old were you?' she asked, leaning forwards.

'Oh, it wasn't me,' he replied, attempting to look serious. 'It was a friend of mine... *Charlotte*. "Charlotte Homiltan". She was a very bad girl. She did all of that before she was eighteen.'

Valentina laughed. 'Then what happened to her?'

'Her parents shipped her off to the army and she's been a model citizen ever since.'

'No more tattoos? No more streaking? No more wild monkey... business?'

He held her gaze as energy crackled between them. 'It's the army. Tattoos and streaking are part and parcel of life. As for the wild monkey sex? I don't think anything has beaten the top of the bus shelter.'

She blushed. 'It sounds uncomfortable and embarrassing.'

'Those words pretty much sum up being a teenager,' he replied with a grin. 'On your days off, I think you should channel Charlotte. Have your teenage years in your twenties.'

A shadow passed over her face and she shook her head. 'That chance passed long ago.' She glanced at her watch and stood. 'I need to get back to bed. It's so late.'

He took her mug. 'You go on, I'll wash these up.'

She stifled a yawn. 'You sure?'

He nodded and took the mugs to the sink. 'Yep, go get your beauty sleep. Not that you need it.'

She smiled shyly and opened the door, turning her head as she passed through. 'Goodnight, *Charlotte*,' she said with a mischievous grin. 'I hope you have wild monkey sex again one day.'

She closed the door and he heard her feet pitter-pattering along the corridor as she ran away. Charlie leaned against the sink and groaned. Valentina Valverde was going to be the death of him.

10

After a few fitful hours of sleep, Charlie knocked on Valentina's door, Bandit by his side for emotional support. She opened it and stood in the doorway.

'What are you hiding behind your back?' she asked as she stroked Bandit.

His neck pricked with heat. 'A present. May we come in?'

Her eyes narrowed, but there was a sparkle of interest in them. 'Be my guest. Did you bring Bandit with you to soften me up?'

The heat spread to his cheeks. 'Maybe. You're very intimidating.'

'Ha! Says the enormous man with all the muscles.'

'Do you want to see them?' He flexed an arm.

She pushed it down, her cheeks flushing. 'Put the guns away. I want my present.'

Taking a large glass jar from behind his back, he presented it to her.

'Pickled gherkins?'

'Oh no, sorry.' He turned it so she could see the label he'd stuck on.

'"Teenage kicks"?' Her brow furrowed. 'What is this?'

He unscrewed the lid. 'Look inside. I thought you needed some ideas of what to do with your time off. You can pick one and then do it.'

She raised an eyebrow, already appearing unconvinced.

'Or not,' he said hurriedly. 'And I thought I could help you out. I'm extremely well-qualified.'

She arched an eyebrow and the god of lust kneed him in the groin. 'Well-qualified at being a drunken idiot?'

He nodded. 'Definitely. I undertook years of specialist training. I'm a Jedi Juvenile Master.'

'And I'm your Padawan?'

'Yes. And when your training is complete, you can be my master and teach me how to become a mature, responsible adult.'

'And how long do I have for that? It could take years.'

He bowed. 'I will put myself in your hands for a lifetime.'

There was a sudden silence as they stared at each other.

She pulled the jar from him and sat on the floor by the fire. Bandit settled next to her.

'Come on then,' she said, beckoning him forward. 'Let's see what amazing ideas you have for regressing me.'

Charlie sat facing her, unable to stop himself staring. Valentina was so beautiful. Her hair was pulled over one shoulder, leaving one side of her neck exposed. He wanted to press his lips to it, feel her heartbeat change, kiss along her jaw, hear her—

'What is it? Have I got something on me?' She was frowning and rubbing her neck.

'No, there's nothing, sorry.' *Get it together, dickhead!*

She reached into the jar. 'Okay then, here we go.'

He'd written all his ideas on A4 paper, then folded them up. They'd only filled the bottom centimetre of the jar, so he'd added more.

His stomach flip-flopped as her hand rummaged around and he prayed she didn't pick the worst ones first. She pulled one out and opened it, an excited smile on her face. Charlie held his breath.

'Write bad poetry.'

He relaxed. They were off to a safe start.

She looked confused. 'Bad poetry?'

'Yes. All teenagers think they're tormented literary geniuses experiencing depths of human emotion never felt before or since. Your job is to write the very worst love poem ever.'

Smiling, she put it to one side. 'Okay, that one can stay.' She pulled out another and unfolded it. 'Steal something? No. I am a good Catholic girl.' She threw the piece of paper into the fire and took another out. 'Play strip poker.' She glanced up. 'And who am I meant to play it with? You?'

He held out his hands. 'Whatever the sacrifice, I'm here to help.'

She gave him a dark look and consigned the idea to the fire.

He swallowed, remembering everything else he'd had the balls to write at two in the morning. This was not going to end well.

She unfolded another. 'Go on a pub crawl. Okay, yes, that we can do.'

Charlie gave himself an invisible high five.

'Take drugs? No, no, no.' She threw the suggestion into the fire. 'Streak through the castle? Me? Are you crazy?'

'This is what teenagers do,' he argued. 'It's meant to be stupid and crazy.'

Valentina tore it up theatrically and chucked the pieces in the fire.

'Oh, come on now,' he protested. 'At this rate, all you'll be left with is drunken poetry.'

She fixed him with a stare. 'How many of these involve my clothes coming off, Charlie?'

He swallowed. 'Er, the teenage years are about your changing body and, er, exploring your sexuality,' he mumbled.

'Is "wild monkey sex" in here?' she asked suspiciously.

He nodded. When he'd run out of ideas, he'd put "wild monkey sex" in another ten times.

She sighed. 'At least you didn't specify who the wild monkey sex had to be with.' She selected another piece of paper. 'Have sex with Charlie Hamilton?' she squeaked, her face flushing.

'You never know, you might enjoy it?' he asked hopefully. Her hand moved slowly towards the fire. 'Couldn't you have a "maybe" pile? A grey area you don't have to make a decision about yet?'

Her pupils dilated. She dropped the paper to the floor. His heart gave a jump of joy. She hadn't completely shut the door on him.

She picked out another. 'Go skinny-dipping. Where?'

'In the loch.'

'But it's freezing! Anyone could see!'

'We could go at night.'

'*We?*'

'I won't look. Scout's honour.'

She rolled her eyes but dropped the suggestion onto the newly created 'maybe' pile.

'Eat something strange, or something for the first time. Okay, I can do that. Next. *Blow something up?* Are you serious?'

'It's fun. And I'm a professional,' he said proudly.

She arched an eyebrow, dropped it onto the 'maybe' pile and picked another. 'Have wild monkey sex. Okay, I will allow that to be a "maybe".' She pulled another from the jar. 'Have wild monkey sex? We've just had that one.'

'Aha. But after experiencing it once, you'll definitely want to do it again.'

'Humph,' she said, dropping it. She took another, then immediately threw it into the flames.

'Stop! What did that one say?'

After another couple ended up in the fire, Valentina sighed dramatically.

'How many times have you written "have wild monkey sex", Charlie?'

He knew when he was rumbled. 'A few,' he admitted.

She took a big breath, then let it out in a rush. 'Okay, just so I know what I'm dealing with.'

Pulling out a few more, she consigned them to fiery deaths as Charlie winced with each ball of flame as if she were kicking him in the nuts.

'Stay up all night and watch the sunrise.' She smiled, and his chest filled with light. 'I like that one, and I've never done it before. That can go on the "yes" pile. Get a tattoo? Abuelita would go crazy.' She held the piece of paper towards the fire, then gazed at the ink spiralling down his arms. 'I suppose it could be a small one, where no one could see.'

She dropped the suggestion onto the 'maybe' pile. 'Graffiti something.' She paused. 'That could also be small, where no one could see.'

Charlie rolled his eyes.

She ignored him and turned the pickle jar upside down, the last few ideas falling into her lap. 'Play truth or dare. Okay, I will allow that to be a maybe. Have wild—' She tossed the piece of paper into the fire. 'Play spin the bottle. With how many people?'

'Four.'

Her eyes were saucers. 'Who did you have in mind?'

He ticked off on his fingers slowly. 'You, me... *Charlotte*, and Bandit.' He grinned at her and she laughed.

'Okay, *Charlotte and Charlie...* that can be a maybe.' She opened the final few and tossed them all onto the fire. He pretended not to notice and picked up the 'yes' pile.

Charlie cleared his throat. 'So, drumroll please...'

Valentina drummed her hands on the floor.

'In the "yes" corner we have... write bad poetry, go on a pub crawl, eat something strange or something for the first time, and stay up all night and watch the sunrise.' He sighed. 'Is that all you chose?' He reached over to snatch the pile of maybes before she changed her mind about any of them. 'And in the "*definitely* maybe" corner, we have... HAVE SEX WITH CHARLIE HAMILTON!'

She rolled her eyes and he laughed.

'Okay,' he continued. 'I'll be serious. Ahem. Go skinny-dipping, blow something up, have wild monkey sex, have wild monkey sex many, *many* more times—'

'Hey! It did *not* say that.'

'Get a tattoo, graffiti something, play truth or dare, and last but not least, play spin the bottle.'

'So,' she began. 'One list is about poetry, wine, food and watching the sunrise. The other is about blowing things up, defacing property, getting naked in public, having a tattoo, having lots of sex, and playing games with the intention of having more sex.'

Charlie couldn't help laughing out loud.

'Yep.' He grinned. 'That just about sums it up. When do you want to start?'

11

Valentina paused at the edge of the precipice, her heart thumping. Was she really going to take this leap?

'Er... maybe tomorrow? I can't do anything today. I have filming,' she stalled.

Charlie leaned back, resting his hands on the floor behind him.

'Are you sure?' he asked with a smile that ignited her underwear.

She recrossed her legs in an attempt to alleviate the burn. It didn't help. He was the killer combination of hot *and* charming.

'I don't think you've got any filming planned until tomorrow.'

She stood and went to the desk. 'I have things to do. Email, exercise, you know.'

Valentina wanted to speak to her sister, her mamá, her abuelas. Speak to someone who might help her decide if she was crazy to even consider his suggestions. She glanced at her watch.

'It's four thirty in the morning in Colombia,' he said, casually. 'What time does your family usually wake up?'

She gritted her teeth. How could someone so gorgeous be so perceptive? It was like he could read her mind.

Valentina stared out the window at the low grey clouds shrouding the hills in the distance. 'You are an insufferable man, Charlie,' she said, her fingers drumming on the leather inlay. He laughed, and she tried not to smile.

'So I've been told. Give it a couple of days and you'll be calling me far worse.'

She heard him stand. A wave of goosebumps fluttered across her skin.

'You can't be a teenager if you ask your family for permission before you do anything,' he said, opening the door.

She stalked back to face him. 'Huevón!'

He laughed and she tried not to laugh with him. 'See, I've gone from insufferable to dickhead in less than a minute. Soon you'll be calling me setenta hijueputa, seventy times a son of a bitch.'

'How do you know those words?'

'I told you, I've been to Colombia, so I had to learn the basics. You know, ordering a beer, throwing my mates under the bus.'

'You threw your friends under a bus?'

'Not literally. It's a phrase. You know, slagging them off, dissing them.'

She crossed her arms, digging her fingernails into her skin to offset the excitement fizzing through her. 'Well, Charlie. I am not ready now. But when I am, I will let you know.'

'Okay. Why don't I give you my number? Then you can message me when you're ready.'

She squeezed her lips together and he stepped into the corridor.

'Or you could put a note under my door?' he said over his shoulder. 'It's the last room on the right before the stairs to the attic.'

Bandit was still inside her room, seemingly in no hurry to leave.

'You too,' she said, pointing to the door.

Bandit ambled slowly out, standing beside Charlie and barking. Valentina took one last look at Charlie's sparkling green eyes, then closed the door and threw herself onto the bed, huffing into the pillows.

Charlie Hamilton.

Valentina had met hundreds of gorgeous men in her life, but none of them had affected her the way Charlie had. The men she came into contact with were attractive on the outside and vacuous on the inside. Tanned skin, veneered white teeth, glossy hair, manicured nails, toned and hairless bodies.

They were the ubiquitous Ken dolls of Hollywood and utterly unappealing to her. She'd acted with them, posed on the red carpet holding their hands, done press junkets claiming they were her new best friends, but it was controlled and contrived. Just another act. None of it was real.

Charlie was *so* real, he was his own law of physics, inexorably drawing her into his orbit. She was spun off her feet, turned inside out, thrown into disarray.

He was too alive. Too much.

She closed her eyes and pictured his. They were like sunshine through leaves. An ever-changing, swirling kaleidoscope of greens and golds. His jaw was strong with a faint shadow of stubble.

His chestnut hair was short and thick, almost a buzz cut, and looked soft as silk. She wanted to feel its velvet softness under her fingers, his stubble against her cheek, his full, firm lips on hers, his hot tongue slipping inside her mouth.

And as for the rest of him...

She moaned, rolling onto her back. Stroking her breasts, her nipples hardened. Her hips bucked of their own accord as she remembered his pull-ups in the gym. His naked back, his shoulders, his arms. His muscles would have made Michelangelo weep.

Valentina wanted to trace every line, every tattoo with her fingers, her tongue. Lower and lower as she followed the dragon south. She let out a cry of frustration. She had no control around him. Opening her eyes, she stared at the bed canopy. *Focus!*

She had goals, a plan. If the cosmetics contract finally came through, she'd have enough money to make *it* happen. Her foot had been pressed to the floor since she was a little girl and she was almost there.

But now, stuck in the Highlands of Scotland with nothing to do for the first time in twenty years, she felt rudderless. Could she take a holiday from her life? Allow herself to go a little crazy for a couple of weeks? Maybe even have a fling?

She swallowed a lump of loneliness in her throat. It had been so long since she'd been intimate with a man. Her bedroom experience was pathetic. An immature fumbling disaster with one of her co-stars on *La Vida Familiar,* then the flash and burn betrayal of stuntman Bryce. The longest sexual relationship she'd ever had was with her vibrator.

Valentina curled on her side into a ball. Charlie was so confident, so good-looking, so experienced. She was an amateur; she would only disappoint him.

She reached for her phone. Her younger sister, Isabella, would still be asleep, but she could send her a message. She sent a series of selfies pulling the worst faces she could. This was their private joke, Valentina seeing how against-type she could be.

Being beautiful was her job. It didn't feel real and it didn't make her happy. Making her sister laugh *was* real and *did* make her happy. It helped ease the pain of being away from her for so long.

Four photos in and Isabella rang.

Valentina winced at the screen. 'Did I wake you? Sorry, chica.'

'Oh no, I've been awake for hours,' her sister replied, pulling the phone back to show her sitting on a sofa. 'This baby...'

'He's getting you in training for when he's born. How are you feeling?'

'Like a cow. A big fat cow.' Isabella puffed out her cheeks and put the phone below her belly so it filled the screen. 'I hate being pregnant. I can't put my shoes on. I can't drive because I can't reach the pedals. I need to pee, like, all the time. And Matias is driving me crazy.'

Valentina smiled. Her brother-in-law was one of the sweetest men she knew. 'What's he done wrong now?'

Isabella frowned. 'He eats too loudly and sleeps too well.'

'Has he started snoring?'

'No. He just lies there. Asleep. While I'm awake. I want to kill him.'

Valentina laughed. 'Baby girl, you cannot kill your husband. He's one of the good ones.'

'I know. I just want this over. I want to meet our baby.'

'It's only a few more weeks. It won't be long.'

They gazed at each other. Valentina's heart tugged. Neither of them wanted to talk about the bigger issue.

Isabella wanted her there for the birth, but she was contracted for another film straight off the back of shooting

Braveheart 2. It was such a painful subject it couldn't be mentioned.

Her sister broke the silence. 'Anyway, this is boring. I want to talk about Charlie. Oh. My. God. He is so hot.'

'What?' she spluttered. 'How do you know?'

'So you *do* think he's hot.' Isabella looked smug. 'I knew it.'

'Wait, you've seen a picture of him? How? There are no photos anywhere on the internet.' Valentina groaned and pulled a pillow over her face as her sister shrieked with laughter. She'd walked straight into that one.

'Abuela took screenshots during their call and sent them to me and Mamá. Did you know they got him to do a "gun show"? His biceps are the size of my head.'

Valentina dropped the pillow in horror and stared at her sister. 'No, no, no, no, noooo!' This was mortifying.

'Big sister, you deserve this. You need to ride that man like the stallion he is.'

'Isabella!' she gasped. 'I can't believe you said that. If Abuelita heard you—'

'She'd agree with me. Honestly, sometimes you're such a prude. You're not still thinking about that Bryce asshole, are you?'

She shook her head. 'But I can't just sleep with Charlie.'

'Why not? If I wasn't the size of a house and married to Matias, I'd be all over him in a heartbeat.'

'Isabella! But I won't see him again after this.'

'Exactly. It's perfect. Think of it as a holiday fling.'

'But—'

'Ugh. Are you sure you're my big sister and not my little one? You've had more fake sex in front of the camera than real sex behind it.'

Valentina raised her eyebrows. 'Am I allowed any secrets?'

'No. You need to tell me everything. I'm a heavily pregnant

woman who can't move. You're my sole source of entertainment. Now, tell me, when are you seeing him again?'

HALF AN HOUR LATER, VALENTINA GOT OFF THE CALL AND turned her phone off completely. Isabella had been beside herself with excitement at Charlie's idea and Valentina knew she only had an hour or so before the news reached her mother and grandmothers.

She left her room and went the short distance down the corridor to the last door before the attic stairs. Her heart was hammering up into her throat as she tentatively knocked.

Charlie opened the door, and his smile made her heart ricochet inside her. He waited for her to speak.

She swallowed. 'I need a new suitcase,' she began. There was a flicker of surprise in his eyes, but his smile didn't waver. 'And I don't know where to get one.'

'Two seconds,' he said before disappearing into the room. He emerged with Bandit and his jacket in his hand. 'I'll drive you to Inverness. Kinloch's too small.'

They walked down the corridor, Valentina's fingers curling into Bandit's fur.

'Do you have a car?' she asked.

He smiled and she imagined a flash of light on his perfect teeth like a toothpaste commercial. He was ridiculously good-looking.

'For you,' he replied, 'I'm going all-in.'

12

'Oh no. No, no, no, no, no.' Valentina crossed her arms. She was standing outside the front of the castle, Bandit at her side, staring at Charlie as he parked in front of her.

He leaned out the driver's window, a shit-eating grin on his face.

She shook her head. 'A Rolls-Royce?'

'Do you want me to dress up as a chauffeur? I look really good in uniform.' He wiggled his eyebrows. Bandit barked in agreement.

'Could this be any more—' She uncrossed her arms, describing larger and larger circles with her hands.

'Cool?'

'Obvious. Ostentatious. Over the top,' she replied, her hands coming to rest on her hips.

Charlie stroked his chin, his brow furrowing as if lost in thought. 'All I heard there was oh, oh, ohhh. And that sounded good to me.'

Her insides combusted. 'You are an obstinate, overgrown, oaf!'

He held her gaze. 'Oh, oh, ohhh,' he replied with a devilish smile.

There was a pause as energy hummed between them, then Valentina gave up and laughed. 'You are impossible. Now please tell me why this is the only option?'

'Rory's grandfather bought it back in the fifties. Rory refuses to use it—he says only dickheads drive them, and his mum thinks it's too big. Someone needs to keep it ticking over.'

'But won't everyone stare?'

'I'll park at the back of the Tesco car park and we can walk from there. It's massive and half empty at the best of times. No one will notice, I promise.'

He got out and went around to the passenger side, opening the door for her. Valentina's cheeks heated as she passed him and sank into the cream leather seat.

'I'm just going to drop Bandit back with Rory. Back in a bit.'

She nodded and he strode off, whistling for Bandit to follow.

Valentina let out a sigh. The car was almost as big as her apartment in LA. She ran her fingers over the polished walnut dashboard and took photos to send to Isabella later.

Before she knew it, Charlie was back and they eased out of the courtyard. She wrung her hands and winced as he drove through the narrow streets of Kinloch, convinced he was about to scrape the car into another or bash into a building.

'Have a little faith. It's not my first time,' he said with a smile.

She sat on her hands and stared straight ahead.

'I've driven tanks through streets narrower than these.'

'And did the streets survive?'

'Most of the time. There was one incident involving a wall, but no one was hurt.'

She gave a harrumph in return and tried to relax. The car was luxurious, but she felt like an undersized doll inside it. Stretching out her legs, they didn't even reach the end of the footwell.

As Charlie drove, she sneaked glances at him. He fitted in perfectly. He had the same size, looks and attitude as the car. He'd thrown his jacket on the back seat and was only wearing a T-shirt.

Her mouth watered as she took in his arms—the corded muscles moving under the skin, the swirls of tattoos snaking up his biceps. She could see a pulse in his neck. She counted his heartbeats, feeling them deep inside her.

He was too hot, and now so was she. She'd dressed for Scottish weather, with a bobble hat and a big scarf. Now she couldn't breathe. She ripped off her hat, unwound her scarf and ran her fingers through her hair.

'So, tell me about Inverness,' she said wanting to take her mind off him.

He cleared his throat. 'A few nice old buildings and all the shops you need. It's not London or LA, but we'll definitely get you a new bag.'

'Are there any thrift stores?'

'Huh? Charity shops? Yeah, sure.'

Valentina didn't want him asking why. She didn't want to get into a long and personal explanation. It was her business. Nothing to do with him. All her past rushed up uncomfortably inside her. She didn't want to think about it, or her life outside of this moment, so stared ahead at the road.

Focus on the now. Everything else can wait.

'Do you want to listen to the radio?' he asked.

'I don't mind.'

He flicked a switch and the car filled with classical music. 'Want me to change the station?'

She shook her head. 'I love it.' The lyrical sounds of a piano danced around them, and Valentina closed her eyes. It took her back to a tiny dressing room as a teenager.

'Clair de Lune,' she said. 'Abuela used to play me classical music and make me learn the composers. There was never time to learn an instrument, so this was second best.'

'You like Debussy?'

She glanced at him. 'Do you?'

His eyes looked different. The flecks of gold seemed brighter.

'It's okay. I'm more of a Russian romanticist myself. Rachmaninoff, Prokofiev. That or early twentieth-century English composers; Vaughan Williams, Elgar, Holst.'

Valentina shifted in her seat to face him. 'Are you making fun of me?'

'You're the mind reader. What do you think?'

She frowned. She'd never met anyone like him before. He could be so cocky, so sure of himself. But those moments were outnumbered by the times when he didn't seem quite so self-possessed.

'You play the piano?' she asked.

He nodded.

'Are you any good?'

He shrugged.

'Why did you learn?'

'I fancied the piano teacher.'

Valentina giggled. 'Oh, Charlie. Did she fancy you back?'

He shrugged again but it was tight and forced.

She felt the tension running through him. 'Is there a piano in the castle? I'd love to hear you play.'

He nodded. 'But it's out of tune. It hasn't been played in a long time.'

His hands were tight on the steering wheel, so she gave him the space he seemed to want and stared out of the passenger window at the roadside heather and grasses flying by. There was silence for the rest of the journey until he pulled to a stop at the end of a large car park.

He turned to her with a smile. 'We're here. Ready to hit downtown Inverness?'

THEY STROLLED SLOWLY DOWN THE HIGH STREET DRAWING second glances and stares. But they weren't for Valentina. Her hat was pulled low and her scarf pulled high. She knew from experience she wouldn't be recognised.

The appreciation was all for Charlie, yet he appeared completely oblivious to all the attention. Every time she turned to look at him, he was looking at her. It was electrifying.

Despite having a job that required her to be the centre of attention, she'd never before felt so seen. It was as if Charlie saw her as a person *and* a woman. As if he could see through all the layers of her being, right down to her core.

She paused outside the windows of every shop, using the time to calm the butterflies in her stomach.

'There's a shop over the road that sells suitcases and bags if you want to start there?'

An ancient and familiar knot formed in her stomach. 'Can we try the thrift stores first?'

She glanced at his face. There was barely a whisper of a change of expression. He hid his thoughts well.

'Sure. There's a big one coming up in a bit. It sells the usual second-hand stuff but also work by local artists. It's really cool.'

He led her to a double shop front. The windows were filled with rugs, scatter cushions, teddy bears, glass, china, books, and toys.

She raised her eyebrows. 'Wow. There's a lot going on here.'

'Go in, knock yourself out.'

'You're not coming?'

'I'll be back in a bit. I just need to pick up a couple of other things. I won't be long. You okay for five minutes?'

Valentina nodded. She'd quickly become used to having him next to her. The thought of him being absent, even for a moment or two, was strange, as if she'd lost her anchor.

She gave herself an internal slap.

'Yes, of course.'

The shop was an Aladdin's cave of treasures set over two floors. Rather than a big open space, there were a myriad of small rooms, some only big enough to fit one person, with bookcases from floor to ceiling and stools provided for smaller people to stand on.

Valentina found a suitcase and left it by the till to pay for later. She then took her time, first looking at the clothes, then moving on to the crafts.

A pile of sheepskin rugs on a table in rich browns and pale creams drew her attention. They were so beautiful. She ran her fingers over the soft fleece.

Inside her raged the usual war. The war she always won but with no pleasure. She could hear her family telling her to buy them. Telling her she could afford them, how she needed to treat herself. But this wasn't a suitcase. It was a luxury. A want, not a need. And every cent mattered for *the plan*.

She glanced at the price tag, then dropped it and turned away. Straight into a wall of heat and muscle.

'You should get one,' Charlie said. 'The cream would work well in your living room.'

'What?'

He stepped back, holding up his hands. 'I didn't know who you were at the airport, so I googled you. I read an interview, and there were photos in your Malibu mansion, er... house, and your living room is all cream and... I'm sorry.'

'So, you know everything about me now?'

He shook his head. 'No, no, of course not. I stopped looking after that. It wasn't right. I'm sorry.'

'That wasn't my house,' she whispered fiercely. 'It was borrowed for the shoot. I rent an apartment smaller than this shop. Happy now?'

She saw the confusion on his face and the hurt. *Fuck.*

She sighed. 'I'm sorry. That was unnecessary and rude.'

The green of his eyes seemed muted, darker.

'There are some things I am not comfortable talking about,' she continued. A wave of suppressed emotion moved through her and she gritted her teeth. She would not let it out.

He smiled as if to put her at ease. 'No worries. I now know the subject of your living room is completely off limits.' He put his hands behind the back of his neck and puffed out his chest. 'However, where do you stand on discussing your bedroom?' he asked innocently.

Her stress dissolved and she giggled, pushing on his chest. 'Have I told you lately how insufferable you are?'

His chest was hot, and she could feel the fast thudding of his heart. She didn't want to stop touching him.

'I think you need to remind me at least once every hour,' he replied softly.

Heat rushed down Valentina's arms into her body. The noises from the shop faded away, replaced by a roaring in her ears. She was lost in space, spiralling around a nebula of green and gold, being pulled faster and faster towards the centre.

Wrenching her hands away, she went to a display by the window, breathing heavily, trying to centre herself. In front of her was a child's mobile. Fluffy clouds and sheep made from wool hung in the air.

She didn't look at the price. This would be for Isabella's baby. It was a gift for her family, not for her, so it didn't count. She took one that was already boxed up and went to pay.

Charlie hung back and met her at the door. 'You hungry?'

'Um, I don't know. What time is it?'

'Lunchtime. I thought you might like to cross something off your list.'

Her cheeks burned. 'What?'

He grinned. 'Not one of the ones involving,' he looked around furtively, *'nakedness,'* he whispered.

Her face was on fire. 'Huevón!' she whispered back.

He burst out laughing as she strode out onto the cold street. He caught up to her and took the suitcase from her.

'Have you ever had fish and chips?'

'Yes, in LA.'

His face fell. 'But have you ever had a deep-fried Mars bar?'

'A fried candy bar?'

He nodded.

'Is that a thing?'

'It's a very rare Scottish speciality.'

'You're making it up.'

He grinned. 'Follow me.'

He led her to a small chip shop. Inside, she saw the menu written on a big board behind the counter. At the very bottom, written in pen, were the words: 'Today Only! Deep-Fried Mars Bar – £5'

'Five pounds?' she hissed at him.

'My treat. Fish and chips to start?'

She wavered, then pulled her purse out of her pocket. 'I want to pay.'

He shook his head. 'No way. My idea, my treat.'

Charlie turned to the counter where a skinny teenager with bright-red spots and even brighter red hair was staring at Valentina, his Adam's apple bobbing erratically.

'*Ahem,*' Charlie began.

The boy dragged his eyes to him.

'I would like two large fish and chips—'

She elbowed him. 'Small please,' she whispered.

'One large and one small fish and chips,' he continued. 'And a deep-fried Mars bar.'

'We don't sell them.'

Charlie stared at him intently. 'Yes, you *do*,' he said, emphatically. 'Remember?' His eyes flicked to the menu. 'Just for today? And they've been so popular you only have one left?'

Valentina stifled a giggle as realisation fell onto the boy's face.

'Oh, aye. Just for today.' He glanced at her and drew himself up. 'It's a very rare Scottish speciality,' he said firmly.

She managed to keep a straight face. 'Then I can't wait to try it.'

The boy dropped the tongs he was holding and his mouth fell open. 'It *is* you. You're Valentina Valverde,' he stammered.

Her body stiffened.

'No, she's not,' Charlie replied. 'Her name's Deirdre and she's from Falkirk.'

She elbowed him and gave a dazzling smile to the boy, whose face was now redder than his hair.

'Yes, I am. Would you like a selfie after you've cooked our lunch?'

He nodded so hard she wondered if his head might fall off.

'Aye, that would be braw.'

He turned to the counter and pulled out a Mars bar, taking the wrapper off and dipping it in batter. As he worked, he kept glancing up at her and muttering 'I cannae believe it!'.

'How come you never smile at me like that?' Charlie grumbled as they sat down to wait.

'You're special.'

'Good special or bad special?'

She paused. '*Special* special. You're in a category all your own.'

The smell of fried food filled the air as they watched their lunch being cooked. 'I was thinking we could do a pub crawl tonight,' he said.

She sat up straighter. 'Tonight? With you?'

'Yeah, unless you've got anything else you want to try? Skinny-dipping? Spin the bottle?'

'No! A pub crawl? Like one drink in every pub?'

'Yep, that's the general idea.'

'Okay.'

His smile made her tummy hiccup.

'Alright then. It's a date,' he said.

'It's not a date,' she replied hurriedly.

'Oh no. It's not a date,' he agreed, his eyes alight. 'It's *definitely* not a date.'

13

'You're going on a date with him!' Isabella squealed through the screen.

'You must wear a dress, my baby,' said Abuelita.

'And make-up. You have to wear make-up, sweet girl,' added Abuela, shoving Abuelita out of the way.

'It is not a date!' Valentina cried in frustration.

'It *is* a date,' came another voice from off-screen. 'Don't forget to brush your teeth between drinks. And don't eat spinach.'

'Mamá? You're there too?' Valentina sat on the edge of her bed with a thump. 'Does everyone know about him?'

Her mother's face appeared on screen. 'Baby girl, we only want you to be happy. Charlie seems kind. And if your grandmothers approve, then so do I. When was the last time you had some fun, eh?'

She saw the concern etched on her mother's face and bit her bottom lip, feeling an upswell of emotion. She missed them all so much. She dropped her chin and squeezed her eyes tightly as a tear slipped out.

'Hey, don't cry, my little girl,' said her mother softly.

'No, no, no! Don't cry! It will make your face all puffy,' Abuela called out. 'Go get a cucumber. Put slices on your eyes. Quick, quick!'

Abuelita appeared. 'And an avocado. Mash it up and put it on your face. For at least ten minutes.'

'And then eat them,' added Isabella, behind them. 'Don't go out on an empty stomach.'

Two hours later, Valentina was pacing nervously in front of the fire, her hands smoothing over her dress. She had only packed one, a simple black bodycon number she'd bought at Target on sale. She didn't own many, usually borrowing them from designers before awards ceremonies. Ceremonies where she never got nominated.

She'd only ever been nominated for one award: a Razzie, for worst supporting actress. Thankfully, she didn't win, but it was a humiliation right at the start of her Hollywood career and confirmation of all her fears.

Don't go there. She would not let her past ruin this evening.

There was a knock at the door and her breath quickened. He was here. They were going out. Together. At night. To drink alcohol.

A nervous laugh burst out. She took a long, slow breath in, counted to ten, put her jacket over her shoulders, and opened the door.

'Valentina,' oozed Vlad, his eyes flicking up and down her body like a lizard's tongue. Bile rose into her throat. 'You're looking extremely...' His mouth opened slowly in an approximation of a smile, his thin lips stretching over his yellow teeth '...succulent this evening.'

She zipped up her jacket and crossed her arms in front of her chest.

'Can I help you?'

Vlad glanced over her shoulder. 'Why don't we go inside and discuss this in more comfort.'

She pulled the door half closed. 'I'm about to leave. What do you want?'

Vlad inclined his head and gave a little huff, as if laughing at his own joke. 'I wanted to discuss the earth meal I am planning with Kirsten. I'd like you to play a bigger part.'

Valentina gritted her teeth. Her co-star, Kirsten, was a nightmare of a narcissist. She was organising a meal for the most important people of the shoot, the menu based on whatever fad diet she was currently championing. Valentina wished she had a way to get out of it without offending Brad.

Vlad's face filled the gap between the door and frame. 'The spirits tell me your primaeval essence is needed.'

'Really? According to you, the "spirits" said I spent my past lives as slaves and prostitutes.'

His eyes gleamed and he swallowed. 'Indeed. We need this sensual energy to ground the spiritual aspects of the meal. Your yang to our yin.'

He suddenly disappeared from view.

She opened the door wider to see Charlie standing behind Vlad, pulling his arm up behind his back.

'Hey, Valentina,' Charlie said. 'I found this outside your door. Is it bothering you?'

'He was just leaving,' she replied, her voice wobbling.

Charlie's face hardened and he spun Vlad around. He whispered something in his ear, then released his arm.

'Off you fuck,' he said in a voice laced with steel.

Vlad turned to look back at her, but she ducked inside the room and sat on the end of the bed, breathing heavily.

A few seconds later, Charlie poked his head around the door. 'You okay?'

She started shaking.

He rushed in and knelt in front of her, holding her hands. 'Hey, hey, it's okay love, he's gone,' he said softly, kneading her palms with the pads of his thumbs.

'Malparido, hijo de puta, gonorrea, huevón!' she hissed, her body shuddering.

Charlie bracketed her legs with his forearms, holding her tightly. 'You can't call him huevón, sweetheart. You're only allowed to call one man a dickhead, and that's me.'

She let out a short laugh. 'I hate him. I want to kill him.'

He squeezed her hands. 'That's my job. You can't have all the fun.'

There was a pause.

'Do you want to talk about it?'

She shook her head as she welled up.

He frowned. 'Has he ever…?'

She shook her head more violently and tears ran down her cheeks.

'Do you want him to die slowly and painfully or very slowly and extremely painfully?'

Valentina smiled and sniffed. 'I'm sorry, Charlie. I was so looking forward to tonight, but I think I should just go to bed. I've got filming in the morning anyway.'

He released her hands and dug in his pocket for a folded handkerchief. She took it and dabbed at her eyes.

'If you stay in, he'll have won. You can't let that malparido ruin your evening. Your call time isn't until ten tomorrow. What would your abuelas say?'

She sighed. 'You're right.' She smiled shyly at him, the handkerchief twisting in her hands. 'As long as you don't mind me looking a bit…'

'A bit what?'

She shrugged and glanced away, allowing her hair to fall in front of her face.

'Valentina.' Charlie brushed the hair back and tucked it behind her ear. 'Look at me.'

She shook her head.

'You're beautiful. Inside and out. You couldn't look bad if you tried.' He stood. 'Now, unless you want to skip pub crawls, sunrises, and poetry, and head straight for wild monkey sex with Charlie Hamilton, I suggest we vacate your room immediately and head to The King's Arms. Where I intend to introduce you to my friends, Mr Buckfast and Ms Midori.'

He went to the door and held it open for her. 'Shall we?'

'So, let me get this straight,' said Valentina, half an hour later as they sat in a secluded corner of The King's Arms. 'Kinloch only has one pub.'

Charlie nodded. 'Yup. And the locals are under strict orders to leave us alone.'

'So, this pub crawl is more of a pub... sit?'

'I can take you for a walk around the village in between drinks if you like?'

'No need. I like it here. I feel normal-sized.'

He gazed dolefully up at the low beams and rubbed his head.

She giggled. 'Did it knock any sense into you?'

'Not a chance. What do you think of the whisky?'

She pulled a face. 'It's not really my thing.'

He smiled. 'You're a teenager tonight, so you're going to hate most of the things you drink. The trick is to pretend you like them. The whisky is just a warm-up.' He gestured to a tray of glasses on the table between them. 'These are the main event.'

The shot glasses and tumblers were filled with all the colours of the rainbow. 'What are they?'

'Well, I thought you could combine two of the items on your list: pub crawl and trying something new. So, I've got a selection of the weirdest things the bar staff could provide.'

'But I've already tried something new. That disgusting fried candy bar.'

'Aha! But that was food. Now we're moving on to drinks. We've got Pernod and black, Midori, Advocaat, Pimm's, cider, Buckfast, crème de menthe, Baileys, Kahlúa, Cinzano, vodka and Red Bull, and the pub's own dark ale. There's also Scotland's second national drink for you to try, but I'm saving that as a hangover cure tomorrow.'

She arched an eyebrow. 'I'm working tomorrow. I can't have a hangover.'

'Where's your fighting spirit? Being a teenager is about turning up late and drunk for work, then breaking the chocolate eclair machine.'

'Huh?'

He handed her a glass. 'Here. You only get my secrets if you drink.'

She sniffed. 'It smells like aniseed?'

'Pernod and blackcurrant. Tastes like cough medicine.'

She took a sip. 'If you think it's cough medicine, then it's actually quite nice. Now, tell me your secrets.'

Charlie leaned forward, darting his eyes back and forth to make sure they weren't overheard. It was unnecessary, as no one was near them.

Valentina moved in closer. She could see the flecks of gold amongst the green of his eyes. A heavy heat was building inside her.

'It was a dark and stormy night,' he began.

Her mouth watered and she took a large gulp of her drink.

'My parents were out playing bridge and my older sister, Tabbie, was away at Sandhurst.'

'You have a sister?' she interrupted. 'What is she like? Do you have any other siblings? What's Sandhurst?'

'One question per drink. Do you want to know about my chocolate eclair catastrophe or my family?'

She took another drink. 'Catastrophe, then family.'

'My family *is* a catastrophe,' he replied. 'Although, in fairness, they all think I'm the problem.'

She raised her eyebrows again.

'Okay, okay, the story of Charlie and the Patisserie Peril. The house was dark. The house was empty. The house was mine. I crept to my father's liquor cabinet and picked the lock. Once in, I decanted an inch from every bottle, replacing the stolen liquid with water. I was left with a glass of what could only be described as drain cleaner. However, I was a young man on a mission. A mission to get as drunk as possible in the shortest amount of time. My dad had made sure all the local pubs and shops knew I was underage, despite being six foot four, so I was going to drink this and go hang out with my mates in the park.'

'Sounds fun.'

'Hey, this was the high life in Chumleigh Underbottom.'

She snorted with laughter. 'Chumleigh what?'

'Underbottom,' he replied with a straight face. 'It's a village that predates the Norman Conquest. Only the very best people live there. Not like the riff-raff who live in South or East Underbottom.'

Valentina snorted again, leaning back and holding her tummy. She laughed with the story and she laughed with the telling. She couldn't remember the last time she'd felt such giddy joy.

She took another drink. 'Thank goodness your Underbottom was the best. But where do the eclairs come in?'

'So, I'll skip all the boring stuff about hanging around in the park sharing a cigarette and pretending we liked it whilst talking about all the girls we definitely weren't shagging. Suffice to say, Jack had a bottle of vodka from his cousin and we necked the lot. I managed to get home and into bed before my parents returned, but woke the next morning, late for work, having slept through my alarm. I ran out the house as Dad was yelling that I smelled like a brewery and demanding to know what I'd done, got on my bike and made it to the factory only half an hour late for my shift.

My job was to fill the eclairs. I had to stand in front of a conveyor belt on which they trundled. There was a nozzle in front of me, dishing out exactly the right amount of cream. I had to lift off an eclair, stick it on the end of the nozzle, take it off and put it back on the conveyor belt, all within five seconds.'

'Sounds complicated.'

He gave her a look that sent an electric shock through her. 'Mock not. It was harder than defusing a bomb. If you got behind with your timings, the nozzle would squirt you with cream, and the eclairs would continue on the belt unfilled.'

She finished her drink. 'Is that what happened?'

'Partly. Within five minutes, I was covered in cream. Then I broke the machine by fiddling with the controls, panicked and puked over the conveyor belt. I cost the factory thousands of pounds that day and went home jobless, covered in cream and vomit, and still wearing a hairnet. Even now, I can't look at a chocolate eclair without experiencing PTSD.'

She wrapped her arms around herself as she laughed.

He grinned and handed her a glass. 'Baileys. You've probably had this before. Chocolate and cream to go with the story.'

She got herself under control and took a sip. 'Oh my god, this is amazing!'

'Try it on your porridge in the morning. It's a religious experience.'

Closing her eyes, she let the taste and the alcohol amplify the desire for him surging through her. Every part of her body was buzzing with heat and need.

She opened them to see him staring at her, his lips parted. She held her breath, then let it out with a rush.

'Your family, your sister, Sandhurst.'

He started as if woken from a dream. 'Three of the biggest passion killers known to man. I need more alcohol.'

He downed a shot of whisky.

'Right. I only have one sibling—my older sister, Tabitha. She's perfect and graduated top of her year from the Royal Military Academy Sandhurst, where army officers are trained. She's now a colonel and runs the Royal Signals Camp in Blandford. She thinks I'm an arsehole.'

He took another glass and drank. Valentina finished her Baileys and picked up another brown drink.

He gestured at her glass. 'Same same, but different. It's Kahlúa, coffee liqueur. Okay, my folks. Let's make this quick. You know how you and your family are joined at the hip?'

She frowned. 'Joined at the hip?'

'Close. You like each other.'

'We love each other.'

His face hardened. 'Yeah, well, if you're close, we're as far apart as planets in different galaxies. My dad was in the army and my mum was the archetypal army wife. Her life was his life. They're cold, they're distant, and I'm their biggest fucking disappointment.'

She gasped. 'Charlie! That cannot be true. You're incredible.'

He gave her a small smile and shrugged. 'Everything I touch turns to shit.' He drank another shot. 'Anyway, that's enough about me. Now it's your turn to answer some questions.'

14

Valentina grabbed a green drink and gulped it down. She didn't want to talk about her life. She couldn't hide herself around Charlie. He saw everything.

'Ugh, what is *that?*' she asked, looking at the glass suspiciously.

'Midori. Melon liqueur from Japan. The other green one is crème de menthe, so you might as well have that one next.'

She took the glass and sipped it. She was now feeling properly drunk, wavering on the edge between fun and crazy—between smiling goofily at him and crawling across the table and ripping off his clothes.

'So,' he continued. 'Tell me more about you and your family.'

She shrugged and took another drink. 'You've googled me. You should know it all.'

'Yeah, because the internet is always right.'

She finished the drink and started another, staring into the glass.

He gestured at it. 'Vodka and Red Bull. So you'll be drunk

and awake. All I know is that you come from a large family and you're twenty-nine. Correct?'

She met his gaze and held it, frantically putting up walls between them, which fell down with every bat of his lashes.

'By the way, my birthday is on July the twenty-eighth as well,' he said with a smile.

'Really?' she replied, her voice breathy.

'Yep. So this summer you'll turn thirty and I'll be thirty-three.'

Her stomach tightened.

He paused and looked at her. *Really* looked at her.

The room was tilting. She grabbed the table.

'You're not twenty-nine,' he stated.

She stood, pushing her chair back. 'I have to use the bathroom.'

THE LADIES' TOILET IN THE PUB WAS SMALL, WITH ONLY TWO stalls. Valentina washed her hands and stared at her reflection. She looked sad and felt old before her time. She'd already lived a lifetime of work. She had no choice. She had to make enough money before forty—the magical cut-off time in Hollywood when most roles for women dried up.

She might prolong the biological clock with Botox and fillers, but that was a line in the sand she wasn't sure she could cross. For now, she would rely on genes and clean living.

Clean living? She let out a laugh. Her life was clean, but there was no 'living'. Now her cheeks were flushed with alcohol and desire flooded her body. This felt like living but it could never last. She owed him at least that truth.

Running her fingers through her hair, she gave herself a nod in the mirror, and went back out.

She sat opposite him and finished the vodka and Red Bull.

He was gazing at her warily. 'You okay?'

Putting the glass down, she nodded. 'Charlie...' she began.

'Ye-es?'

'I want to be honest with you.'

He nodded slowly.

'This thing...' She gestured between them. 'It has no future. It's just for now. For when we're in Scotland. You and I could never work.'

She stared at his face, trying to read the emotions that flitted across it. Shit, she was drunk. Was he sad? Relieved? Indifferent?

His face was a mask. 'Of course. As a wannabe teenager, it's your job to have a fling with someone completely inappropriate. I'm the last person you'd want to be with.' He took a drink without looking at it and knocked it back in one.

She smiled as if happy, but inside there was a yawning chasm of disappointment. Why did the truth hurt so much?

Now veering from happy-drunk to miserable-drunk, she needed to snap out of it. She brought out her phone, turned the camera on, and passed it to him.

'Would you take some photos of me for my sister? We have this thing, just between us. I send her the worst pictures of me I can to make her laugh. It's like an antidote to all the bullshit of my job.'

He grinned at her, and her heart told her it was genuine.

'Yeah, sure.' He lifted the phone. 'Knock yourself out.'

She picked up two of the glasses, put them either side of her face and went cross-eyed.

He laughed. 'That's awesome.'

The sound of his laughter was like sunshine, pulling her mood out from behind the clouds. She pulled another face, and another, every laugh from Charlie spurring her on. She lifted the two pint glasses of dark ale and held them in front of her breasts, sucking her cheeks in and raising her eyebrows.

He pulled a face. 'Woah, hang on. How am I meant to hold the phone still when you're doing that?'

She giggled, put the pints down, and picked up a shot glass of something yellow.

'Advocaat. Alcoholic custard,' he explained.

She nestled it between her breasts and stuck out her tongue, as if trying to reach the glass.

'Fuck's sake, Valentina. You're killing me here,' he muttered.

She glanced at him, took her finger and dipped it in the drink. He kept the camera still, but his lips were parted, his eyes glued to her hand. She raised her finger slowly, then stuck it up her nose, a look of surprise on her face.

He took the picture, then they both dissolved in hysterics. She downed the drink, pulled out the handkerchief he'd given her earlier and blew her nose.

'See if they're any good,' he said, passing her the phone.

Valentina stared at the screen, joy filling her. 'These are absolutely awful. They're perfect—she'll love them. Thank you, Charlie.'

He smiled and shifted in his seat. 'They're not awful. They're funny. You're beautiful *and* funny. You should be doing comedy. You should post these on Instagram.'

A lurching sickness rolled through her, and she put the phone down. 'Are you crazy? If these got out, no one would take me seriously. It could kill my career.'

'Why?' He looked confused.

'I only get offered one role: I'm the sexy girl who ends up dead in the first act. *Braveheart 2* is the first film where I almost get to the end before being killed. I know my limits and have to work within them before I'm too old.'

He shook his head. 'It can't be that simple.'

'It is. I've been doing this for nearly twenty years. It's ninety-nine per cent bullshit and one hundred per cent misogyny. Do you really think I would be sitting here now if I didn't look like this?'

'Maybe, but there are millions of beautiful people out there who can't act. You've got something they don't.'

'That's not true. My career is based on looks, being at the right place at the right time, and never saying no to a job. A good work ethic and reading people are the only talents I have.'

'I don't believe that for a second. Don't you want to do something different?'

'Of course I do. The film I'm doing after this is a small art house one. A chance to try something different. But I have to be pragmatic. I also have a cosmetics contract I'm about to sign. I can't risk that by having photos like this in the public domain.'

He lifted two glasses of fizzing pink liquid and handed one to her. 'Let's drink to that then. Pimm's and lemonade. Meant to be drunk in the summer with a slice of cucumber.'

They clinked glasses and she tried to ignore the thoughts and feelings fighting for her attention.

'So, you have a sister. How old is she?' he asked.

She rolled her eyes. 'This is meant to be a night off from my family.'

'Ah, come on. Just the basics.'

'Okay, there's Manny, my older brother. He's thirty-six. He's married to Maria and they have four kids. Then there's me.' She hesitated, her heart wringing. 'Then my younger sister, Isabella. She's twenty-six, married to Matias and seven months pregnant with her first child.'

She saw his forehead crease, as if trying to solve a puzzle.

She didn't want him to spot the gap in her family portrait so offered herself up instead.

'I'm thirty-two, okay? The producers on *La Vida Familiar* told us to lie about my age when I started on it.' She finished the drink and put it down, feeling more and more unsteady. 'Happy now?'

'Ecstatic,' he replied with a grin. 'We're exactly the same age. So, you never had a big party for your thirtieth?'

She shook her head. 'I was working. They brought out a cake which had a big "twenty-seven" iced on it. I felt like such a fraud.' She reached for another glass, her fingers fumbling to hold it. She took a sip and grimaced.

'Buckfast. Grape juice, sugar, ethanol, caffeine and chemicals. Made by monks, banned in the US, and the drink of choice for young offenders. "Buckfast. Gets you fucked fast" is the unofficial slogan.'

Valentina knocked it back in one, squeezing her eyes shut and shaking her head. She wanted oblivion. Tonight was about the present, not the past. She kept her eyes closed, focusing on the waves of drunkenness, the pounding desire. A swell of nausea moved through her and she opened her eyes, using his as a point of balance.

He was studying her. 'You okay?'

She nodded and unsteadily got to her feet. She went around the table, leaning on it for support. Charlie moved his chair, as if to stand, but she gripped his shoulders, pushing him back down as she sat on his lap. Her face so close to his, their noses touched. She saw the black of his pupils flooding the green irises till only a rim of gold remained.

'Valentina...' He broke off, his voice low and rough.

She could feel his breath against her lips. She ran her fingers up the back of his neck into his hair, rubbing against the grain.

He shivered under her touch. 'I don't...'

She continued stroking into his hair and brought her lips to his ear. 'What is it, Charlie?' She bit down gently on the lobe and he jumped as if shot, breathing heavily. Why wasn't he touching her?

'Valentina, I don't want to—'

She stilled, shock freezing her body to numbness. He didn't want this. He didn't want her. Oh god. What had she done? Her stomach rolled with the shame of rejection. She clamped her hand to her mouth.

She was going to be sick.

Stumbling up, she ran for the bathroom. Yanking the door open, she tripped forward to the toilet and dived for the bowl, making it just in time as her guts emptied. Her body heaved, again and again, the pressure watering her eyes.

Warm hands at the back of her head lifted her hair out of the way as she gripped the sides of the seat. She reached the end of a gag and gasped for breath.

'Lift your head a bit,' Charlie said.

She complied and he flushed the toilet.

'Now hold still for a moment,' he continued, braiding her hair, then tucking the end under the back of her dress. He kissed the top of her head. 'Stay put,' he murmured. 'I'm going to get you some water.'

As soon as the bathroom door closed, Valentina moaned and threw up again. A minute later, Charlie was back and passed her a glass of water. She swilled out her mouth and spat in the bowl, keeping her gaze away from his.

'Think there's any more to come up?' he asked.

She shook her head and started crying.

He crouched behind her, taking the water off her with one hand whilst pulling off sheets of toilet roll with the other. 'Don't cry, sweetheart. Take this and let's get you out of here.'

She shook her head and sat on the floor, covering her eyes.

'You can go now,' she said between sobs. 'You don't have to stay.'

He stroked down her back and kissed the top of her head again. Why was he doing that? Did he feel sorry for her?

'I'm not going anywhere, sweetheart.'

Her shoulders shook with her tears. 'Just leave. I've had enough humiliation for one night.'

'Do you think I rejected you back there?'

She nodded.

'Dickhead,' he muttered under his breath. 'Valentina, listen to me. I want you so badly it hurts. Whatever blood is needed for my limited intellect is permanently rerouted to my dick when you're around. But I don't want you doing anything *you* don't want to do, anything *you* regret. I'm not in your league, Valentina. And I don't want to take advantage of you when you're drunk.'

She lifted a hand and he gave her the toilet paper. She wiped her face and blew her nose. 'I'm sorry,' she whispered.

'For what? You've ticked off more teenager boxes than I intended tonight. You're on fire.'

Despite herself, she smiled.

He held out her phone. 'Want me to take a picture to show Isabella? You left this on the table when you ran, so I picked it up.'

Valentina nodded. 'She'll love this. She is always telling me I'm too well behaved.' She unlocked it and passed it to him.

He stepped out of the cubicle and snapped some photos of her sitting on the floor looking sorry for herself.

'Charlie?'

'Yes, love?'

'I feel terrible.'

'You going to be sick again?'

'I don't think so, but my head is being crushed by a rock.'

He handed her the glass of water. 'Drink this, then we'll go home. When we get back, have two paracetamol and a pint of water. Then bed.'

'I need to settle the bill. My purse. It's in my jacket pocket.'

He took her purse out of his pocket. 'I picked it up with your phone. The bill's sorted.'

'Charlie, no,' she moaned. 'I was going to pay.'

'No way, José.'

She opened her purse. 'How much was it?'

He took it and put it back in his pocket. 'We're not going to have our first argument in a public toilet. You can pay me back in kisses.'

Glancing up at him, she tried to frown, but it turned into a smile.

He grinned back. 'Your half of the bill came to eleventy trillion pounds. You can start repayments tomorrow.'

She groaned. 'I feel like death.'

He stood and held out his hands. 'Come on, you'll feel better in the morning. I promise.'

15

Valentina wasn't at breakfast, so at nine o'clock Charlie knocked on her door, figuring she'd need an hour to prepare herself for starting work at ten. She opened it a crack and looked at him through a curtain of hair.

'How are you doing?' he asked.

She groaned in response and opened the door for him, then stumbled back to the bed and flopped on it, face down.

He followed her and put a bowl of porridge on the desk along with a can of drink. 'Well, you're awake, and a dressing gown means you're half dressed, so that's a start.'

She raised her head an inch. 'What's that smell?'

'Porridge. Do you feel hungry or sick?'

'I don't know.' Her head dropped back down. 'I think I'm dying.'

He laughed, opened the can, and poured her a glass.

'What's that?' she mumbled into the duvet.

'Irn-Bru. Scotland's second national drink after whisky. Also called "fizzy juice". It's the best hangover cure there is.' He sat on the edge of the bed. 'Want to give it a go?'

She pushed herself to sit and glowered at him.

'If that's a dirty look, I'm afraid it only gets a three out of ten.'

She stuck her tongue out.

'That's the spirit. Now, drink this. In five minutes, you'll be back to calling me a dickhead.'

Taking the glass, she sipped. Her nose wrinkled. 'It tastes like candy.'

'Well, it is almost one hundred per cent sugar. You've got just under an hour before your call time. Try and drink it all.' He stood. 'I'll come by the set later to see how you're doing.'

'How are *you* feeling?'

He grinned. 'Eleventy trillion out of ten.'

She blushed. 'Huevón,' she muttered.

'Told you so.' He hesitated, then kissed her on the top of her head before he could stop himself. 'I'll see you later.'

CHARLIE STROLLED DOWN THE CASTLE CORRIDORS FEELING lighter than air. She liked him. Valentina Valverde liked *him*. It was like discovering there really was a pot of gold at the end of the rainbow. Nothing could beat this high.

His phone buzzed in his pocket. He pulled it out and crashed back to earth.

> Tabbie: We know you're not in Angola. When you're not licking Brad Bauer's backside, call me.

Familiar feelings of guilt and inadequacy crawled up inside him. Of course his family would find out. Barbara would have rung his mum, using his presence as an excuse for a catch-up. How long did he think the Angola lie would run?

He put the phone away. He'd rather be back on the front

line than speak to his sister right now. *Chickenshit*, his conscience berated him. *Fuck off*, he replied, selecting another box in his mind to cram this subject into. *Dickhead*, his conscience yelled faintly as he sealed the box and buried it at the back of his mind.

Collecting Bandit from the workshop, he patrolled the castle from top to bottom, scoping out Vlad simpering over Kirsten in the great hall. That evening the two of them were putting on an 'earth meal' for the stars and heads of each department. Of course, the hard work was being done by others, but it was their concept, so they were taking the glory.

As the Earl of Kinloch, Rory couldn't get out of it and had asked him to come along for moral support. Charlie doubted his ability to keep his cool around Vlad, so told Rory he needed to grow a pair, and that he'd rather disembowel himself with a spoon than spend an evening pretending to like Vlad, or lentils.

After Charlie had put Valentina to bed the previous night, he'd crept to Vlad's room to try and get in whilst he was asleep and remove whatever drugs were in his man-bag. But Vlad had been prepared and the wardrobe was wedged in front of the door. So Charlie had a think about what else he could do to slow him down and took Bandit for a walk to Kinloch's pharmacy for some laxatives.

That afternoon, he drove to Inverness with Bandit, his eye on a present for Valentina, and returned just after her wrap time, meeting her in the main corridor downstairs.

She was wearing her character's tight, beaded leather dress, her big parka draped over her shoulders. She blushed when she saw him and pulled the coat over her chest.

'How did it go?' he asked. 'Hangover gone?'

'*Shh*, Charlie,' she whispered. She glanced around. 'I feel a lot better, thank you. And I ate some lunch as well.'

He moved closer, noticing her pupils dilating and her lips parting. 'That's the power of Irn-Bru. It's made with girders,' he whispered.

Her forehead creased and her cheeks flushed.

'You make bridges out of them. They're big. And long. And hard.'

She blinked rapidly, then pushed him away. 'Will you behave?' she hissed.

He opened his arms. 'What? I'm talking about Scottish infrastructure. Civil engineering.'

Her eyes narrowed and he started to laugh.

'You are so immature.' She pulled her parka tighter around her, breathing heavily.

'I did warn you, I'm a Jedi Juvenile Master...' He cleared his throat. 'I was wondering if you wanted to do anything before your posh dinner tonight.'

'Are you going to be there?'

He shook his head. She looked disappointed.

'But I thought when it was over, you might want to cross something off your list?' he asked. Her eyes widened till he could see all of the white around the dark irises. 'No, not that, I thought you might like to go skinny-dipping. It'll be dark,' he added, as if that would sell it.

'Naked?' she whispered, her voice going higher.

'Yep.'

Valentina's head shook so fast he could hear the beads on her dress clinking together.

He put his hand on his heart. 'I promise I'll keep my eyes closed. And I'll get naked first.'

She took a breath, then started coughing. Had she just choked on her own saliva?

'You okay?'

She nodded.

'And anyway, once I get in the water, the cold turns me into Charlotte. Remember?'

'Charlie. You are intolerable.'

He grinned widely. She smiled back and every feeling inside him ramped up.

'I was wondering,' she began. 'If you could take me—'

'Yes,' he interrupted. 'Whatever you want, the answer's yes.'

She raised her eyebrows. 'Really?'

'Yes.'

'Anything?'

He nodded.

'Go to a karaoke bar with Brad?'

He nodded again more hesitantly.

'Sing "2 Become 1" by the Spice Girls with him?'

His smile was slipping but he nodded again, trying to remember if anywhere within a fifty-mile radius of Kinloch had a karaoke bar.

'Share a spa day, including hot tub and couples massage, with ...'

This was more like it.

'...Vlad?'

He retched and stared at her in horror as she laughed.

'Have I found your hard limit?' she asked, her eyes alight with mischief.

He nodded. 'And it's also been banned by the Geneva Conventions.' He shuddered and shook his head. 'You've scarred me for life. There are some things, once thunk, can never be unthunk.'

She giggled. 'I was actually wondering if you could take me for a run in the countryside. I need some exercise.'

Charlie resisted the temptation to suggest a spot of horizontal jogging might be preferable, and tried to keep his features blank.

'Yeah sure. Do you want to get changed and I'll meet you by the front door in ten?'

She smiled. 'That's perfect, thank you. I need to get out of this thing.' She glanced down at her costume and scrunched her nose. 'When the shoot is over, I want to burn this.'

FIVE MINUTES LATER, CHARLIE STOOD IN THE CASTLE hallway gazing out the windows at the angry black clouds. They spat out rain that gusted horizontally across the court-yard, buffeting the cars and slapping at the castle as if fighting to get in. He felt the warmth of Valentina behind him and turned to see her uncertain face.

'That's a lot of weather.'

A flash of lightning and an explosion of thunder split the sky. She jumped and grabbed his arm. He instinctively flexed his muscles.

'Gym?'

CHARLIE UNLOCKED THE GYM AND FLICKED ON THE LIGHTS. There was a pile of clean towels by the door, so he grabbed one to hide his arousal. He kept his gaze focused on the equipment whilst his peripheral vision ran around the mirrors trying to get a lock on Valentina.

It didn't need to find her. Her image was already burned into his brain. He briefly closed his eyes and saw her black leggings accentuating every curve, moulding to her incredible body. Her arse. *Fuck me.* Half his mind threw him a kaleido-scope of sexual possibilities whilst the other half fought back with images of Vlad in a hot tub as he screamed at his dick to go down.

He thought back to the last time they'd been here. His

shirtless pull-ups. The look on her face as she scoped him out in the mirrors. The feel of her last night as she sat on his lap. *Fuck!*

'I... I have always wanted to do a pull-up,' she said hesitantly.

So her mind was in the same place as his. He kept his back to her, focusing on the line where the wall touched the ceiling.

He cleared his throat. 'They don't have a pull-up machine here.'

'Oh. So what do you suggest?'

Charlie gritted his teeth. He could think of some ideas but they all involved touching her. He shrugged, clenching his fists around the towel.

'Maybe, I could stand on a bench?'

He moved, grabbed the nearest one, plonked it underneath a rack, then stood to the side like a sentry, his eyes averted. He heard her stepping onto it.

'Charlie, I still can't reach. Can you help?'

He turned slowly to face her. She looked unsure, chewing on her plump bottom lip. He moved behind her and dropped the towel to the bench. Placing his hands on her hips, he lifted her.

Valentina's fingers found the bars and he took some of her weight as she pulled. He stared at the small of her back, the curve of her spine as it disappeared under her leggings. The heat from her skin scorched through his palms.

She made soft little grunts as she pulled, sounds that sent surges of blood to his cock. Desire raged like wildfire through him. It was too big, too all-consuming to control. He was frantically trying to put out the flames, but she was gasoline.

She let go of the bar, breathing heavily. 'Thank you.'

He lifted his hands away, grabbed the towel, and took a step back. If he didn't put some distance between them, he wouldn't be able to stop himself reaching for her, turning her, pulling her to him, showing just how hard he was for her.

'Maybe I should do some free weights?' she asked breathily.

He stalked to the dumbbells and selected one. There was a bench next to them facing the mirrored wall. Valentina straddled it and faced the mirror. He handed her the weight. She sat up straight, lifting her arm up and down.

'Not that way,' he said, his voice rough and tight. 'Your upper arm needs to be tucked into your body.'

She tried again.

He shook his head. 'Not like that—you'll hurt yourself.'

'I don't understand.'

His feet moved before his brain caught up. He sat behind her, leaving an inch of space between their bodies. She turned her head and the hair from her ponytail tickled his neck.

'Face forward.'

Folding his hand around hers, he lifted the weight, showing her the correct move. As her elbow came up, her arm grazed across the side of his chest. She sucked in a breath.

He glanced up, his eyes meeting hers in the mirror. Her pupils were huge, her cheeks flushed, her mouth open. He felt her fingers relax around the dumbbell and it dropped to the floor with a thud.

He couldn't hold back any longer. He had to touch her.

Keeping hold of her hand, he lifted it onto her thigh. She offered no resistance. He interlaced his fingers with hers and squeezed. She held his gaze and her legs widened slightly.

Heart thumping, he brought his free hand to her other thigh, barely touching. He stroked slowly up and down the inside of her leg. Her eyes fluttered closed and she dropped her head to his shoulder with a sigh. He shunted his body closer, pulling her back flush with his chest.

'Charlie,' she whispered.

He nuzzled the soft skin of her neck, her pulse beating fast under his lips. 'Hmm?' He inched higher up her leg. She twitched as if shocked and reached her arms back to grab his legs, pulling him closer.

'Fuck,' he exhaled. His muscles were tense, his cock harder than steel.

She rubbed back against him.

'Fuck, Valentina. Tell me.' He kissed up her neck. 'Tell me what you need.'

She was breathing heavily, making soft whimpering sounds. 'I, I...'

He gently scraped his fingernails higher as she trembled under his touch. Feeling her arousal soaking through her leggings, he sucked in a breath. She let out a low moan.

Blood roared through him. His skin was on fire, his cock throbbing, demanding to bury itself in her. He could feel the hard nub of her clit through the thin Lycra and scraped his nails across it.

She jerked.

He rubbed over it. 'Here?' he whispered.

She bucked against him. 'Oh god. Charlie, yes,' she gasped.

He continued to circle it as he lifted his head and stared at their reflection. Her body nestled in his, her head thrown back on his shoulder as he circled the centre of her pleasure.

Her breasts were pushed forward, her nipples poking through the fabric of her top. His cock pulsed at the sight. He lifted his free hand from her leg and slid it under the material, cupping her full breast, rolling the hardened nipple between his finger and thumb. She moaned again and arched her body into him.

Never had he felt such hunger for a woman. The urgent need to get her off, to have her fall apart under his touch. He growled and nipped at her neck. She was shaking now, breathing erratically, driving her pubic bone into his hand.

He needed to feel her. He nudged under the waistband of her leggings, through her curls to her wetness. She pushed him closer.

'Charlie,' she gasped. 'I want you. In me.'

He plunged his finger deep inside her, rubbing her clit with his thumb. 'Oh, oh, oh,' she gasped as he thrust, her voice getting higher until she suddenly stiffened, her last 'oh' turning into a sharp cry as she detonated around him.

He held her tightly as her hot centre contracted and she thrashed in his arms. In the mirror, he watched her come undone, rushes of power flooding through him.

He had done this. He had brought this pleasure out of her.

As her body relaxed against him, he gently kissed down her neck. She opened her eyes and he lifted his head, imprisoning her gaze in his. As she watched, he pulled his fingers slowly out of her, then sucked them into his mouth.

Her body jerked and she gasped again, her cheeks flushing. She turned around so she was facing him, her head bent. He lifted her chin and lost himself in her endless dark eyes. She was so beautiful.

'That wasn't on the list,' she said softly.

'It was on mine.'

'I, I've never done anything like that before,' she said, looking away.

He moved his lips to her ear. 'Neither have I,' he whispered back. He felt her smile against his cheek.

'What, um, er, about you?' she asked shyly.

He was about to speak when a shrill voice echoed down the corridor outside the room.

'Hurry up. You're so fucking lazy.'

They leapt up and away from each other, Valentina taking

the dumbbell she'd dropped and Charlie grabbing the towel and holding it in front of himself.

He needn't have worried, as his erection deflated rapidly as Kirsten stormed in. She stopped short when she saw him. She was wearing pastel coloured, tie-dyed Lycra hot pants and a crop top with the words 'Hot Yoga Bitch' emblazoned across the chest. Shauna staggered in after her, breathing heavily, two bags hanging off her arms.

'Hi, Shauna. Hi, Kirsten,' Charlie said. 'We were just leaving.'

Kirsten's eyes narrowed and her face went through the contortions necessary to approximate a smile. She dropped her head to one side and twirled a strand of blonde hair around her fingers.

'It's my earth meal tonight,' she said coquettishly. 'Are you coming? His Holiness and I want to share our spiritual gifts with everyone.'

Behind her, Shauna was lifting pink dumbbells out of the bags and setting them on the floor. Charlie looked at them quizzically.

'They're plant-based,' Kirsten explained. 'And blessed by His Holiness.'

'Ah,' he replied blandly. Valentina went to the door, giving Shauna a squeeze on the shoulder as she passed. 'I'm afraid I won't be able to make it to your meal,' he continued. 'However, Ms Valverde is very much looking forward to attending.'

Valentina froze as Kirsten turned to look at her. She gave Kirsten a tight-lipped smile and disappeared out the door.

Charlie nodded at Kirsten and sprinted after her.

CHARLIE MET VALENTINA IN THE CORRIDOR. THERE WAS NO one else around. She faced him, a shy smile on her face. He smiled goofily at her and reached out his hand. She took it and squeezed. They stood in happy silence, his heart overflowing.

She leaned a little closer. 'Why did you say I was looking forward to the meal?' she whispered. 'Have you seen the menu?'

'That's half the reason I'm not going,' he whispered back. 'The rest is that I won't be able to stop myself from punching Vlad.' He grinned. 'Want me to cook for you now? Line your stomach with some real food?'

'What's on your menu?'

'Steak and chips?'

'Sounds perfect.'

16

The castle dining room was ornate and beautiful, with high ceilings and wood panelling. An open fire was burning, and candles and flowers decorated the long table.

Valentina was warm, full, and fizzing with happiness. Even the fact that Vlad was sitting to her right didn't dampen her mood. He was ignoring her, focusing instead on Kirsten, Zoe, Brad, and Barbara.

The meal Kirsten had planned looked pretty, but tasted disgusting, and Valentina was glad she'd eaten half an hour before with Charlie.

She absentmindedly moved each course around her plate and sipped champagne as she thought of him, each memory bringing a new rush of delight. She'd only ever been intimate with two other men, and the experiences couldn't compare to what she'd just shared with Charlie, the way he'd made her feel.

Sparks jolted up her legs and she trembled, picking up her glass and gazing into it as the bubbles rose and popped.

Sex with her co-star, Santiago, had been awkward, unpleasant, and disappointing. Both of them had been virgins and he'd decided to educate himself by watching pornography. By the time Valentina had realised sex didn't have to be like that, she'd been put off trying it again for years.

After they'd split up, she became deliberately standoffish with any man who approached, her walls impregnable.

But then she'd met Bryce, a stuntman. He was an Australian wanting to make it big in LA and had the looks: sun-bleached blond hair, bright blue eyes, washboard abs. He also had the moves, a seemingly laid-back attitude, and the ability to charm man, woman or beast.

She was a steppingstone for him, a way to advance his career, but she'd fallen deep. That was until he'd tried to make money by selling photos he'd taken of her. They weren't nudes, but they were candid and intimate. She felt like he'd ripped out her soul.

After Santiago, sex with Bryce had seemed amazing. But now, thinking back, even that had been another act, a performance. He'd never made her feel an ounce of what Charlie did.

Valentina squeezed her legs together. She was certain that anything Charlie did to her would be mind-blowing. But what could she do for him? How could she be good enough?

A pang of unease pricked her happy bubble. What if he didn't like what was under her clothes? What if he thought she was too small, her breasts too big? Did he expect her to shave her pubic hair? Santiago and Bryce wanted that, but it made her uncomfortable. The regrowth was itchy and the ingrowing hairs were annoying and painful.

And if Charlie didn't mind what was under her clothes, how could she give him pleasure when she didn't know how to do it right? She'd tried her best with Bryce, and he'd been helpful, but most of his instructions started 'no, not like that'.

Her stomach tightened. She couldn't allow herself to go

through that humiliation again. She'd talk to Charlie later. Explain things couldn't go any further. She sighed. Now it was her heart that squeezed.

She picked up a chocolate from her plate. At least *this* tasted good. If in doubt, chocolate was always the answer.

Rory stood and addressed their end of the table. 'Please excuse us and continue your evening. Zoe's not feeling well.'

Zoe's face was pinched and she was holding her stomach.

'What's wrong?' Valentina asked.

'I've got a bit of a tummy ache. I think I just need to lie down,' Zoe replied through gritted teeth.

Kirsten waved her hand in a dismissive gesture. 'Oh, I get bloating all the time. You need a peppermint tea and a massage from His Holiness. He's trained in Howanda massage. It draws out toxins.'

Vlad raised his arms and Valentina instinctively recoiled.

He waved his spindly fingers at Zoe. 'I will come to your room and give you my healing touch.'

Her face went white, and Rory's hardened.

'That won't be necessary,' he replied brusquely, putting his arm around his girlfriend and ushering her away.

The moment Rory and Zoe had gone, the nexus of power that bound the table together collapsed like a dying sun. Brad usually liked to be the centre of the universe, but when Rory left, he turned his attention exclusively to Barbara, leaving a vacuum that Vlad expanded to fill.

Vlad stretched out, manspreading as far as his cassock would allow, and every cell in Valentina's body screamed at her to flee. She made her excuses and left.

Wanting to keep some of her boundaries up, she still hadn't given Charlie her number, so had no idea how to get in touch with him if he wasn't in his room. Outside his door, she knocked nervously, her stomach twisting.

He flung it open, and her jaw dropped. He was shirtless, a pair of jeans slung so low on his hips she could see he wasn't wearing underwear.

'Ready to go?' he asked with a grin.

TEN MINUTES LATER, VALENTINA WAS WALKING THROUGH Kinloch engulfed in her winter clothes, a bag containing towels over her shoulder. Her stomach turned over with every step.

'You *promise* you won't look?' she implored.

Charlie stopped and took her hands in his. 'Yes. For the—' he glanced up, scrunching his face, then back at her with a smile '—*fifty-fourth* time, I promise I won't look at you.'

She gave a *'humph'* and carried on, still holding one of his warm hands. She felt so safe with him, even though sensation was rushing up her arm like sparkles of light.

'I can't believe I'm doing this,' she babbled nervously. 'It's crazy. I must be out of my mind. What would my...' she broke off, pressing her lips closed.

'Your mum? Your sister? Your grandmothers? What would they say?' She didn't need to look at him to know he was smiling broadly. 'Shall we give them a call and find out?'

'My phone's stopped working and my tablet's back at the castle,' she replied grumpily.

They reached the edge of the village and stepped off the side of the road onto the loose shingle by the edge of the loch.

'Ah,' he replied. 'How convenient.'

She shot him a filthy look and he laughed.

'You know full well that all of them would approve, and Abuela would ask for photographic evidence.'

'You're right. She keeps asking if I know where your dragon tattoo ends.'

He squeezed her hand. 'You can see in a minute if you like?'

'Charlie!' she hissed, looking around in case anyone was about. 'I will not look.'

'You're more than welcome. After years in the army, I'm perfectly fine with my own nakedness.'

'Well, I am not fine with mine,' she whispered back.

He stopped abruptly and gazed down at her. The rain that had bucketed down earlier had stopped, and the skies had cleared. Pale moonlight illuminated his face.

'It's okay if you don't want others to look at your body, but you've got to be happy in your own skin.'

She pulled at his hand, trying to get him to walk on. It was like trying to move an intractable bull. 'Come on, let's get this over and done with.'

He wasn't budging, so she dropped his hand and set off alone along the shore, the loose stones crunching under her boots. He jogged to reach her.

'Woah, hang on, back up a bit.'

She ignored him.

'Valentina, wait, por favor.'

She stopped, hot and embarrassed. 'What?'

He sighed. 'Lo siento. I just want to ask, are you happy with your body?'

She glanced away and shrugged. 'I do what I can with what God gave me.'

'Valentina,' he said softly. 'You're a fucking goddess.'

She shrugged again. She didn't want to be having this conversation.

'It will not last. And in Hollywood, I'll always be fat.'

There was silence, then he let out an incredulous laugh. 'What the fuck, Valentina? That's bullshit. Fat? Jesus Christ.'

She crossed her arms.

He stared at her. 'Whatever dipshit said that to you is blind, jealous, has a tiny dick, or all of the above. Fuck my life.

What's wrong with the world? I'm never going to LA if it's full of people like that.'

A hole opened inside her heart. Their lives were so very different, and Charlie was only in hers for a short time. Whatever she shared with him was fleeting—soon they would go their separate ways. Expecting any more from this situation was like trying to hold onto a beautiful dream when you're waking up.

She took a deep breath. Her life outside of Kinloch could wait. She wanted to stay in this dream for as long as she could.

'This is why I keep asking you to keep your eyes closed.'

He nodded. 'I may be a dickhead, but you can count on me. I won't look.' He paused. 'Valentina, you don't have to do this if you don't want to. You never have to do anything you don't want to. This is meant to be fun.'

She glanced behind them. The lights of Kinloch were far enough away. 'We *are* doing this.' She lifted her chin. 'We are going skinny-dipping.'

He grinned. 'Alrighty then!' He shucked his jacket to the ground. 'Last one in's a wazzock!' He pulled his T-shirt over his head and threw it behind him.

'Wait! Stop!' She darted forward, putting her hands on his bare chest, then lifting them off as if scalded. She blinked, trying to avoid looking at his chest. *Oh god, his body.* 'Er, I thought we could do this slowly?'

He raised an eyebrow. 'It's pretty cold. Better just to jump in. It's like removing a plaster—best to rip it off.'

She licked her lips. 'I'm also, er, a bit scared of what's in there.'

Now both his eyebrows were raised.

'You know. The monster...'

His face contorted as he suppressed a smile, then he gave up trying and laughed. 'This isn't Loch *Ness*.'

She frowned at him, but the corners of her mouth twitched.

He took her hands. 'The biggest things in there tonight will be us. How about I go in front and you follow behind?'

She nodded and squared her shoulders. 'Okay, I can do this.'

She moved away from him, farther up the slope towards a line of trees, then glanced back. He was facing the loch. He toed off his boots and pulled off his socks. Her mouth ran dry, all the moisture in her body rushing south.

He popped the top button of his jeans, then paused.

'Are you taking off any clothes or are you just watching me take off mine?' he asked casually.

She spun on her heels and tugged off her jacket, her face burning. 'I'm taking them off,' she replied. 'Don't look.' She heard him laughing softly and quickly removed her clothes. The cold air shocked her body, sending goosebumps rippling over her skin and pebbling her nipples.

What in God's name was she doing?

'Okay,' she called out. 'I'm going to turn around now. You need to look at the ground.'

'Roger that.'

She stepped gingerly over the cold stones down the slope to the water. They felt like lumps of ice. She stopped when she saw his bare legs in front of her.

'You ready?' he asked.

'Yes. But go slowly.'

He stepped into the black water without a sound.

She inched forwards.

'¡Mierda! It's so cold!'

'You're doing great,' he reassured her as he continued deeper.

'Wait! Charlie, stop.' She balled her hands into fists,

breathing in and out through clenched teeth as she shuffled forwards.

Come on!

She took a bigger step, stumbled over a rock, and pitched forwards with a cry. Her arms flailed. She was too far away to reach his back, so she caught him around his hips, planting her face firmly into one taut arse cheek which stifled her scream.

Oh fuck. She felt the tremors in his body as he laughed. Part of her died, while the other parts had never felt so alive.

'You alright back there?'

She'd started to shiver but her face was on fire. She inched her feet closer and stood, reluctantly removing her hands from him.

'I apologise,' she said stiffly, staring at his peachy backside. 'For attempting to eat your bottom.'

He flexed one butt cheek, then the other and she drew in a sharp breath.

'You checking out the Hamilton buns of steel?' he asked, still laughing.

Valentina groaned. 'I don't think I've ever been so embarrassed. When I tell Isabella, she's going to laugh so hard she'll probably pop her baby out.'

He reached his hand behind himself, and she took it.

'Hey, don't be embarrassed. I can't remember the last time I've laughed so much. You're a comedy genius.'

'Humph.'

'Come on—let's get a little deeper before I turn completely into Charlotte.' He continued slowly forward.

She followed, wincing and hyperventilating with every step.

'Try to slow your breathing. Breathe in and out through your nose.'

'I'm smaller than you, so it's deeper for me,' she replied

through chattering teeth. 'How can you be so calm?' She gripped his hand tightly. 'And I'm scared.'

He stopped. 'Okay, how about I carry you?'

She froze. Even her teeth stopped vibrating for a second.

'I won't look. I promise. I'll have one hand under your legs and the other on your back.'

By now, she was so cold she'd do anything to feel some warmth. Her brain was clearly reaching the delusional state of hypothermia as it screamed at her *Yes! Do it!*

She moved in front of him and glanced up. His eyes were tightly closed as he reached and lifted her into his arms. The relief of being out of the water was outmatched by the feeling of being held by him.

He was so big and strong she didn't even need to hold around his neck for support. If she died now, it had all been worth it. She tucked her arms into her body and snuggled into his chest.

'Better now?'

'Yes, thank you.'

'Excellent. Now let's get a little deeper, shall we?' He strode forward and the ice-cold water lapped at her bottom.

She grabbed around the back of his neck, clinging to him.

'I promise I won't drop you,' he reassured, but she held on even tighter as the water crept up to her stomach.

'That's enough!' she cried, and he stopped.

She stared at his upper chest, his neck, his face. He was the most incredible-looking man she'd ever laid eyes on. Suddenly she wasn't cold at all. All she felt was an overwhelming heat, a need to be closer to him.

'Valentina.'

'Mmm?'

'Skinny-dipping usually involves swimming around. Would you like to try that?'

She held on tighter. 'No, I'm not moving.' She hesitated. 'Do you want to swim?'

He pulled a face. 'You're giving me the choice of swimming on my own in a freezing loch or holding a naked you in a freezing loch. Which one do *you* think I'd rather do?'

She smiled. He was so lovely. He hadn't tried to peek once. She moved closer, blinking next to his cheek, brushing it with a butterfly kiss.

He jerked. 'Valentina?'

She gently held the sides of his face, the rasp of his stubble under her fingertips. He inhaled sharply. She kissed each closed eyelid, peppered kisses down his cheek, then pressed her lips to his.

He groaned. She took that as encouragement and parted her lips, angling her head and kissing him harder. The tip of his tongue darted into her mouth and the second it touched hers, light exploded, electrifying every nerve.

She opened further, allowing him in. He pulled her closer, his hot tongue caressing hers as pleasure rushed through her, coalescing in her core. She could feel the strain of his muscles as he tried to hold back. She wanted to take in everything he had to give.

Suddenly, she felt something in the water. They were not alone.

She pulled away from him and screamed, climbing up his body to get away.

His eyes snapped open. 'What is it? What's happened?'

'Close your eyes!'

He did. 'What's going on? Are you okay?'

'There's something in the water!' she yelled as she panicked. 'It touched my bottom!' By now she'd pushed herself over his shoulder, her legs kicking out of his grip. 'Oh my god —it's still there! Charlie! I stood on it!'

She lifted her legs up behind her so she was now completely out of the water, balancing across his shoulder. She was shaking with fright and veering into tears.

'Oh my god, Charlie, you have to get us out of here!'

He was shaking beneath her. Had he been bitten? Hurt?

'Charlie? Are you okay?'

He gulped in a breath, then guffaws of laughter fell out.

'What is it?'

He continued to laugh uncontrollably.

'Charlie!' she yelled, slapping at his back.

He tried to stop laughing, but each time he tried to speak, it started up again.

'Huevón! This is serious! There's a monster in the lake!'

At the word 'monster' he bent forward, doubling over, laughing so much he was almost silent, making little wheezing sounds every time he tried to draw breath.

She relaxed a little. If it was this funny, could it really be that bad? Eventually his laughs petered out and he stood straight, holding the back of her legs against his chest.

'Are your eyes still closed?'

'Yes, Valentina, they are.'

'What is so funny, Charlie? There was something in the lake. I felt it.'

He kissed the side of her bottom as she lay over his shoulder.

'Valentina, my love. The "monster" was awakened by you. The "monster" you felt, was my, er...' He cleared his throat. 'My, er...'

She sagged over his shoulder in mortification and groaned.

He walked them out of the water and gently lowered her to the ground, his eyes still closed.

'You've got the towels. Use them all. Get dry and dressed as quickly as possible. I don't want you catching a chill.'

'What about you?' Her teeth chattered as she spoke.

'I'll use my T-shirt. Now go before I open my eyes.'

She limped to her clothes and pulled a towel out of the bag. She was so cold she couldn't feel her skin as she rubbed it. Her limbs were shaking violently, and she could barely control her breath.

She pulled her clothes on and ran to the water's edge. Charlie was facing away, his clothes back on.

'Are you dressed?' he asked.

'Yes, and I can't stop shaking.'

He opened his eyes and gazed at her with concern. 'Let's get you back and warmed up.'

❀ 17 ❀

Valentina's teeth were still chattering uncontrollably when they arrived back at the castle.

Charlie rubbed her freezing hands in his. 'I'll grab the thermometer from the first aid kit in the kitchen. Go straight to your room and get into bed.'

She stared at him in shock.

'Fully clothed,' he grinned. 'Keep your hat and gloves on too.'

Back in her room, she left the door unlocked, took off her boots, and got into bed, pulling the covers up so only her nose was showing.

Charlie strode in a minute after and sat on the edge of the bed. 'I just need your ear.'

She turned her head to one side and he brushed her hair out of the way, sending tingles down her body.

'Friends, Romans, Colombians, lend me your ears,' he proclaimed as there was a beep and he put the tip in her ear.

'You are so silly, Charlie,' she shivered. She heard another beep and turned to look at him.

He was frowning. 'Let me do that again.' He put it back and there was another beep followed by a sigh. 'Thirty-four point five. You're clinically hypothermic. Fuck!' He leapt off the bed. 'Don't move. I'm going to get the fire going, then get you a hot drink.'

She pushed herself up. 'What's *your* temperature? What about you?'

'Back under the covers,' he ordered. He fiddled with the controls on the radiators. 'I'm fine. No one would miss me if I was gone, but the universe would implode if anything happened to you.'

She pulled a face, but he wasn't smiling.

'I'm serious. You're the centre of so many people's worlds.'

He laid the fire, and when it caught, put the guard in front and passed her tablet to her. 'I'll be back as soon as I can.' He kissed her lightly on the lips and left.

Valentina closed her eyes, feeling the sensations in her lips, yearning for more. She was so needy for him.

She rang Isabella, the family member least likely to freak out at her current state.

'Chica, that is not your best look. Is it that cold in Scotland?'

Valentina giggled, her teeth chattering. 'We went skinny-dipping.'

'¡Madre Mía! How far did the dragon go?'

What little warmth there was in her body rushed to her cheeks. 'I didn't see.'

Isabella let out a huff and looked up. 'Oh, for love of all that is holy, what is *wrong* with you?'

She smiled. 'But...'

'Yes?' replied Isabella, eagerly.

'We kissed, I accidentally bit his bottom, and I woke the Kinloch monster.'

. . .

Fifteen minutes later, Isabella was still laughing as Charlie returned, holding two mugs. He put them on the bedside table and picked up the thermometer.

'Good evening, Charlie,' Isabella called from the screen.

He put the thermometer in Valentina's ear and grinned at her sister. 'Hello, Isabella, nice to meet you.'

Valentina's heart beat faster as the threads of her life continued to weave together.

Charlie stared at the thermometer as it beeped. 'Thirty-four point nine. Heading up, but not good enough. Sit up, and let's get some hot fluids in you.'

She suppressed her smile as he fussed, and Isabella smirked with unrepressed delight. He held the tablet for her so she could see her sister, then passed her a mug. She smelled it and sighed with delight.

'What is it?' Isabella asked.

'Chocolate caliente.'

'Marry him!' Isabella cried in Spanish. 'Marry him now!'

Her eyes flicked to Charlie. His face was blank. Did he understand?

'I'm going now,' she replied in English. 'I'll speak to you tomorrow.'

'Okay. I love you. Goodbye, Charlie. Don't forget, we all want to know where the dra—'

Valentina ended the call.

'Ugh. My family is so embarrassing,' she muttered, passing him the tablet. 'Please turn that off and throw it out the window.'

He chuckled, put it on the desk, then sat on the edge of her bed and lifted his drink. 'Cheers.' They chinked their mugs together. 'Here's to crossing another item off your list.'

'How are *you* feeling?' she asked.

'A bit cold, but I'll be okay.'

'Take this.' She handed her mug to him and shuffled sideways on the bed, dividing the pillows. She pulled back the covers.

He hesitated.

'Come on, I won't bite.'

There was a pause, then one of Charlie's eyebrows lifted. Her face flushed.

He kicked off his boots and climbed into bed beside her. 'I'd be a "completa idiota" if I turned that offer down. Even though you're wearing more layers than a mummy.' He tucked the covers around her and passed her mug back.

They sat in happy silence, sipping hot chocolate and watching the flickering flames of the fire. Valentina couldn't remember ever being so content outside the embrace of her family.

As the drink started to warm her from the inside out, she sneaked glances across at Charlie. He was in her bed! Butterflies fluttered in her tummy.

'Where did the last fifty years go?' he mused.

'What?'

His green eyes were dancing. 'Well, it would appear we've bypassed the "falling in love" phase, the "settling down and having children" phase, and have fast-forwarded to the "sitting fully clothed in bed together drinking hot chocolate" phase of our lives. You're even wearing a woolly hat.'

She smiled shyly. 'So, we've managed to have children without, er, you know, um...'

He tilted his head and waited for her to finish, the corners of his mouth twitching.

'You know,' she whispered. '*Doing* it.'

His shoulders shook as he unsuccessfully tried to hold back

his amusement. Sparkles fizzed through her. His face was gorgeous without expression, but when he laughed, it shone brighter than the sun.

'Yes,' he said. 'We've got four, maybe six kids. I told you earlier you were a goddess. You've created them without...' He paused, then whispered, '...*Doing* it.'

She stared into her mug.

'Your powers are limitless. You even managed to turn Charlotte into Charlie in a freezing loch. That's more challenging than turning water into wine.'

'You're...' She broke off, shaking her head.

'Good-looking? Witty? Charming? Or still a dickhead?'

She gazed at him, trying to sum up everything he was in life and to her. 'You're all of that and so much more. You're extraordinary,' she replied softly.

She saw the surprise on his face, the slight tension around his eyes as they became liquid, the set of his jaw. He swallowed. She finished her drink and set it on the bedside table, then snuggled up to him, snaking her arm under the covers and hugging across the expanse of his chest.

He carefully put his arm around her. By the side wall she saw her new suitcase, and beside it on the floor, her rucksack. Her heart was too full to hold everything in anymore. She needed to release the pressure.

'Alejandro is my younger brother,' she said quietly. 'He died because of me.'

She felt his chest stop moving as he held his breath. The sound of the crackling fire filled the silence.

He put his drink down and held her with both arms, stroking one hand slowly up and down her back, his breath returning. There was nothing hurried about his touch, no interrogation. He just waited for her to speak.

She couldn't remember the last time she'd told the story

out loud. Maybe she had never truly articulated her version of events.

'He was born ten months after me, an unplanned surprise. We grew up like twins. We were...' She crossed her fingers together against his chest and he hugged her a little tighter. 'We were so close. And we were crazy. Oh, we were wild.'

She paused, allowing the memories to come trickling in.

'Ale grew his hair longer, and I cut mine short so it matched his. Abuelita would tie ribbons in my hair and I would run outside and rip them out. We were the same size, so I wore Ale's clothes. We fooled everyone, sometimes even Mamá and Papá. We ran around barefoot, knocking on doors and running away. Stealing fruit, knocking over trash cans. We were known locally as "los pequeños salvajes", the little savages.'

Valentina closed her eyes and saw Ale's fierce face, his sun-browned skin, his black eyes, his tousled hair. She felt him grab her hand, the two of them running together through the back alleys behind the village houses, kicking up clouds of red dust. They were going to take on the world and win.

'My parents despaired,' she continued. 'They thought we were going to get into serious trouble. Then Abuelo died and we got even worse, stealing money, skipping school, riding the buses all day eating candy. So, when we were eleven, my parents sent us to different secondary schools. Ale had to take a bus for over an hour each way to his and I went to a very strict, all-girls school. Things were never the same again. Just over a year later, in a school play, I was seen by one of the producers of *La Vida Familiar* and went with Abuela to live in Bogota.'

Charlie kissed the top of her head through her hat. She hugged him tighter, a yearning pain in her heart for what once was and what could never be.

'The school he went to was rough. He fell in with a bad

crowd. We didn't know until it was too late, until he was arrested for selling drugs to other kids. My parents took him out, but he was angry. He wanted freedom. He wanted to travel the world.'

She opened her eyes and indicated the bag with her head.

'The rucksack is his. He was going to go to every country and cover his bag with their flags.' She paused, staring at the Colombian flag Charlie had fixed. 'I was becoming famous and people thought my family was rich. It was a dangerous time in Colombia... One day Ale got in another fight over me. But this guy had a gun. The producers allowed me one day off for the funeral. I hardly remember anything about that day. It was so quiet. Nobody cried. We were all paralysed with shock. But I remember speaking to God. I stood in the church and promised I would not be bad ever again. I would dedicate my life to getting my family out.'

She glanced up at him; the gold streaks in his eyes were like flames.

'And I almost have. I'm almost there.'

He raised his eyebrows slightly as if asking how.

She shuffled out of his hold and brought her tablet back to the bed.

'I still send them money, but not as much as I want—they so get so cross when I do.' She shook her head in exasperation with them. 'So, I've been saving to buy this.'

She found the website and passed him the tablet.

'Angel Park estates?'

'Yes. It's a new gated community in LA. When the money for the cosmetics contract comes through, I'll finally have enough to buy houses for my parents, my grandparents, my sister, my brother, and a small one for me.'

He looked at her.

She couldn't read his expression.

'A *small* one?'

'Yes. I don't need anything big. I could live with any of my family, but I want them to have their privacy.'

Charlie ran his finger along the scuffed edge of her tablet, then put it on the bed. 'So, every penny you earn goes into this fund?'

'Yes.' She was beginning to feel uncomfortable. Was it a mistake to have told him?

'And what does your family think of your plan?'

Her stomach squeezed and she looked away. 'We don't talk about it.'

He put the tablet on the bedside table. 'Come here.' He reached out and she snuggled into his chest. 'You're the most incredible person I've ever met.' He kissed her forehead. 'Your family are blessed to have you.'

She slid her hand under his jacket, feeling the warmth of his skin through the T-shirt. She scraped her nails down the ridges of his abs and he tensed.

'Valentina?'

'Yes, Charlie?'

'If you keep doing that, there's going to be trouble.'

She smiled and kissed the side of his neck. 'Maybe trouble is exactly what I need.'

❧ 18 ❧

Charlie tensed, then stretched and grabbed the thermometer. He put it in Valentina's ear and pulled it out as soon as it beeped. 'Fuck!'

'What is it?'

He showed her the small screen. 'Thirty-five point two. You're not getting naked until it's at least thirty-six.'

The swarm of butterflies inside her took off, batting their wings on the inside of her ribs. 'Maybe kisses would help me warm up?'

He stared at her, his eyes shining with green fire, then threw his jacket to the floor. She scooted under the covers and he followed, bracketing her body with his, his forearms braced either side of her head. He pulled off her hat and sank his nose into her hair.

'Fuck,' he exhaled. 'You smell so good.'

She tentatively touched the sides of his chest. He groaned, his hot breath sending prickles of excitement through her. She tugged his T-shirt up and ran her fingers across the muscles of his back.

He was still, but vibrating with tension. She scored her fingernails up his spine to the back of his neck. He broke away, pushing his face into the pillow and breathing heavily.

'Jesus Christ, Valentina,' he cried, his voice muffled.

Her body hummed with delight and she brought her mouth to his ear. 'Is the monster waking up, Charlie?' she whispered.

He huffed out a laugh, then put his knee between her thighs, pushing them apart. Before she could think, he wrapped his arm around her right leg, opening her to him.

His face was millimetres away, his eyes a dark, stormy green. Thrills rushed across her skin like popping champagne bubbles.

'Valentina,' he growled, pushing his hips into her. 'The monster's been awake since I saw you at Heathrow.'

She pulled his head down, mashing his lips to hers, darting her tongue into his mouth. He responded by holding her tightly, devouring her.

Pleasure crashed through her so fast she lost all sense of anything except his hot, urgent kisses and his rock-hard cock rubbing against her jeans. Aching desire pooled in her lower abdomen. Her body cried out to be stretched, filled, loved by him.

For the first time, she felt the alchemy of true passion—the crazy chemical cocktail of hormones driving her to want him bare inside her, filling her with his seed. She undulated her body, rubbing herself against him.

He broke away. 'Valentina. Jesus Christ.' He was breathless, his voice wavering as if he were about to faint. He scrunched up his face and yelled into the pillow.

'What is it? Are you okay?' she asked, her own voice breathy and light.

He raised his head and stared at her. The intensity in his eyes made her heart stop and her body tremble.

'Valentina.' He brought his forefinger and thumb towards each other until they were almost touching. 'I am *this* close to coming.' He shook his head. 'You're so fucking sexy, I'm literally about to come in my pants.'

Her cheeks burned as nervous laughter bubbled out. 'Well, isn't that what teenagers are meant to do?'

'You're the one being a teenager. I'm meant to be experienced enough to make it good for you.'

Her tummy clenched around his words, setting off a time bomb of worry, ticking down the seconds till she disappointed him.

Charlie was experienced—that was an undisputed fact. And she'd never got sex quite right. She heard Bryce's voice echoing from her memories: *No, not like that*. How could she please Charlie when she'd failed the only two men she'd ever been with? What if all the passion in his eyes disappeared when she took off her clothes?

She chewed her bottom lip.

He didn't notice as he was reaching for the thermometer to take her temperature. 'Thirty-five point eight.' He threw the thermometer away and she heard it hit the floor. 'Fuck it. We're getting naked.'

Her heart sped up. The worry bomb went off, sending splinters of anxious shrapnel shooting out.

She put her hands on his chest. 'W-wait,' she stammered.

He stopped.

'Can you please turn off the lights?'

He looked askance at her, as if she'd suggested they dress up as clowns. 'Why?'

Her eyes darted away from his. 'I... I would feel more comfortable.'

He knelt and pulled her legs either side of his, stroking up and down her thighs. 'You don't want to see me?'

'No! No, it's not that,' she said hurriedly.

She felt wretched and ashamed. He slowly pulled off his T-shirt and dropped it to the floor. She stared at him. *Holy mother of God.* She'd never seen such raw and powerful perfection. His face was symmetrical, beautiful, yet utterly masculine. A jaw you could strike a match off and lips that were made for sin.

And as for his body... Valentina's mouth watered. Charlie was the lovechild of a supermodel and Satan. Shredded and sculpted, every muscle perfectly outlined. But it was the body of a real man. The hair in the centre of his chest and leading down from his naval told her he was virile, not vain. Tattoos and scars told of stories she was yet to learn.

He stroked again up her inner thighs. 'Then what is it?' he asked. 'Because I'm fucking desperate to see you. To kiss you, lick you, taste you.'

She clasped her hands over her face. If she wasn't up to temperature before, she was now.

He gently pulled them away and kneaded his thumbs into her palms. 'What is it, Valentina?'

Her anxiety was boiling up, the pressure rising until she couldn't bear it any longer. 'How many people have you had sex with?' she blurted.

He seemed shocked, then embarrassed. His eyes shifted away and her heart sank. How could she ever please a man who'd been everywhere and slept with everyone?

He gazed back at her, squeezing her hands. 'Is this relevant to us, here, now?'

She nodded.

'Do you want me to include one-night stands when I was so drunk, I might as well have been shagging a piece of furniture?'

She nodded again. She could see his cheeks reddening.

'Is this important to you?'

Oh god, no wonder Rory joked he had syphilis. Could

Charlie even remember how many women he'd been with? She nodded, bracing herself for his answer.

'Five.'

'Five hundred?' she whispered, her throat tightening.

He shook his head.

'Five thousand?'

He shook his head again.

She was lost, bewildered. How many more could he have slept with? Five million?

He held up a fist, extended his thumb, then the rest of his fingers in turn. 'Jennifer, Katie, Lisa, Caitlin, and Caroline. Five.'

Her mouth opened but her brain failed to find any words.

He brought his hands back to the insides of her legs, scoring his nails up and down the fabric of her jeans. 'Is that a problem?'

'Er, ah!—' She broke off as he grazed the apex of her thighs. How could she think? How could she process what he'd said when he did *that*?

'Fuck!' he exhaled roughly.

He took a breath and held it, the muscles of his face and neck straining. He looked in pain. He let out a long, slow stream of air as if trying to hold onto his sanity.

'Do you think, Valentina, that once I see you naked, I won't want to be here anymore?'

Uncertainty flickered like a flame and his expression changed.

'Have men treated you badly in the past?'

She didn't know how to respond. Had Bryce? Or had it been her fault?

'Those arseholes didn't deserve you.' His face was tight. 'But I'm glad they fucked up.'

She sucked in a shocked gasp.

'I'm glad,' he continued, 'because it means I'm here with you now and they're not. And if those wankers have set the bar so fucking low that you're worried about me seeing your insanely hot body, anything I can do is an improvement.'

He took her hand and put it on the outside of his jeans. She trembled. He was so hard, so big. His length reached the waistband of his trousers.

'Do you doubt how you make me feel?' he asked. His large hand covered hers, squeezing, stroking. The heat was burning through the thin layer of denim.

'I *want* to see you,' he growled.

She swallowed, adrenaline coursing through her.

His eyes held hers. 'I want to see your skin flush. I want to watch you lose control. I want to watch you come.' He squeezed harder over his rock-hard shaft and she laboured to breathe. He looked on the edge of losing it. 'Do you believe me?'

She nodded.

He shuffled back and her hand fell to rest on his thigh. He bent one of her legs. 'Would you be okay if I took off a sock?'

She nodded again, watching, mesmerised as he pulled it off and massaged her foot with warm, strong strokes. She offered her other leg for him and he removed the sock, taking a foot in each hand. Both legs were bent, her feet centimetres from where he was pressing against his jeans.

Her heart hammered as she pushed back against his touch, bringing the soles of her feet either side of his cock. It was longer than her foot. He held the tops of her feet lightly, letting her lead, his breathing shallow.

She stroked her feet up and down his hard length, then brought her big toe over the top of his jeans, touching the hot, wet head, the slit soaked with precum.

Panting now, his hands were balled into tight fists, digging into the front of his thighs. She made a soft, needy sound in the back of her throat and felt his cock twitch. He closed his eyes tightly and lifted his chin, the tendons in his neck vibrating like piano wire.

'Fuck!' he growled.

Valentina took her chance and reached forward, snapping the top button of his jeans and pulling the zipper down. She fell back into the pillows as his cock sprung free. He let out a guttural cry and her breath caught in her throat.

She stared. It was long and thick—the head large and engorged, the skin tight and glossy with his arousal. His balls were drawn up into his curly brown hair and she could now see the head of the dragon. Its mouth was open and it looked like it was about to bite down on the base of his shaft.

Without thinking, she brought her feet either side of it and dragged them up and down. She ran her toe through the deep slit at the top, coating the whole of his cock with precum. His eyes were still tightly closed, his face scrunched up.

Her heart was beating fast, pounding against her chest. She couldn't believe she was doing this. She was bringing him pleasure. And with her *feet*? Nervous thrills spiralled and spun inside her.

Charlie wrenched away; his arms braced on his thighs.

'Please, can I take off your jeans?' He sounded desperate.

Her heart thumped into her throat. She nodded.

He undid the top button, tore down the zipper, and pulled her jeans down and off. He brought them up to his face and breathed in her scent. Her breath stopped with a gasp. *What is he doing?* He took another long breath, then dropped his eyes to her plain white panties.

Her hands shot to cover her crotch. He brought a finger to the outer edge of her hip, pushing it under the side of her knickers.

'Breathe,' he whispered.

Her breath returned in deep gulps. Was it possible to feel so much and not die?

Charlie tugged at the underwear. 'Can I take these off?'

She panicked and shook her head.

He smiled as if to reassure her. 'I can work with that.'

She wanted to close her eyes, but they remained stubbornly open as she watched him drop her jeans to the floor. He lay between her legs, kissing her ankles, stroking his fingers up and down her lower legs.

Over the sound of her own laboured breathing, she could hear him humming with pleasure. With each stroke, desire rushed up her legs, adding to the heavy pulse throbbing in her core. Between each devastating kiss he whispered endearments into her burning skin, telling her how beautiful she was, how hot she made him.

She tried to keep still, but the pleasure was too much to contain. She needed to move to release it.

By the time he reached the apex of her thighs, her body was vibrating. She desperately wanted to keep covering herself, but her fingers were twitching like tethered birds wanting to fly.

His nose pushed between them and he hummed into her sex. Blinding pleasure shot through her and she cried out, her hips bucking up into his face. His hot wet tongue pushed through the sodden cotton of her panties, dragging over the material, sucking at her through it.

'You taste so good,' he groaned.

'Oh god,' she cried, unable to hold back. 'Charlie!'

He dragged again and again across the cotton of her underwear as she rocked against him. Her hands fluttered away and settled on the back of his head, fingers splaying through his hair as her orgasm started to build.

He found her swollen clit and sucked on it, pulling at the nub through her panties.

'Oh, oh, *oh*...' she sobbed, clutching his hair, tugging him closer.

He pulled back, resting his forehead against the inside of her thigh, breathing heavily. Why had he stopped? Just as she was building the courage to ask, he started again, licking up the length of her slit. Long, hot, wet pulls of pleasure, every third one ending with the tip of his tongue vibrating against her clit.

His hands were on the insides of her thighs, pushing them wider. She felt the tendrils of her orgasm gathering at the outer edges of her being. They swirled around each other, whirling strands of pleasure weaving together into a tapestry of coloured light, getting brighter, thicker, bigger, building until—

He stopped again. Frustration boiled inside her as the promise of her orgasm ebbed. She bucked her hips into his face and he chuckled.

He knelt above her and touched the buttons of her jacket. 'Can this come off?'

Her body was heavy with desire, her nervousness beaten back. She nodded. He took her hands and sat her up. She stared at his swollen cock and blushed, letting him tug off her jacket.

'Are you ready to lose the jumper?' he whispered into her hair.

She nodded again. He tucked his fingers under her jumper but lifted off her T-shirt as well in the same move. She looked at him in surprise.

He grinned. 'Oops...'

She crossed her arms in front of her large breasts, anxiety and desire fighting inside her. She felt naked, despite the underwear.

Charlie kissed her lips gently and she softened into his touch. 'You take my breath away,' he whispered. He laid her back on the bed and stroked down her torso between her breasts.

She shivered.

He tilted his head. 'Are you warm enough, sweetheart?'

She nodded, not wanting to speak in case she wept with emotion. He looked relieved and kissed down her neck, suckling at her skin. A low moan escaped her as he scored his nails across the cup of her bra, finding her tight nipple and pinching it.

His mouth found the other and pulled at it through the lace material. She held onto his back, holding him to her. His cock bumped against her inner thighs, and she clamped her legs around it. He growled over her breast, thrusting his hips forward once, then leaping back as if burned.

He took a ragged breath in, his whole body tensed, then he fell on her. His mouth captured hers, one hand on the outside of her bra, the other returning to her panties. He pushed under the side of her underwear and into her tight heat, his thumb moving in circles over the top of the fabric, zeroing in on her clit.

She clenched around him, the promise of her orgasm whipping inside her like the winds of a storm, gathering for a cataclysmic release. His fingers slowly fucked her, building her pleasure as she moaned into his mouth and writhed against him.

He stilled and pulled his head away.

'Charlie, no! Don't stop,' she begged.

He gazed down at her, his eyes hooded and dark, his breathing ragged. 'Valentina. Do you want to come around my fingers or my cock?'

At his words, she clenched and light tore up her body. She looked down at his cock, weeping with precum.

'You need to tell me,' he said, his voice husky. 'I need to know what you want.'

She swallowed. This was it.

'Your cock,' she said, her voice scratchy and desperate.

His eyes widened as if he couldn't believe her. He grabbed a condom from his back pocket, ripped the packet open and unfurled it over his enormous length.

'Before you worry, I bought them earlier from the local pharmacy in a fit of optimism,' he said quickly, heading off her question before it arose.

She clutched at him, wanting him inside her before her insecurities changed her mind. He pulled her pants to one side, settled the head of his cock at her entrance, then looked at her as if seeking reassurance.

She opened her legs wider, angled her hips up and grabbed onto the side of his jeans, tugging him closer. They both cried out as he began to push into her resistance. He stopped, his arms braced either side of her.

'Valentina. You're so fucking tight,' he hissed.

She looked down, her mouth dry as he nudged further in. He was so big.

He paused. 'You okay?'

She nodded. Her previous experiences could never have prepared her for this. His size, the intensity in his gaze, and the feelings in her heart. She bucked her hips as she pulled him deeper. She wanted this more than anything in the world. She wanted him. Her life, her problems, her dreams, all faded to black. The only things in existence were her and Charlie in a blissful bubble of light.

He bottomed out and they breathed together, their eyes locked. She felt seen, held, wanted. Emotion boiled inside her, cracks appearing in the walls she'd erected around her heart for so long. She pushed everything down and closed her eyes, gyrating her hips up to him.

'Move, Charlie,' she whispered.

He thrust, sending sparks of pleasure shooting through her. She felt him dragging slowly out, then the hard, shattering pleasure as he buried himself inside her with a grunt. His pace was slow but intense, as if he could read her mind and her body, making tiny adjustments to ramp up her pleasure.

Her orgasm built again, flickers of light spiralling from the outside of her body inwards, whirling together faster and faster until her body reached the cresting point of no return.

'Open your eyes,' he commanded. 'Valentina, look at me.'

She wrenched them open and the sight of him sent her tumbling over the edge. Her chest arced off the bed, her head following. Everything went black as her orgasm hit. Wave upon wave of ecstasy rolled through her as she thrashed with overwhelming, blinding pleasure.

Over the ringing in her ears, she heard a high-pitched, keening scream, which she vaguely realised was coming from her. Her inner muscles contracted around his thrusting cock, detonating more shocks of pleasure. She heard him roar as he shuddered inside her, pumping his release.

She held him tightly as he collapsed on top of her, burying his face in her hair, breathing heavily, repeating her name over and over like a prayer.

She stared blankly up at the curtained canopy of the four-poster bed, her body humming at a new frequency.

Nothing would ever be the same again.

Charlie woke with the cool morning light on his face, holding a pillow tightly in his arms. He stared at the clouds, glowing with streaks of pink and gold through the diamond-paned window.

Last night Valentina hadn't said a word after she'd come apart around him. She'd seemed shocked and overwhelmed. He'd held her until she fell asleep, then carefully extricated himself from the bed, tucked her in, turned off the lights, and crept back to his own room.

She was working the next morning and he knew if he stayed the night, he wouldn't be able to stop himself from reaching for her again and again.

Now, awake and alone, it was his turn to be overwhelmed. His heart thumped loudly, pushing up into his throat. His skin was hot and itchy, stretched tight, trying to hold in emotions too big to constrain.

A hot wind twisted through his mind. It rattled in the dark corners, disturbing dust-covered memories. It poked him to feel things he didn't want to feel.

Throwing back the covers, he sat on the edge of the bed, head in his hands, trying to ignore his erection. It jerked impatiently, slapping against his stomach, demanding to know where Valentina was. *Fuck!*

He couldn't get carried away. He couldn't let thoughts of her lead to thoughts about Caroline. About the baby. About even darker memories.

Focus, dickhead!

He had no future with Valentina—she'd made that abundantly clear. So why make more of this than what it was? A fling. A bit of fun. Notch number six on his bedpost. He shook his head in disgust at his thoughts and headed to the bathroom for a cold shower.

As the water battered his body, he thought of how Valentina was last night: nervous, shy, unsure. But she'd still laid her body, her life, her soul open for him. She'd blown his fucking mind.

He'd never met anyone like her before. Someone so responsible, so compassionate. She'd given up her whole life for her family, made them her life's mission whether they wanted it or not.

He sighed, letting the icy water run down over his face. He'd met her grandmothers, her sister. They wouldn't want her blaming herself for Alejandro's death. They wouldn't want her working her life away to buy them a dream.

He turned off the shower and dried himself, staring in the mirror at his scars, his tattoos, his history. He rubbed the towel over a black puma, remembering Caroline's name written underneath, then over a string of musical notes on his arm.

He felt a sudden rush of loss. Everything he touched turned to shit.

Valentina was a saint. What the fuck could he bring to her life? The only thing he had to offer was his body.

He moved into the bedroom, throwing on clothes. In what brief time they had together, he was going to worship her. He was going to leave her so pleasured, so well fucked, she'd have no doubt she was a goddess. He had to undo the damage done by whoever made her feel less than she was.

The thought that some prick had made her think she wasn't desirable, wasn't perfect just the way she was, made his blood boil.

A quiet knock at his door had his heart tripping. He yanked it open.

Valentina gazed up at him, her dark eyes anxious.

'You left,' she said, her voice small.

'Do you think I didn't want to stay?'

He could see the answer on her face.

Pulling her inside, he shut the door, drawing her into his arms, burying his nose into her hair.

'Valentina,' he exhaled, holding her tightly to him. Heat pulsed in his cock. He cupped her face, falling into her liquid eyes. 'I left because you're working this morning. You needed to rest, not have me bothering you all night.'

Her eyes widened and the flush in her cheeks spread. He reached down and kissed her, running the tip of his tongue along her plump bottom lip. She shivered and his blood ran thick with desire. Holding her tighter, he kissed her deeper, his tongue stroking hers. Sparks turned into flames as she pressed into him.

He lifted her and she wrapped her legs around his waist, rubbing against his jeans. The friction on his cock was excruciating. He sat on the edge of the bed, grabbed her bottom, and pulled her closer to him with a grunt. She moaned into his mouth, running her hands into his hair, setting off more fires to rage through his body. All he could think of was burying himself inside her again.

She pulled away, breathing heavily, her eyes hazy, her lips puffy.

He bucked his hips.

'Charlie?'

Her voice sent another jolt to his cock. That soft accent saying his name, breathy with need.

'Huh?'

'I have to eat some breakfast, go to set.'

He blinked himself back into a world that rudely chose to exist outside of their bubble. 'You're incredible. You blow me away.'

She smiled at him, shining with happiness.

He would do anything to keep that smile in place. 'I've had an idea.'

She raised a perfectly shaped eyebrow. 'Another one? Don't we have enough on our plate, Charlie?'

He kissed the end of her nose. 'True, but we're motoring through your list of teenage kicks. I think we'll have ticked everything off in the next twenty-four hours.'

'Really?'

He ran his fingers up and down her back. 'This idea is about fundamentally altering the fabric of your cognitive universe.'

She giggled. 'Those are big words.'

He pulled her closer to his cock. 'It must be because they're coming from *this* brain.'

Her mouth dropped open, and she blushed. 'Charlie!'

He grinned. 'So, wanna hear my cunning plan? It actually intersects with some of your teenage tasks.'

'Does it involve getting naked?'

'Yes!'

Her cheeks were now on fire. He tucked his fingers in the back pockets of her jeans, feeling the warmth from her skin.

'So, Valentina. There exists in this room someone who does not fully comprehend the extent of their beauty and blindingly hot body. We all know that person isn't me. Because...' He flexed his arms as he held her. 'Check out the gun show.'

She giggled.

'So, I have taken it upon myself, until we say goodbye, to dedicate my body to pleasuring yours until you know how truly mind-blowing you are.'

'How selfless of you,' she said, trying to hold back her smile.

He raised his eyebrows. 'I know, right? I'm like the Dalai Lama of sex.'

There was a pause.

He held his breath, waiting for her, his body tense.

'Okay, Charlie.'

He felt his eyes bugging out. Was this for real?

She gave him a mischievous grin. 'I hope you've got stamina.'

CHARLIE MADE VALENTINA LATE. THERE WAS NO TIME FOR sex, but once he started kissing her, it was impossible to stop. Eventually, when they heard a runner calling her name down the corridor, he opened the door to his room and pushed her through, promising to come find her later.

Rory was out most of the day running errands for Zoe with Bandit, so he did a walk-through of the castle, went for a run, then worked out in the gym. It was late morning when he went to find Valentina.

Passing by the front door to the castle, one of the twenty-four-hour security guards called to him.

'Charlie?'

He stopped. Standing beside the thick-set man was a courier, holding a package. 'Hey Greg, what's up?'

'This chappie's got a package for Ms Valverde, but he has to give it to her personally. Can you take him to her?'

'Yeah, sure, no problem.' He turned to the courier. 'Follow me.'

He led the way to the great hall, the young man beside him turning his head at every new sight.

'Do you know her?' the courier asked. 'Valentina Valverde?'

He couldn't help a grin spreading across his face. 'Yeah, a bit.'

'What's she like?'

'Amazing.'

In the great hall, he spotted Valentina chatting to Zoe. He stood back, his hand on the courier's arm, waiting for her conversation to finish before interrupting, happiness warming him from the inside out.

She made her way over to them, her face composed but her eyes smiling.

He nodded at the man beside him. 'Valentina, this young man has a parcel for you.'

The courier thrust a bag at her, swallowing nervously. 'Is it a script?' he blurted.

She smiled, but seemed uncomfortable. 'Yes. For my next film.'

'Wow. Er. Wow.' It looked like he was going to pass out with excitement.

Her smile broadened but didn't reach her eyes. 'Would you like a picture?'

CHARLIE ESCORTED THE COURIER BACK TO THE FRONT OF THE castle, listening to his non-stop chatter about how this was the greatest day of his life, then returned to Valentina. She had the package wedged inside the big bag she carried everywhere with her.

She turned to him. 'I'm going to get Zoe some lunch. She's still not feeling great after last night. Then I've got an appointment for a couple of hours. When I'm done will you be free?'

He nodded. His to-do list had been culled to only one task —pleasuring her.

'Should I come and find you around three? Will you be in your room?'

He nodded again.

'Charlie, have you lost the power of speech?'

His cheeks heated as he nodded again.

She grinned and turned on her heel, returning to Zoe, the beads on the bottom of her dress swishing with every step.

He limped away stiffly. Maybe he needed to offload some pent-up sexual energy to stop himself putting in a premature performance later. The run and the gym hadn't done anything to take the edge off.

His phone rang and he answered without checking who it was, expecting Rory. 'Mate, what's up?'

'It's me,' his sister replied. 'How's Angola?' Her voice dripped with sarcasm.

Guilt flooded through him, pushing out every bit of happiness. He opened the door to the library. It was empty and quiet. A grand piano stood in the corner, a dust cover over it. He turned his back to it and sat in an old leather wingback chair with a sigh.

'Hey, Tabbie.'

Silence. He could hear his sister taking a breath as if to speak, then changing her mind. Years of shame bore down on him. Decades of disappointing both her and their parents. He didn't know what to say. Sorry didn't even begin to cover it.

'I'm ringing about a couple of things,' she began, her voice brittle. 'It's Mum and Dad's ruby wedding anniversary in a couple of weeks. They're having a garden party.'

Charlie's stomach twisted. He'd rather have his teeth pulled out without anaesthetic than attend. All those happy couples, people who'd known him from childhood, who'd watched his every fuckup. All asking if he had a 'special someone' in his life.

The last time he'd seen his parents' friends, one of them was even tipsy enough to ask if there was a special 'gentleman friend' in his life. If Charlie went, he would stand there, the odd one out, a rictus grin stuck to his face, as parts of his soul broke off. Until all that was left of him was dust.

'Barbara told me the shoot will be over by then and you won't be needed. I've also spoken to Mack, and he says you don't have any work lined up.'

He let out a huff. His sister, as ever, had all his exits covered.

'You need to be there, Charlie.'

'And the other thing?' His voice sounded cold and flat.

Another long silence. *Don't be such a fucking dick!* He could tell his sister was trying to keep her cool, trying to be the bigger person. But instead of being his best self, he shrank back, becoming all the worst parts.

He could hear her trying to start sentences again, trying to find the right words.

Irritation flared inside him. 'What is it? I've got to go.'

'It's nothing—forget it,' she said in a rush. 'We can talk at the party.'

He sighed. 'Oh, come on, Tab... out with it. It can't be worse than having to spend a day with the great and the good of Chumleigh Underbottom.'

There was silence, then she spoke. 'I'm pregnant.'

Charlie laughed. It sounded manic and forced. 'Very funny.'

'We've just had the twenty week scan. We're having a little girl.'

The news was a punch to the gut. He was going to be sick. 'But you don't want kids.'

'How do you know?'

He didn't reply.

'How the fuck do you know that, eh?' Now his sister was shouting. 'You don't know the first thing about what I want and don't want. You even think my marriage to Miles is some sort of joke. What the fuck is wrong with you, Charlie? Why are you such a fucking arsehole? Why can't you just be happy for me?' He heard her voice break.

'Tab—'

'We're *done*, Charlie.' He could hear her trying not to cry. 'Don't call me back. Don't ever speak to me again.'

'Tab—'

But she'd hung up.

❧ 20 ☙

Charlie stood at the edge of the loch. He was far from the village and utterly alone. He tugged off his clothes and walked into the water.

The cold pricked at his body and he fought to control his breathing. He wanted the pain. It was no less than he deserved. He'd never felt so ashamed, so worthless. He'd had a privileged upbringing, been afforded every opportunity, and this was the man he'd become.

He sank under the water. Knives of ice stabbed at his forehead, his eyes, his ears. Should he stay here? Let go? Make a clean break from this life? *Coward.* He pulled his head up and ran his hand over his face. He'd never walked away from his comrades in the field. It was about time he grew up and stopped running away from his family and his past.

Out near the middle of the loch an osprey swooped and soared. It glided down, then snatched at the surface with a splash, flying upwards and away with a fish in its talons.

It was a moment in time, a moment of now, which became the past as soon as it had happened. Charlie flexed his hands, suddenly hyper-aware of the constantly unfolding present. He couldn't undo the past. He couldn't let it blight his life, his relationships, and his future.

He strode out of the water and dried himself with his T-shirt. His mind was full of boxes containing past mistakes. Boxes he should have dealt with years ago.

The longest journey starts with a single step.

He could do this.

BACK IN HIS ROOM, HE FINISHED VALENTINA'S PRESENT AND put it in the wardrobe, then picked up the embroidery of the cottage garden that Barbara had started. She hadn't done much, but her stitching was immaculate. He sat on the bed and threaded a needle.

He was making headway when a knock at the door pulled him out of his meditation. He dropped the panel, threw a pillow over it and went to the door, his legs stiff and sore. He was surprised to see Valentina on the other side. 'You're done already?'

'I'm actually a little late.'

He glanced at his watch. He'd been sewing for over two hours. No wonder his legs hurt. She gazed at him expectantly.

'Shit! Sorry, come in. I, er, was, um, reading.'

She cast her eyes around the room. 'What book?'

'Er.'

She went to the bed where a strand of embroidery thread was sticking out from under the pillow.

'*War and Peace.* I was reading it on my phone.'

She moved the pillow aside and picked up the embroidery panel.

'Hmm. This doesn't look like *War and Peace* to me.' She

grinned. 'If Abuela sees this, she'll definitely want to fight me for you.'

His cheeks burned. He'd rather be naked than have her look at this part of his life.

'Did you do all of this?' she asked.

He cleared his throat. 'Barbara, Rory's mum, started it, but she's given it to me to finish. I was thinking of giving it to my mother when it's done.'

She smiled and his heart squeezed. 'Charlie, it's beautiful. I'm sure she will love it. You're such a caring man.'

Shame burned like acid in his throat. 'I'm not,' he replied thickly. 'I'm not a good person.'

She stared at him, her gaze appraising and assessing, then laid the panel carefully on the bed. 'If I can be hot, then you can be kind.'

He rolled his eyes.

She tilted her head at his reaction. 'Just because you believe something doesn't mean it has to be true.'

'That's not a fair comparison, Valentina, and you know it. You're objectively hot as fuck. It's a fact. Like gravity. Or taxes. I, on the other hand, can point you to a long list of people who think I'm a thoughtless prick.'

Her expression was blank. 'Hmm. If you say so.' She paused. 'I've spent the last two hours overseeing a present for you. Would you like to have it?'

'What?'

She smiled. 'I had an idea. To do something for you.' She took his hand. 'Shall we go and see it?'

She had done something for *him*? He felt uncomfortable and embarrassed. He already knew he didn't deserve it.

'Come on, Charlie, if it makes you feel better it's also a present for me.'

Now he was even more confused. 'Have you bought a sex swing?'

She pushed at his chest. 'No! Charlie!' She looked shocked and a little bit aroused. 'Is... *sex*,' she whispered, 'all you ever think about?'

He shrugged. 'If you're around, then yes.'

Her nostrils flared. She put her hands on her hips and lifted her chin. He couldn't help his eyes dropping to her magnificent chest.

'Charlie!' she hissed, crossing her arms in front of herself.

He pouted.

'Do you want your present, or not?'

Valentina led Charlie through the castle until they reached the door to the library.

'Come on,' she said, tugging him inside. 'It's in here.'

He followed her through. The room looked the same as it had earlier, but the dust cover had been removed from the grand piano and the lid was raised. His stomach clenched with unease.

She pulled him towards it. 'I found a piano tuner in Inverness and he came and tuned it this afternoon.'

His legs felt wooden. Sickness rose into his throat. She sat him down and he stared at the keys, his eyes blurring.

She sat next to him. 'So it's really a present for me because I want to hear you play.'

His head turned slowly towards hers. He felt dizzy. She looked so excited. So expectant.

'I can't,' he said hoarsely.

She frowned. 'You don't really know how to play?'

'No, I can play.' His throat was closing. 'I *could* play—once.' He looked down. 'I haven't for fourteen years.'

'Charlie?' Her voice was soft. Her hand covered his and he flinched. He couldn't go there. He just couldn't. She squeezed. Emotion strangled him. Pain stretched up into his face, his eyes pricking. Hers were full of compassion he didn't deserve.

'What happened, Charlie?'

He shook his head.

She held his gaze. 'I haven't talked to anyone outside my family about Alejandro. I thought it was impossible. That if I did, my heart would break open and I would die from the pain. But I felt safe with you. I could do it.' She smiled at him. 'And I didn't break. I want you to feel safe with me. I'm not going to judge you.'

His heart stretched inside him. To move on from the past, he had to acknowledge it. Valentina was his Samaritan—a passing stranger on his journey through life. Someone he could unburden himself on, then never see again. If she could tell him about her brother, he could tell her this.

He turned his palm up and clasped her hand, staring down at their fingers entwined, then took a deep breath.

'We moved a lot when I was growing up because of my dad's different army postings. Whenever we moved, the piano came with us. My mum doesn't play much herself, but she loves classical music and wanted me and my sister to learn. My sister was more like my father, into sports. She was Daddy's girl and I was Mummy's boy. Playing the piano made Mum happy, so I kept doing it.

'When I was twelve and Tab was fifteen, my dad got a more permanent posting and we moved to Chumleigh. My hormones were raging and I was fed up with Dad telling me what I could and couldn't do. I was growing so fast and it was really hard on my mum. It was like I went through puberty in a couple of months and her little boy had been stolen and replaced by a grumpy man.'

He brought his other hand to stroke Valentina's fingers, using them as a distraction whilst he opened the darkest box in his mind.

'I was angry,' he continued. 'And resistant to the life I thought my parents had chosen for me. My dad became stricter, my mum confused, hurt, and distant. I'd won a music scholarship to an exclusive local school, but intended to stop playing as soon as I got there. It was going to be another form of rebellion, a way of punishing my mother for always siding with my father. But then I met my new piano teacher.'

Charlie paused.

'Her name was Jennifer,' he said with a thin smile. 'She was twenty-one, just out of music college and working as a piano teacher until she worked out what she wanted to do with her life. I fell in love during our first lesson. I didn't say anything to anyone, but from that moment on I practised every day. I wanted to please her, impress her.

'And the more I practised, the more time there was in the lesson to talk. For one hour a week I would play a bit, to show I'd done whatever she'd asked me to, then we would talk. At home I was just as difficult as before—a typical teenage arsehole. But with her it was different. I was happy.'

Valentina was silent as his mind slipped backwards in time.

'She was my teacher for five years. She thought I was a prodigy.' He let out a short laugh and shook his head. 'She was so proud of me. I even applied to music college, partly for her, but mostly to piss off my dad. I never intended to go. I didn't want to leave her.

'In my final year of school, when I was seventeen, I made my move. I'd been in love with her for years and wanted her to fall in love with me. I was the same height I am now, almost the same weight and had been shaving every day since I was fourteen. I knew almost everything about her and was overflowing with confidence and testosterone. Seducing her was easy. I took her to bed without any thought of what I was doing to her life.'

'Charlie,' Valentina said gently. 'She was what, twenty-six? A grown woman. In a position of trust. She took advantage—'

'No,' he said sharply. 'No fucking way. Absolutely not. She was innocent and clueless. She lived at home with her elderly parents and was a fucking virgin, for Christ's sake. I was the bad guy. I took advantage of her. I was thoughtless and selfish, and when it all went wrong, it was her who paid the price.'

He felt like his chest was being crushed. He couldn't breathe.

Valentina moved closer and held onto his arms. 'It's okay, Charlie.'

His breathing was laboured and he fought to get it under control. He wasn't going to shy away from showing her just what kind of a person he was. Let the scales drop from her eyes.

He held her gaze. 'It was a fucking miracle we got away with it for so long. I think mostly because her parents were deaf as posts and went to bed at eight o'clock. But two weeks after my eighteenth birthday, the exam results came out. I got straight A's. We went out in Chumleigh and got wasted. I persuaded her to climb on top of the bus shelter at three in the morning.

'We had sex, too drunk to notice the noise we were making. The police were called and we were arrested. Then it all went to shit. We were charged with public indecency, and during the interview it came out we'd been having an affair. Jennifer was then charged with sexual offences against a minor. She was sacked, banned from teaching for life, and demonised by the press.

'My parents went ballistic. I told them I was never going to give her up. My dad and I fought in front of my mum as she screamed at us to stop. After beating the living shit out of me, Dad gave me a deal. He'd back my claim that I only ever had sex with her once, when I wasn't legally a child, if I joined the army and never saw her again. I went along with it. It was the only way I could attempt to salvage the mess I'd made.

'That night I climbed out the window and cycled to her parents' house. I told her what we should do. She couldn't stop crying. She kept apologising, over and over, as if it were her fault and it was my life being screwed over, not hers. It felt like my heart was being ripped to shreds. I made her promise to go along with my dad's plan, then left. I joined the army and didn't see her again. I haven't played the piano since.'

Charlie bowed his head, exhausted and empty.

'Do you know what happened to her?'

He nodded. 'I asked my friend Mack to check up on her. He found her on Facebook. She's living in Kent. Married with four kids. He said she looked happy.'

'Charlie, look at me.' Valentina lifted his head. 'If she can move on and be happy, maybe you could too?'

The sound of her tablet ringing jolted them both. She lifted it from her bag. 'It's Isabella.' She hesitated.

He stood. 'Answer it. It's important. I've got to go and find Rory anyway.'

He walked out without looking back.

Valentina curled up on a sofa by the empty fireplace to take the call, hidden from the door by the tall back of the seat.

She made an effort to smile when Isabella's face appeared on the screen, even though her thoughts were still with Charlie. 'Hey, sexy mamá, how are you doing?'

Her sister tried to smile in return but immediately dissolved into tears.

'Bella, what's wrong? Where's Matias?'

Isabella's face was puffy, as if she'd been crying a while. 'At work,' she sobbed.

'Where's Mamá? Abuela and Abuelita? You shouldn't be alone if you're sad!'

Isabella blew her nose. 'I'm sorry, Tina, I thought I'd be okay if I talked to you. I didn't mean to cry.'

'Sweetheart, it's okay. I'm glad you rang. What's going on?'

Isabella wiped her eyes and smoothed her hands over her face. 'I keep getting these pains. They're called Braxton Hicks contractions. My belly goes tight like a drum. But, Tina, they hurt so much. It's getting real now and I'm scared.'

'Have you spoken to Mamá? Your midwife?'

Isabella nodded. 'They say everything's fine.' She puffed out her cheeks. 'I'm sorry. I didn't mean to dump all this on you.'

Valentina glanced at her bag which contained the script that had arrived earlier. It was the reason she wouldn't be at the birth, holding her sister's hand.

She felt sick with guilt. The role wasn't even paying much, but it was so different from anything she'd ever done before. She was gambling on it being the catalyst for new and more interesting jobs.

'Remind me when you're coming home?' Isabella asked.

This was a rhetorical question. They both knew when.

'I'll be back for my birthday.'

'You never told me about the film you're doing next. What's it about?'

More shame scratched at Valentina's skin. Even her agent said the role was a risk. 'It's just a small independent art house. The story's about London life,' she lied. 'It's not important.'

'Then why do it?' her sister asked bluntly. 'Pull out. It won't affect anything. Just come home.'

Irritation flared inside her. She couldn't. She'd never pulled out of a contract. She'd never missed a day's work. 'I can't.'

Isabella was silent, staring at her.

Valentina shook her head. 'I *won't*. I won't walk away from my responsibilities.'

Her sister's jaw was trembling. 'What about us? Aren't we more important than some little film?'

'I'm doing this for you!' she cried. 'Everything is for you!'

Her sister shook her head. 'It's not what I want. I want you here.'

· · ·

WHEN THE CALL ENDED, THE DAYLIGHT WAS FADING AND the library was getting dark. Valentina lay on the sofa in a ball, her body numb and her mind blank. She was in a prison of her own making and couldn't see a way out.

The door opened and someone crept in, crying. She lifted her head over the back of the sofa to see Shauna, her shoulders shaking as she held her face.

'Shauna?'

She shrieked. 'Oh, Valentina, I'm sorry. I didn't know you were here.'

'Chica, it's okay. Come sit for a bit.'

Shauna glanced from the door to her watch. She crossed the room and sat next to Valentina. 'She's eating with His Holiness. I've got a few minutes.'

'Rough day?'

'I've had better.'

'Want to talk about it?'

'There's no point.'

'You could get another job?'

Shauna shook her head. 'She'll blacklist me. Like she did all the others. I was so dumb. I thought I could do better than them. Of course, I was wrong. So now I've made my bed, I have to lie in it.'

'There's always another way.'

Shauna looked at her bleakly. 'Is there?'

Valentina's throat tightened. 'Want to go grab some dinner? The caterers told me tonight is "Colombian night", so you can learn from an expert how wrong they've got it.'

She checked at her watch again, then nodded.

VALENTINA AND SHAUNA WERE EATING WHEN CHARLIE joined them. He looked as devastatingly hot as ever, but

Valentina could see the tension on his face.

'Ms Valverde, Ms Merritt. May I join you?'

Shauna blushed and looked to Valentina.

'Yes, of course,' she smiled. 'You are most welcome, Mr Hamilton.'

The three of them ate in silence as if lost in their own thoughts, with no one possessing the energy to lift the mood. After a few minutes, Shauna had cleared her plate and was checking the time.

'Congratulations, Shauna,' said Charlie with a grin. 'That's a new record. My money's definitely on you for the next Coney Island eating contest.'

She blushed again and Valentina rolled her eyes.

He grabbed the edge of Shauna's plate as she stood. 'I'll sort it. You go attempt to please the unpleasable. Let me know if you succeed as I've got some water I'd like you to turn into wine.'

Shauna let him take her plate. 'Thank you,' she said to both of them before dashing off.

As they watched her go, Valentina felt Charlie's leg touching hers. Heat spread up her thighs. She reached under the table for his hand. His fingers stroked hers, nudging into the creases, circling her palm. His touch was electric.

'Are you busy this evening?' she asked, her voice breaking slightly.

He shook his head and her internal temperature shot up.

She swallowed. 'I wondered if you could give me a guided tour?'

His eyebrows raised slightly.

'Of your tattoos.'

He let go of her hand and grabbed the bottom of his T-shirt, pulling it up.

'Charlie!' she hissed, yanking it back down and glancing

around. 'Not here!'

He stared at her, a pantomime look of confusion on his face. 'Where do you suggest? The guided tour normally starts here around seven.'

She glared at him.

He leaned forward and smiled. 'Your room or mine?' he whispered.

As soon as she entered her room, Valentina shut the curtains.

Charlie turned the main lights on.

'Could you turn them off please?' she asked. 'I thought we could light a fire.'

'Good idea,' he replied. 'It's far too bright in here.' He covered his eyes as if to shield them. 'Fuck, I think my retinas just burned out.'

He turned the light off and the room darkened, then raised his arms, waving them about as if feeling his way.

'Yes, this is much better.' He stumbled straight into the fire guard, kicking it over with a crash. 'Oops, hang on.' He knelt and knocked over the log basket.

'Charlie!' she yelled. '¡No seas tan idiota!' She put her hands on her hips as he crawled across the floor towards her. 'Okay,' she huffed. 'You've made your point.' She tapped her foot impatiently at his theatrics. 'You can put the light back on.'

He reached her feet and grabbed her ankles. 'No problem. I've found a floor light. Give me a sec.' He felt up her legs and excitement fizzed under his touch. 'I just need to find the button to turn it on.' He roamed higher. 'I think this model has two.'

She shrieked with laughter and tried to wriggle out of his touch. He pulled her down to him and their lips met. She kissed him without hesitation, angling her head, her tongue darting into his hot mouth.

He groaned, running one hand into her hair, the other down to grab her bottom, yanking her against the hard length of his cock. She tugged at the bottom of his T-shirt, needing his hot skin on hers. He released her and pulled it off as she removed her own top and unsnapped the clasp of her bra, letting her breasts fall free.

He stared at her in the half light, the shadowed planes of his body heaving with every breath. 'Christ, Valentina.'

She was feverish with need, burning with an urgent desperation to get him inside her, to rock herself to a blinding climax. She lifted his fingers to her hardened nipples and sharp pleasure shot down to her clit as he rolled and rubbed the tips. She dug her nails into his muscled thighs.

'Jesus fucking Christ,' he exhaled, his breathing harsh and ragged.

She felt wet heat on her nipple and cried out again as he sucked on her, pulling out more pleasure. She fumbled to open his trousers, then pulled his cock free from his boxers. He groaned against her breast, the vibrations pulsing down her body. Grabbing his cock, she stroked it as she rocked her hips.

It wasn't enough. She stared into his luminous green eyes shining in the darkness. 'Charlie. I need you.'

He blinked.

She moved back, pulling her trousers, knickers, and socks off. He pulled a condom out of the back pocket of his jeans.

'Hurry,' she whispered.

She watched his shaking hands as he sheathed himself, then kneeled above him, straddling his thighs and slowly sinking down. They cried out together as he entered her. She held the back of his neck, his tendons taut as she stretched around him. Shocks of pleasure radiated through her centre.

He bowed his head to suck at her nipple. Pleasure flooded through her, helping ease her all the way down. She sat, feeling the fullness of his cock, the fabric of his jeans on the backs of her thighs. He jerked inside her and she squeezed hard around him. He let out a strangled cry, his body vibrating.

She wanted to lose herself with him, leave the rest of the world behind, surrender to the intense pleasures of his body. She locked her arms around him, lifted, then dropped with a sigh.

Her orgasm was already spiralling deep inside, so she chased it, riding him, grinding herself against his rigid abs. The shudders started, then they smashed through in thunderous waves of pleasure. She screamed his name, pulsing around him as she shook in his arms.

The sensations continued, rippling out beyond her skin until she lost sense of where she ended and the rest of the world began. He released her breast and held her tightly as he thrust up into her, hard and fast. More shocks of pleasure shot through her as he came, his body shaking as he cried her name.

They clung to each other as if holding on for dear life, gasping in unison. Her whole world was this moment. Her whole world was him. Her heart opened like a flower, the petals unfurling towards his light with a fragile, yearning sweetness.

She pushed them closed. She couldn't open herself up to him. She wouldn't.

He was kissing her face now, stroking her hair, repeating her name over and over. The flower inside her bloomed, filling her chest with longing for what she could never have.

She kissed him, stopping the sound of her name, trying to focus on the physical and block out the emotion. His kisses were languid, his tongue tasting her, stroking her mouth.

It was too good, too much. She broke away and rested her forehead on his.

'What happened to the grand tattoo tour?' she asked breathlessly.

He let out a huff. 'I don't know. One moment I was crawling around on the floor, the next I was jumped by a light fitting.'

She giggled.

'Valentina...'

'Yes?'

'Do you think at some point in the future you might allow me to take off my jeans?'

She let out a throaty laugh.

He arched an eyebrow. 'You know, when we...' He brought his mouth to her ear. '*Do it*,' he whispered.

'Are you teasing me?'

She felt his smile against her cheek. 'Only a little.'

She rested against him as their breathing slowed, feeling him still thick inside her. In the dim light she could see their bodies entwined. She shivered with nervous excitement.

He kissed her shoulder. 'I need to get something from my room. Can you give me a couple of minutes?'

She nodded and climbed off him, suddenly shy. He stood, took care of the condom, and redressed.

He held his hand out to her. 'Stand on my feet.'

She looked at him, confused, then did as he asked. He walked her to the door, her feet on top of his.

'What are you doing?' she giggled.

'Keeping you close. I understand if you put clothes on when I'm gone, but I want you to know that naked you is my favourite you.' He leaned down and kissed her. 'I'll be back in a bit.'

❦   22   ❦

Charlie knocked on Valentina's door ten minutes later, showered and unsure, her present behind his back.

She opened the door and he took in her outfit.

'Tartan pyjamas. In pink, no less. Very nice. I think they're the colours of the McGhirlie clan.'

She poked him. 'They were a gift from my sister and they're very soft and warm.'

He kissed her. 'Just like you.'

She whimpered as their lips touched and his cock throbbed in his jeans.

She pulled away, her cheeks pink. 'Can I have my tattoo tour now?'

He glanced over her shoulder into the room. The fire was lit and the side lights were on. 'In a minute. I want to get your present ready first.'

'My present?'

'Yes, but you have to sit on the bed and close your eyes so I can set it up.'

'O-kaay,' she replied dubiously, then did as he asked.

He opened the door a little further and her eyes snapped open.

'Hey, come on now. No peeking.'

When she did as instructed, he put the fireguard in front of the fire and laid his gift on the floor. He then gently peeled her hands away from her face. 'You can look now.'

She opened her eyes and he felt a familiar tug in his heart as he held her gaze. She was utterly captivating. Each time he saw her he tumbled deeper and deeper into—

'Where's my present?' she asked, interrupting his thoughts before they got out of hand.

He led her to the fire, his palms beginning to sweat. What if she didn't like it? What if she liked it but didn't want to accept it? He gestured at the floor, looking for her reaction. 'There's your present.'

She dropped to her knees, her fingers running into the soft, pale wool of the sheepskin. 'Charlie, it's beautiful. Thank you.'

His shoulders slumped with relief.

She frowned at him. 'How big was the sheep?'

He knelt beside her. 'It's a Hamilton. A heritage breed designed for size and stamina.'

'A *Hamilton*,' she replied with a grin. 'So where are all the branding marks?'

'On the back.'

She turned the edge of the giant rug over. 'Oh, Charlie!' she gasped. 'You've used four.' She touched the stitching holding the fleeces together. 'Did you sew this?'

'Yes.'

'But, Charlie, it's so expensive. I...' She broke off and he swallowed. She'd noticed the embroidery in one of the corners. She traced the letters. 'You've sewn my name.'

He cleared his throat. 'Yeah. I embroidered your name into

the back of every sheepskin. So you know it's yours. Every bit of it is yours.'

She dropped her head and let go of the edge of the rug so it fell back into place. Her cheeks were red.

He'd anticipated she might try to turn his gift down, so had embroidered her name on the back. Then he thought she might unpick the four sheepskins and give away the other three. He'd be fucked if he was going to let that happen, so he'd sewn her name into the back of every one.

'Valentina?'

She nodded, still gazing down.

'I can afford it. It's my money and I want to do this for you. At the end of the shoot, I'm going to get it couriered wherever you want. If you don't want to give me your address, I'll get Shauna to arrange it. Please. Let me do this for you.'

He watched a tear run down the bridge of her nose and drop to the cream pile. It held together at the end of a tuft, a perfect sphere, the flames from the fire dancing inside.

'Hey.' He pulled her onto his lap. 'If there's going to be any bodily secretions on this rug, I don't want them to be tears.'

She snuggled into his chest and he passed her a handkerchief. 'Sorry, Charlie. It's so lovely but I'm not very good at accepting gifts.'

He rocked her gently in his arms. 'You know how good it feels to give a present to someone?'

She nodded.

'Then allow me to feel good. If you're happy, then I'm eleventy trillion times happier.'

She wiped her eyes. 'How am I doing paying off my bar bill, by the way?'

He shook his head. 'Terrible. You've got twenty trillion, ninety-nine million, ninety-nine thousand, ninety-nine hundred, and sixty-nine kisses left to go.'

'Huevón,' she said with a smile, her fingers tracing the line of his jaw. She trailed them down his neck to where the first tattoo started. 'So, when do I get my tour?'

'Right now, if you want?'

She nodded and went to her bag. 'I just want to take a picture of the rug first to send to my family.' Her back was to him as she rummaged through the bag, taking out the parcel the courier had delivered earlier.

'Remind me what's in the package?' he asked, shucking off his clothes.

'Just the script for my next job.' She pulled out her tablet and turned around.

He'd stripped down to his boxer shorts and was lying on his side on the rug, one leg bent up.

'Hey, chica,' he said, wiggling his eyebrows. 'Do you think Abuela will like how I've accessorised your rug?'

She bent over, holding the tablet to her tummy as she snorted with laughter.

He put his thumbs inside the band of his shorts. 'Too many clothes? Better to go au naturel?'

'No!' she shrieked and ran towards him, dropping the tablet on the rug and trying to stop him undressing further. Her face was inches from his cock. It twitched against the material. 'Does it ever stay still?'

He grinned. 'Not when you're about.' He scooted off the rug. 'Take some pictures now, without me ruining the shot.'

Valentina snapped a couple, then glanced up at him through her long lashes. 'Can I take some with you too?'

He lay back on the rug. 'You'll have to tell me what to do. You're the expert on looking good for the camera.'

She grinned. 'Well, this is my first time directing someone, so let's see what happens.'

Holding the tablet, Valentina told him how to move his

body. She was effortlessly stunning and Charlie doubted he'd be able to see a pair of tartan pyjamas ever again without getting aroused.

She giggled as he adjusted himself, trying to hide the impossible. 'Charlie, I can't send these to Isabella.'

He lifted his chin. 'Let me see.'

Even though his boxers were covering his shaft, it was obvious he was massive. But that wasn't what made the photos pornographic—it was the look of lust in his eyes as he stared at the photographer. He gave the tablet back to her.

'I don't care who you show those to. But whoever sees them will probably guess that we've...' He brought his hand to his mouth as if to impart a secret and looked around furtively.

'Been having sex?' she asked sarcastically, her hand on her hip.

'Valentina Valverde! I was going to say they'd guess we'd been drinking chocolate caliente.'

She shook her head and laughed. 'Setenta hijueputa.'

He patted the sheepskin. 'Come sit down, Queen Valentina of the McGhirlie clan, and I'll tell you about my tattoos.'

She sat in front of him next to the fire. He remembered the first time they'd sat like this. Then, he'd presented her with a jar filled with ideas. So much had happened since that night. Now they'd been intimate with each other in a way that went far beyond the physical. She held his gaze, and her eyes glowed. Was she thinking the same thing?

'So, what was your first tattoo and why?'

He pointed to his knee. 'This one. To piss off my dad. It's pretty faded now.'

She scrunched up her nose and peered through the hairs. 'A smiley face?'

'Yes,' he replied proudly. 'I'd started wearing ripped jeans, which my parents absolutely hated, especially my dad. Whenever we were sitting across from each other, he always said it looked like my knee was looking at him. So, I took a needle from my mum's sewing basket, grabbed a pen, and gave myself my first tattoo. I would have drawn someone giving him the middle finger, but my artistic ability wasn't up to the challenge, so I did two dots and a semi-circle instead.'

Valentina laughed. 'What did he think when he saw it?'

Charlie grinned. 'He was horrified, of course, which was the desired effect.'

She shook her head, still laughing. 'One day, Charlie, when you have kids, they're going to give you hell.'

He felt like he'd been punched in the guts. *Caroline's baby.* He'd so desperately wanted it to be his. And now his sister was pregnant as well.

She stopped laughing at the instant change in his expression. He didn't want her to ask what he was thinking. The wounds were too fresh and his heart was still raw from talking about Jennifer.

She smiled brightly. 'Okay, what was tattoo number two?'

He pointed to the musical stave around one arm. 'I got this when I was sixteen. My dad hadn't shown my photo to the tattoo parlours, so I got away with it, even though I was underage. The notes are a G and C. It was the closest I could get to Jennifer and Charlie.'

'What did your parents say?'

'They were furious but conflicted. My mum was secretly pleased, thinking it showed my love and commitment to classical music.' He rolled his eyes. 'How little they knew.'

Valentina put her hand on his leg.

He covered it with his and squeezed. 'The third was this.' He touched the design on his left chest. 'The Parachute Regiment badge. It was the start of a new life for me when I joined the army. Getting this ink magnified that change and helped me feel like I fitted in.'

'And the rest? The dragon?'

He blew his cheeks out, embarrassed. 'They're mainly dickhead tattoos. Done to look cool or make some kind of statement I didn't know the meaning of. I haven't had a new one for a few years now.'

She pointed to his right pec which was completely empty of ink. 'Would you ever have anything done there?'

'One day, maybe.' He shrugged, although he already knew exactly what tattoo he wanted. 'May I have your autograph, Valentina?'

She blushed.

He chuckled. 'Have you ever autographed someone's chest?'

She shook her head.

That fact made him deliriously happy. 'Go get your Sharpie then.'

She scrambled up and rummaged in her bag, pulling it out and returning to kneel in front of him. He tried to control his breathing as she put her hand on the front of his shoulder to steady herself. His cock was already throbbing, pushing against the cotton of his boxers.

He felt hot puffs of air against his skin as she breathed. She carefully signed her name, then sat back, gazing critically at her work. She was so beautiful it stopped his heart.

'It's missing something.' She leaned in and placed a soft kiss above her signature. 'Perfect.'

His heart was pounding through his body. 'You know I'm never washing that off.'

She straddled him, their faces nearly touching. She rubbed herself against his cock.

'Fine by me,' she whispered as she brought her lips to his.

❧ 23 ❧

The next few days felt like a surreal dream to Valentina. She spoke to her family as normal, but everything else was different. She let her emails slide, didn't bother posting to social media, and for the first time since she was a child, put thoughts of money and her career to one side.

She spent every moment she could with Charlie and had never been happier.

Charlie was the most incredible person she'd ever met. Being with him was like discovering your house has gold under the floorboards and fairies in the attic. She'd never been so comfortable in her body, so at ease with who she was and what she looked like.

And as for the sex... It was ecstatic and meaningful, intimate yet otherworldly. Part of her was screaming that it was all about to end, that she had a new film and a new challenge to go to, that emails had to be answered. But she ignored the voices and threw herself into every moment with Charlie.

Every second was even more precious because she knew it wouldn't last.

One evening, late at night, she got a call from her agent to say the cosmetics contract had been signed and the first deposit of money placed in the agency account.

She'd done it.

After twenty years of work, she had enough to buy her family a new life. Charlie was thrilled and 'permanently borrowed' a vintage bottle of champagne from the castle's cellars. They drank it in her room, playing strip poker and laughing, then spinning the empty bottle and making love late into the night.

The next morning, Valentina woke with a dry mouth and a sore head. She picked up her watch from the bedside table and groaned when she saw the time. She didn't have to work that day, but wanted to feel a little more human. She rubbed her toes up and down Charlie's leg. He didn't respond. She rolled over to face him and froze.

He was reading the script for her next job.

She saw how much he'd read. He was almost at the end. Her stomach rolled. He gazed at her. At first glance, his face was blank, but she could see his devastation. He set the script to one side and got out of bed, putting on his clothes.

She sat up, pulling the covers tightly around her. 'Where are you going?'

He ran his hands through his hair. 'I'm going back to my room to shower.'

'Why were you reading that?' she demanded. 'It's private. Confidential.'

His eyes were bleak. 'It was by my side of the bed. I woke up a while ago and wanted to let you sleep. I picked it up to pass the time.'

She looked away.

'Has your family read it?' he asked, his voice unsettlingly calm.

She shook her head, embarrassment and shame spiralling inside her. How she felt now would be nothing compared to when her family saw the completed film.

'*Why*, Valentina?'

'I'm trying to build my career. Do something different, get more opportunities,' she muttered, hating herself and hating him for calling her out.

'With that?'

'It's art house.'

'It's bullshit,' he replied angrily.

'It's going to be shot in black and white.'

Charlie slapped his forehead as if coming to his senses. 'Thank god—that'll make *all* the difference.'

'Charlie—'

'This is the kind of shit that critics at film festivals jerk off over. Watching it with one hand stroking their hipster beards, the other wedged down the front of their skinny jeans.'

He gripped either side of his head as if trying to prevent it exploding.

'Christ, Valentina. You told me you've never been topless for a role. You fucking *hate* that stupid dress they've put you in for this job. A week ago, you were too shy to show me your body *in private,* and now you're going to do *this*?'

'It's my body!' she yelled. 'I can do what I like with it.'

'Of course you can, but this is shite. And what about your make-up contract? Have *they* read the script?'

'Yes, they have. They're a French company, and the film's director is a famous French auteur. They don't have a problem with it.'

'But they'd have a problem with photos of you letting your hair down and having fun?'

'That's different. A different context. You wouldn't understand.'

'Clearly.' He took a breath as if to calm himself. 'Look, you don't need the money. You've got enough for your dream now. Cancel it. Tell them to fuck off.'

'I can't. I've never broken a contract before.'

'And you've never done full-frontal nudity with four fucking strangers before either!' he exploded. 'You're so talented, Valentina. I've seen you on set. You're luminous. You could do anything. You're so much more than this.'

'No, Charlie, I'm not. You don't know what you're talking about. I'm not a good actress. I'm not. I'm just tits and ass. That's all I'm good for.'

He shook his head, his face tight.

A wall of pain moved up inside her, obliterating everything. 'Please leave,' she said, her voice wobbling.

He didn't move.

'Get out!' she screamed.

He flinched and left the room.

As the door shut, she crawled under the covers and sobbed.

VALENTINA CRIED UNTIL HER THROAT HURT AND A BOX OF tissues had soaked up her tears. She was furious. How dare Charlie read the script? How dare he judge what she did with her life? Why did he care so much anyway? It wasn't like she was ever going to see him again after she left Scotland.

But no matter how she berated him in her mind, coming up with new ways to castigate him, she felt sick with shame.

She hid the script in the outside pocket of her new suitcase, had a shower, and put on make-up to hide her red eyes and blotchy skin.

Today was meant to be the happiest day of her life. The day

she'd worked towards for so long. It should be a day of celebration. She'd sent a group message to her family last night telling them the cosmetics contract was through and that she'd be sorting out the papers for the house purchases in the next couple of weeks. Now she wanted to see their faces and get excited with them about the future.

Her tablet was ringing when she came out of the bathroom. It was still really early in Colombia.

Isabella?

It was her brother, Manny, still in his dressing gown, unshaven and dishevelled from sleep. He was frowning at the screen and attempting to flatten his unruly hair.

'You look great, Manny,' she said, struggling to smile.

'Tina, I look like shit.' He angled his face up, pulling at his chin as if he could remove the jowls. 'How Maria puts up with being married to this is one of God's many miracles.'

'It's just the angle, Manny. Don't hold the screen so low. You're still the fourth-best-looking Valverde.'

'Hey, thanks, little sister,' he replied sarcastically. 'You sure know how to make an old man feel good at six in the morning.'

'How are you doing? Are the kids awake? Did you get my message?'

'Yeah, I got your message. The kids are still sleeping. I came downstairs so I could talk to you privately.'

Unease prickled in her stomach. 'Is everything okay?'

Her brother glanced away, rubbing his bristly chin.

'Manny? What's going on?'

He looked back at her, his dark eyes crinkled with concern. 'Tina, you know how much we love you, right?'

The unease turned into panic. Where was this going? She nodded.

Her brother sighed. 'Chica, this dream of yours. You've been talking about it since you were a little kid. I know it comes from a good place, I do. But we thought you'd have let it go by now.'

Shards of ice pierced her heart. 'W-what do you mean?' she stammered. 'What are you saying?'

Her brother passed his hand over his face. He looked tired, as if carrying the world on his shoulders. 'Tina, this is *your* dream, not ours. I'm so sorry, chica, but we don't want to move to America.'

Valentina felt like she was falling. 'What? Who? You and Maria?'

Her brother shook his head. 'All of us. Nobody wants to come.'

CHARLIE HEARD THE BANG AND SCREAM FROM HIS ROOM. HE ran down the corridor and pushed open Valentina's door. She was kneeling on the floor, howling, her tablet smashed in the empty fireplace.

He'd never heard anyone make sounds like she was, like it was the end of everything. What the fuck had happened?

He knelt behind her, checking to see if she'd cut herself.

Shauna rushed into the room. 'What happened? Is she okay?'

'I'll handle it,' he replied. 'Could you please stand outside the door for ten minutes and tell anyone else who comes along to fuck off?'

She hesitated, her eyes moving to her watch, then nodded and shut the door behind her.

Charlie cradled Valentina, moving her onto his lap, rocking her. She was gasping, saying his name.

He shushed her. 'It's okay, Valentina. I'm here.'

Her howls turned into sobs. He could hear footsteps

outside the room and Shauna's voice as she sent people away. Eventually Valentina went quiet and still. The only sign of life was the gentle rise and fall of her breathing.

He held her, stroking her back as she huddled in his arms.

'I'm sorry,' she whispered.

He kissed the back of her head. 'There's nothing to be sorry about.'

'Yes, there is. I was horrible to you.'

'No, Valentina, I was a dickhead. I've no right to say anything about your life. I should have kept my big mouth shut.'

She started crying again. The sound broke his heart.

'Hey, hey... don't cry, love.'

She crawled out of his arms and went to the bathroom, closing the door behind her. He could hear her blowing her nose, then running the taps. He checked the floor for any splinters of glass.

When she returned, he held up the smashed tablet. 'Let me guess—Vlad got your number and rang you from the toilet?'

She tried to smile, but then compressed her lips together as if trying not to cry again. She sat on the floor, wringing her hands in her lap, too far away for him to put his arm around her.

'My brother, Manny, called me this morning. He told me...' She broke off, breathing heavily, her eyes raised to the ceiling.

Charlie waited, his stomach filled with lead.

Her gaze moved to the floor. 'He told me none of them want to move to America.'

He shuffled forward and put his hand on her knee. She'd spent her life working for this dream. It was so real to her she couldn't allow herself to question it. He felt for her family too. How awful it must have been to finally burst her bubble.

'He said they are all happy where they were. He told me

they couldn't talk to me about it. That I wouldn't listen.' She looked at him, lost and desolate. 'What have I done with my life, Charlie? What do I do now? My family doesn't want to be with me...'

Her voice broke.

'That's not true. They love you. Why don't you speak to Isabella, your mum, your abuelas?'

She shook her head. 'I'm too angry. I'll just say all the wrong things and make it worse. And anyway...' She indicated the smashed tablet.

'Is your phone still broken?'

She nodded.

He pulled his out. 'Use mine. The only person who ever calls me is Rory, and that's only because he has to.'

She shook her head.

'Go on, take it.' He turned it over to show her signature on the back. 'Look, it's even got your name on it.'

She wiped her eyes and shook her head again. 'I've spoken to my family every day my entire life. I think I need a break.'

24

Charlie tried his best to be a distraction for Valentina, but she was lost in a fog of grief and self-doubt. He'd spent five years as a teenager fixated on his dream of Jennifer, so understood a little about the storm of emotions she was caught up in now that everything had collapsed around her.

In the far corners of his mind, an ill wind stirred. It whispered a story of another woman. Of ten years spent chasing a dream that had finally crumbled to dust. He couldn't face examining this third of his life. He couldn't say Caroline's name, picture her face, or think of the child that could have been his.

So, he focused on caring for Valentina. When she didn't want to leave her room for meals, he brought her food. When she barely touched her plate, he took it away and came back with shortbread, insisting she try the national biscuit of Scotland. And that night he held her until her tears dried and she passed out with exhaustion.

As she slept, he stared up at the canopy above her bed, his

heart full, wondering if it were possible to have a future with her.

She'd made it clear that whatever relationship they had would end when she left Scotland. Could he prolong the dream? Her next film was in London. Could he see her again there?

A wave of nausea rolled into the back of his throat. Her next job wasn't a role—it was soft porn. He imagined her on a set full of men. They had the power, even if that power came from looking at her naked body when they were still fully clothed.

No one should be in a film like that. No one deserved to be caught up in some misogynistic sexual fantasy on camera or off. But what could he do?

He shivered. Who'd told her she was just tits and ass? Those words had been put in her mind by someone else. Someone jealous or punishing her for not sleeping with them.

He gazed down at her sleeping beside him, her plump lips gently parted, her long lashes resting against her soft skin. How could he protect her? He was filled with an overwhelming urge to carry her away, to keep her safe from a world that didn't deserve her.

But he couldn't take away the right to make her own decisions, the right to her own life. So he had to sit back and watch her walk into a situation she'd never truly recover from. An experience that would kill part of her soul.

THE NEXT MORNING, AS VALENTINA SLEPT, CHARLIE WENT to get her breakfast. When he returned, she was awake, staring into nothing, the curtains still closed. He put the tray on the table beside her and opened the curtains with a flourish, promptly falling to the floor with a cry. He heard the bedcovers move.

'What is it?' Valentina called out in alarm.

He writhed on the floor, covering his face. 'The light! It's too bright! I'm melting...'

He heard her slump back onto the bed. He got to his feet and sat on the edge, grinning at her.

She rolled her eyes, but he could see they were wet with the promise of more tears.

Taking her hand, he rubbed his thumb across the back. 'I've brought you some breakfast. I didn't know what you might feel like eating, so I got it all. You've got everything from bacon and eggs to porridge. What do you fancy?'

Her lower lip was trembling, and he was desperate to lift her mood.

'Other than *me*, of course,' he added.

She tried to smile. 'I don't know. I'm sorry, Charlie. I just feel so...'

He suddenly remembered who would cheer her up.

'I know what you need,' he exclaimed, taking out his phone. 'You need Dave.'

'Dave?'

'Uh-huh.' He unlocked it and showed her the home screen. 'Meet Dave,' he said proudly.

'Oh my god, is that a *dog?*'

He slowly shook his head. 'I'll have you know, Dave contains the DNA of at least ninety-seven pedigree prize winners.'

Valentina gave him a questioning look.

'Granted, they were rats, badgers and goldfish,' he continued, 'but still, Dave's a living legend. He's proof that evolution can work backwards.'

'Is he yours?'

'Not yet. He's a long-term resident at a shelter I volunteer at. As soon as I'm properly settled somewhere, I'm going to adopt him.'

She stared sceptically at the photo of him. 'Is he safe? He looks deranged.'

Charlie opened up his videos. 'He's daft as a brush and completely harmless. He's only a danger to himself. Here, take a look.' He handed her the phone. 'They're all taken in the park where he walks me.'

Valentina watched, open-mouthed, as Dave ran around chaotically, his limp not slowing him down one bit. It appeared as if he were chasing a fly with no sense of direction. She giggled. Charlie flicked through to the next one. Dave was standing by the edge of the pond, barking at the ducks. Behind him, unseen, a fat pigeon pecked at a lump of bread. In the video, Charlie called for him. Dave turned his head, saw the pigeon, and jumped back in shock, straight into the pond.

Valentina laughed. 'Oh my god, Charlie, he's amazing.'

His heart swelled. 'Oh, there's so much more. Hang on.' He flicked through the videos.

'How many do you have of him?'

'Tons. I've got no one else to film.' He stopped at a video. 'This one's awesome. I'm throwing snowballs and he doesn't know what's going on.'

He watched Valentina as she laughed at Dave catching the snowballs, then getting confused when they disintegrated in his mouth.

There was a knock. 'I'll get it,' he said. 'You hang out with Dave.'

He opened the door a fraction. On the other side was a young woman wearing a headset. She looked worried.

'Is everything okay?' he whispered. 'Valentina could do with being left alone, if at all possible.'

The woman shook her head. 'There's some kind of family emergency,' she whispered back. 'They can't get hold of her, so her agent rang us.'

Adrenaline shot through him. 'What's happened?'

'I don't know, but she needs to ring her parents immediately.'

'I'll get her to call them now. Can you tell people not to ask her what's happened?'

She nodded. 'Yes, of course.'

He closed the door quietly.

Valentina was wiping tears from her eyes as she laughed at the screen. 'Charlie, I love him. He's too funny.' She glanced up. 'What was that about?'

'I don't know. But you've got to ring your mum. Use my phone. Do you have the number?'

Her face turned white. She tapped on the screen. 'I'm ringing the house. It's what, three in the morning? They'll be there.'

They listened as the number rang out.

'I'll ring her cell.'

He could see her shaking as she dialled again.

The call was answered. '¡Mamá! ¿Qué está pasando?'

Charlie stood back, giving her space, even though he couldn't understand what was being said. Her mother was doing most of the talking as Valentina's free hand clenched the sheet.

There was a break in the conversation and she stared at him.

'Isabella started bleeding and was taken to hospital.' She took a big breath and held it. 'They had to do an emergency C-section,' she said in a rush. 'He's in the special baby unit and she's in intensive care.'

He sat beside her. 'Can I help at all?'

'Can I use your phone now, and can we go and buy me a new one as soon as possible?'

'Yes, of course. I can get the keys for the car. Do you want me to stay with you now?'

She hesitated. 'No, you go. She's just getting Papá.'

Charlie heard her mother speaking, then a man's voice.

'Papá?' Valentina said. 'Soy yo.'

He squeezed her shoulder and left.

In the corridor, Charlie slumped against the wall, breathing heavily. Would the baby survive? Would Isabella? How would he feel if that happened to Tabbie? He had to ring his sister. He had to hear her voice. He scoured the castle for Rory, finally finding him as he drove into the back courtyard with Zoe.

He went to the driver's side as Rory got out. 'Can I borrow your phone?' he asked, giving Zoe a brief wave.

'Good morning to you too,' Rory replied. 'What do you need it for? Prank calling the Prime Minister again?'

He shook his head. 'I need to speak with Tab.'

Rory grinned. 'And she won't pick up if she sees your number? I'll let you in on a little secret, mate. We all think twice about answering when we see your name come up on the screen.'

'Ha ha. That's half the reason. The other is that I've lent Valentina mine. Can I use the car to drive her into Inverness so she can get a new one?'

Rory pulled out his phone, unlocked it and handed it to him. 'Sure. I'll be in the workshop with the keys. Any news on Vlad?'

Charlie shook his head. 'Fuck me, I've slipped him enough laxatives to give an elephant the shits. He must be flushing his food and eating something else. No one's guts are that strong.'

Rory frowned. 'He's been down to the pub again, sniffing around the women and trying to buy drugs.'

'You know, I'd quite happily take care of him permanently.'

'Get in line, mate,' Rory replied. 'Get in line.'

CHARLIE TOOK RORY'S PHONE INTO AN OLD STOREROOM JUST inside the back door of the castle. He pulled a plastic chair off the stack in the corner and sat, staring at his sister's number. He took a big breath and dialled. She picked up after a couple of rings.

'Hi, Rory.'

'Tab, it's me.'

Silence.

'Tab, please don't hang up. I really need to talk to you.'

The silence continued.

'Tabbie?'

'I'm still here.' Her voice was flat. 'What do you want?'

'Tab, I'm sorry. I'm sorry for everything. I'm sorry for being an annoying prick growing up. I'm sorry for being a surly bastard at your passing out ceremony. I'm sorry for getting drunk at your wedding and throwing up as you were leaving the reception with Miles.'

His words tumbled out, tripping over themselves as he tried to think of the million things he had to be sorry for. All the things he should never have done. All the things he'd never apologised for at the time.

He gripped the phone. 'I'm sorry for not making more of an effort with Miles. I'm sorry for leaving you to deal with Mum and Dad and for having to mop up my messes. I'm sorry for being distant, for not stepping up. I'm sorry for lying to you and for what I said on the phone. Tab, I'm so fucking sorry. My life has been one long series of fuck-ups and you've had to witness most of them.'

He paused for breath, head bent, forehead resting on his hand.

'Tab, I know one phone call isn't going to even begin to make up for the hurt I've caused you, but I want to be honest for the first time. I've lied to you and I've lied to myself for so fucking long now, and it's got me nowhere.'

His chest was tight, his heart racing. He couldn't breathe.

'Tab?'

'I'm here, Charlie. I'm not going anywhere. Take your time.'

His head was pounding as all the boxes in his mind opened at once and spewed out their contents. All the pain he'd refused to acknowledge or name was crashing through him at once. He was shaking now, his breath coming faster and faster.

'Charlie!' his sister yelled. 'Hold your breath. Now!'

He followed her order, his head so light he was sure he'd faint. His body and mind were screaming at him, but he tensed his muscles and screamed back. His heartbeat slowed and his head cleared. He let his breath go with a shudder.

'You okay?'

He nodded, then remembered she couldn't see him. 'Yeah, thanks.'

He closed his mouth and breathed slowly in and out through his nose. His sister waited. Finally, he felt more in control. He rubbed his hand over his face and sighed.

'Tab, growing up I was always in your shadow. You were everything Dad wanted me to be and I resented you and him. I acted like a complete dick. The only time I felt true to myself, the only time I didn't hate myself and everyone around me, was when I was with Jennifer.'

He pinched the bridge of his nose.

'I know no one believed me. They thought I was just a kid, but I fucking loved her, Tab. I loved her for five long years. And when it all went to shit, I hated myself and the world even more. When I met...'

He swallowed, the name caught in his throat.

'When I met Caroline, I wanted her to replace the life I'd lost with Jennifer. I wanted to get married and have kids. I desperately wanted kids with her.'

He paused, his tender heart opening to his deepest truth.

'She said we were too young. She didn't want us to live together. She didn't want to get married. Then she wanted me to leave the army. But I had no career to go to. No degree. I wanted to work my way up the ranks, make enough to support a family. So she dumped me, and the next thing I know, she's marrying some wanker from the City.

'I knew it was bullshit, so I waited, and sure enough, she came back. She said she'd leave him if I left the army. So I did. But she didn't leave.' His voice was barely a whisper. 'And now she's pregnant with his baby.'

'Oh, Charlie.' He could hear the pain in his sister's voice. 'Are you sure it isn't yours?'

He nodded again. 'Yes. She'd been withholding sex for a while and we always used condoms anyway. She went away for a holiday to the Maldives. I thought it was with her mum, but it was really with him. She told me she conceived there. She's about twenty-two weeks now, almost the same as you. She's also having a little girl. I'm so sorry, Tabbie. I totally freaked out when you told me. I've always wanted kids and just assumed you didn't.'

'Charlie,' his sister sighed. 'I'm sorry too. And I'm sorry I was away when it all happened. I never knew Jennifer meant so much to you. I never understood why you were so angry all the time or what any of us had done to deserve you behaving like you did.'

He let out a huff. 'I was a fucking prick ninety-nine per cent of the time, Tab. You can still call me that to my face.'

He swore he could hear his sister smile. 'I'm trying to be nice.'

'I don't mind. I deserve it. You can kick this dog when he's down as much as you like.'

'Okay, then—Caroline was a cold-hearted bitch who didn't deserve you.'

A shocked laugh burst out. 'Don't pull any punches, Tabitha.'

'It's true. She used you. She didn't give a toss about your feelings. You were just her pretty pet. She could show you off to her friends, then put you back in a box when she got bored. We all saw through it. And we all fucking hated her for how she treated you. You know why Dad went so mental when the two of you got together?'

Tabitha didn't wait for him to reply.

'He hated your CO. I mean, *really* fucking hated him. Dad had to lower himself and kiss his arse to get you at his table that night. He did it for you. To try and give you a leg up. To give you a chance to prove yourself. When you went off with Caroline, he wasn't mad because you embarrassed him by shagging her. He was mad because he knew what a cunt your CO was and didn't want you anywhere near his family.'

'Tab!'

'Oh, come on, Charlie. You think I haven't heard that word before? I run an army base. I use it every day. Your CO was Cunty McCuntface and his cow of a daughter wasn't far behind.'

'Tab! You're going to be a mum!'

His sister laughed. 'Yeah, a fucking kickass mum who's

going to run the army by the time she's done. Since when did you turn into such a prude?'

Charlie laughed, feeling lighter than air. 'You're right. You can call him whatever you like. He made my life hell.'

He felt a twinge of pain in his heart for all the time lost, for the relationship he could have had with his sister.

'I'm so sorry, Tab. For everything.'

She sighed. 'Me too. I'm sorry I didn't know any of this and I'm sorry I couldn't have supported you more. But it's done now. You need to talk to Mum and Dad. Say all this stuff to them. You're still coming to their party, aren't you?'

'Yeah, I'll be there.' His throat tightened. He thought of his sister having a baby. What an incredible gift it was for their family. 'You're going to be the best mum ever, Tabbie,' he said, his voice hoarse. 'And your little girl is going to have the most devoted uncle in the whole world.'

25

Valentina stared blankly out the window as Charlie drove her to Inverness, his phone clamped to her ear. Whilst she talked and listened to various family members, she worked her way through a box of tissues on her lap. By the time Charlie parked, most lay crumpled around her.

He opened her door and shook his head when she tried to clean them up. 'Leave it.'

As they walked through the centre of Inverness, she held tightly to his hand. Being in public helped control her tears, and the fresh air was like a cold shower, calming the heat of her emotions.

Charlie's hand was warm, strong, reassuring. The only solid thing in a world turned upside down. For the first time in her life, she didn't have a focus, a goal that drove her on, a grand plan that made all the shitty jobs and shittier people worth dealing with. She felt completely adrift and unstable.

She was angry with her family, but also guilty for assuming her dreams were also theirs. When she thought about the reality of taking Manny and Maria's kids out of school, uprooting her family from their friends, their church, their community, their home, she felt sick with shame.

She'd been a child when she'd stood in front of her brother's coffin and had her idea. An idea that, like a dog with a tattered toy, she hadn't been able to drop. And for what?

Her teens and twenties had been lost to work. Rather than pay for an assistant and a manager, she'd taken on those jobs herself, leaving no time to grow as a person and discover who she was. She hadn't found a hobby, hadn't read books or listened to music. She realised with a lurch that she hadn't even made any real friends.

Charlie squeezed her hand. 'You okay?'

She shrugged and managed to smile at him. He was incredible. In the middle of all her turmoil, he was there. Reliable, dependable, unflappable. He was effortlessly kind and thoughtful, and hilariously, stupidly funny.

He also had a brain and the wherewithal to use it, hidden inside a man so good-looking that her underwear was ruined the second she thought about him. She'd assumed he'd slept with half the world, but he hadn't. Just because he had the face of a bad boy and the body of a god didn't mean he was a player.

He stopped outside a mobile phone shop. His golden-green eyes held hers. He reached down and brushed a kiss against her cheek that made her shiver.

'You've got this,' he whispered.

She moved her lips to find his. She wanted to lose herself in him. Use the blinding pleasure he gave her to blot out everything else. She tugged his head closer, her tongue slipping into his hot mouth, her body pressing hard against his. He groaned, sending a pulse rocketing through her, then pulled back, breathing heavily.

'Valentina,' he growled. 'You're killing me.'

A hiccup of laughter bubbled up. It felt so good to be

happy. It was such a sharp contrast to all the tears she'd shed. She welled up again. How could she feel good when Isabella and her baby were in hospital?

'Hey, hey, don't cry, sweetheart,' he implored. 'You need to save your tears. In a couple of minutes, a teenager is going to use words we don't understand and make us feel technologically illiterate. Now *that's* worth getting upset over.'

She smiled as he wiped the corners of her eyes with his thumbs. 'Do you mind choosing a phone and tablet for me?' she asked. 'I just don't have the strength. I can't think straight right now.'

'Of course. Anything in particular you want? Budget? Colour?'

She puffed out her cheeks and shook her head. 'Money's not a problem anymore. Just get one that is easy to use, will last, and I can use straight away. I don't care about the colour.' She blushed, suddenly shy. 'Unless they have one that matches your eyes.'

He swallowed, then cleared his throat.

'Okey dokey,' he said, pulling her into the shop. 'One Kermit-the-Frog-green phone coming right up.'

Valentina sat in a chair by the shop window, watching videos of Dave and sneaking glances at Charlie. He seemed in his element, gathering the shop's staff around him as if briefing them for battle. He was charismatic and confident; the centre of everything.

They bustled about him, eager to be the first to find the perfect solution. Occasionally he'd pop back to where she was sitting, kneel and give her an update. He chose a model that was precharged so she could start using it immediately. He even took her credit card so she didn't need to move.

Her heart overflowed. Why did it have to end in a couple of days? Could they have a future together? As he stood at the counter getting everything bagged up, his phone vibrated in her hands. She glanced at the message without thinking.

It was a picture—an ultrasound scan of a baby.

Was that Isabella's? She stared at it, confused.

Another photo came through, this time of a beautiful blonde woman cradling her neat pregnancy bump. She was tall, slim, willowy, and dressed in expensive-looking clothes. Was this Charlie's sister? She looked like a model, not an army colonel.

A message pinged in.

> Caroline: You're right, Charlie. I love you and want to do this with you. All the pregnancy hormones made me a little crazy. We're meant to be together and you're going to be a wonderful father. Ring me when you get this and we can talk about a plan for when you get home. I love you, Caro xxx

Valentina stared at the message as the world ground to a halt. Her memories dredged up his voice. *Jennifer, Katie, Lisa, Caitlin, and Caroline.* This was the last woman he'd slept with before her.

They were in love.

And she was carrying his child.

'Hey, sweetheart, you're good to go.'

She glanced up to see Charlie holding a bag in one hand, an iridescent green phone in the other.

'It works,' he said. 'And I've already messaged your mum so you can ring her straight away. I'm not sure about the colour, but the guys say it's the best match.'

He grinned at her. She stared back. He looked guileless. Open. Honest.

'Oh, and your new tablet's in the bag too.'

She'd always prided herself on being able to read people. How wrong could she have been?

Now his expression was concerned. 'Valentina? You okay?'

Oh my god. He was a psychopath. He believed his own lies so completely they appeared on his face as pure truth. He crouched down and she flinched.

'Valentina? What's happened?'

She couldn't breathe. She needed to get away. She grabbed the bag and her new phone from him and thrust his into his hand.

He stared at the screen.

She pushed past.

'Valentina, it's not—'

She didn't wait to hear any more. She ran.

OUTSIDE IN THE STREET, VALENTINA LOOKED BLINDLY LEFT and right. *Which way?* She was paralysed in a living nightmare, gripped with fear. She swerved right, in the opposite direction from where they'd come, and ran.

'Valentina, wait!'

She ran faster, but her legs were no match for Charlie's. He reached her and touched her arm. She spun around and stopped, yanking away from him.

'Valentina,' he gasped. 'That's not my baby. Please, let me explain.'

'Then whose baby is it?' she spat, rage boiling inside her.

'Her husband's.'

'What?' Valentina couldn't believe it could get any worse. 'You're having an affair with a married woman? A *pregnant* married woman?'

'No, it's not like that. We split up, then she married him,

then we…' He broke off, shaking his head, then straightened and gazed at her directly. 'Yes, I had an affair with a married woman. Caroline broke up with me again a few weeks ago.'

He wasn't even attempting to hide the ugly truth.

She glanced around wildly. On the other side of the street was a row of taxis. She could have wept with relief. She turned to face him. He looked desolate.

'Do not follow me. And do not look for me. I never want to see you again.'

She ran across the road and jumped in a cab. Only when the car was moving did she allow her tears to fall.

BACK AT THE CASTLE, VALENTINA WANTED TO GET TO HER room without seeing anyone. She couldn't face talking, smiling, or lying about why she was so upset.

A big group of people stood chatting on the main stairs, so she turned right, running for the library. It was empty. She leaned against the wall, gasping for breath as sobs wracked her body. Through her blurred vision, a head popped up from the sofa facing the fire.

'Rough day?' Shauna asked, her own eyes puffy and red.

Valentina nodded and sat beside her.

Shauna held her hand. 'Your turn to cry now,' she said. 'I think I'm all out of tears.'

❧ 26 ❧

Charlie sat in the car, looking at the empty seat next to him. It was covered in tissues full of Valentina's grief. As if she didn't have enough to deal with, he'd now added his fucked-up life to her burdens.

Valentina hated him and rightly so. He hated himself. Could he try and talk to her? Explain the history of his relationship with Caroline?

He dropped his head back and closed his eyes. What was the point? It didn't matter that he'd been with Caroline before she got married. It didn't matter that it had been Caroline who'd made the first move after her honeymoon. He'd always had a choice, the chance to choose the right path. And he hadn't.

No matter how much of a twat her husband might be, Charlie was the one in the wrong.

A yearning sadness engulfed his chest. How badly did he think of himself to be strung along by Caroline for so long? Was it some kind of masochistic punishment for what had happened with Jennifer?

At least he wasn't hiding from his past anymore. He may have lost all chance to be with Valentina, but from now on he could make different choices in his life.

Valentina was extraordinary. She deserved the very best... and that definitely wasn't him.

Charlie needed to sort his life out. And that began with Caroline.

He picked up his phone and called her.

'Charlie, hi! Oh my god, I've missed you so much! I'm just out with Fenella. Can you ring back in a bit?'

He didn't know whether to laugh or cry. 'Caro, I'm not going to call back. What you said when we last met was true. It's best for everyone to call it a day, once and for all.'

There was silence, then he heard a chair scraping back and her exiting onto a street.

'You don't mean that. Just come home and we'll talk about it.'

'No, Caro. I'm done. I spent ten years waiting for you. Wanting what you have with your husband—'

'And you can still have it!'

'Yeah, I can. And I will, one day. It just won't be with you.'

'Charlie, you don't know what you're saying.'

'I do. For the first time in years, I'm being truthful to myself and to you. I should never have got back with you after you married Gareth. I did the wrong thing. But now I'm doing the right thing. And I'm choosing to be happy.'

He heard her huff. 'You'll be back,' she said, her voice hard. 'You'll be *begging* me to take you back.'

She ended the call.

Charlie stared at the screen. He blocked her numbers, her email, and deleted her as a contact. He closed his eyes, exhausted. But he didn't feel relief—just emptiness.

He dialled Mack and left a message.

'Hi, mate, it's me, your favourite dickhead. Just giving you a heads-up. Caroline wanted to get back with me, so I finally grew a pair and ended it for good. I've blocked her number, so if she calls you with some bullshit about getting in touch with me, don't tell her where I am. I've also spoken to Tab and started building bridges. Yeah, I know, I've had a personality transplant. Anyway, I'm done here in a few days and want some work to take my mind off the misery that is my shitty life. Don't care what. Don't care where. Cheers, mate. Speak soon.'

He then rang his sister and left a message, letting her know what had just happened. Telling Mack, telling Tabbie, made it more real. It helped draw the line under his life with Caroline.

He turned his phone off and headed back to the castle. He wasn't going to harass Valentina to try and make her see his point of view. He was going to respect her wishes and leave her alone. She had enough to deal with.

Right now he wanted to puke out all the pain in his guts. He didn't know whether to achieve this by drinking a bottle of whisky or by punishing himself in the gym.

Either way, he wanted it to hurt.

THE GYM IN THE CASTLE BASEMENT WAS EMPTY. FIVE minutes into his warm-up, Charlie heard footsteps outside and tensed.

Valentina?

Brad Bauer strode in with his assistant, Crystal.

'Hey, man!' said Brad excitedly.

As Brad pumped his hand up and down, Charlie bit back a sigh. This level of positivity was not what he wanted. Or any form of interaction with another human.

'Wanna work out together? My trainer ate dinner with His Holiness last night and now he's sick. Can you spot for me?'

Charlie shrugged. 'Yeah sure, no worries.'

He had nothing else to do and lacked the motivation to feel pissed off just because he didn't like a film Brad made years ago. Right now he wanted to move on from everything in the past, and that included disliking Brad for no good reason.

As they started training together, Charlie's mood lifted. Brad was the most enthusiastic man he'd ever met. He was like a puppy that had accidentally eaten a bag of ecstasy and amphetamines. He bounded from exercise to exercise, always wanting to do more, slapping Charlie on the back and whooping.

When Charlie suggested improvements to his form, he lapped it up, listening intently and taking it to heart. He may have been a Hollywood pretty boy, but he knew how to work hard.

After an hour, both men were sweating and pumped, and for a few brief seconds of intense pain during each set, Charlie's mind was free of Valentina.

Crystal had left them to it at the beginning but returned with an enormous camera, which she handed to Brad.

'Sweet. Thanks, babe.' Brad turned to Charlie, who was leaning on a rack, breathing heavily. 'Man, your physique is sick. Can I get some shots?'

What the fuck?

Brad put the camera to his face and snapped away. 'Yeah, that's the look. Perfect!'

Crystal gave Charlie an enthusiastic thumbs up.

'What do you want me to do?' Charlie asked, feeling awkward and no longer at home in his own body.

'Just be yourself, man,' Brad replied over the sound of the camera shutter firing off like a machine gun.

'That never ends well,' he mumbled.

Brad laughed. 'You're funny. Don't sweat it. The Bradster's

here. I got you.' He moved Charlie like a mannequin. 'Yeah, yeah, that's it. Sweet!'

Charlie gave up any hope of resistance and entered the twilight zone of Brad Bauer's flow state. Within twenty minutes, the lighting in the gym had been tweaked and Charlie was topless with his shorts pulled dangerously low.

'Man, that dragon,' whistled Brad. 'I gotta get me one of those.'

He paused, looking off into the middle distance. Crystal whipped out her phone and held it to his mouth.

'*Fight Club* meets *Enter the Dragon*. Jerry on script development, Pam on co-prod with the Chinese. Schedule meeting to discuss in ten days.'

He blinked, then turned back to Charlie with a grin. 'Okay, man, look at me like you wanna rip my guts out.'

Charlie's jaw tensed. Given the right circumstances, this acting lark was easy.

WHEN BRAD FINISHED PHOTOGRAPHING EVERY INCH OF Charlie's body not covered by clothes, he clapped him on the back with a final *'whoop!'* and they went their separate ways.

Charlie paused on his way past Valentina's room, but didn't knock. He showered and went to the catering truck, hoping to catch a glimpse of her there. Even if she wouldn't talk to him, he wanted to see her, to know if she was okay.

Shauna was ahead of him in the queue and left with two plates covered in foil. Was one for Valentina?

His chest felt so empty. His heart yearned not only for Valentina, but what she'd brought to his life. He'd been the best version of himself when he was with her. It wasn't even that he was being someone different. With her, he could be the real Charlie, the one usually hidden under layers of anger and pain.

Returning to his room, he worked on the embroidery for his mother until day turned into night. As he sewed, questions moved restlessly through his mind.

Did he dislike certain things in his life just to piss off his parents? Did he like other things only to please Jennifer or Caroline? If he took away these connections, what truth was left behind?

What actually made him happy?

He left his room, moving silently down the corridor and the main stairs. Few people were around now, and the library was empty. He flicked on a side light and stared at the grand piano. It loomed in the corner of the room and in his memories.

His heart beat faster and his fingers tingled.

No one was here. No one was watching. No one would know.

He lifted the fallboard and sat, adjusting the height of the stool before he realised what he was doing. He stared at the keys. Each one was loaded with meaning and memory.

As soon as he'd met Jennifer at their first lesson together, not a note was played without her in his mind. Every bar written by the composer, every emotion the music could elicit was experienced through the lens of his love for her.

Without her, music was just sound and playing a mechanical action. But now? If he could let go of the past, could he let go of the link between her and the piano? Could he love playing and music for its own sake?

He rested his hands on the keys as long-buried sensations moved down his arms. His heart was racing. He swallowed, checking he was still alone. He didn't know where to begin, so began with scales, remembering the feel and placement of the keys.

He closed his eyes, his fingers limbering up as he systematically went through every scale: major, minor and chromatic. When he finished, he opened his eyes and blinked. He'd done it. He'd played the piano and his mind had stayed on the notes, not on Jennifer or the past.

Going to put the fallboard down, he was seized with the urge to push the boundaries. What would happen if he revisited some of the pieces he used to play?

Before he could second-guess himself, he dived in at the deep end, into Rachmaninoff's second piano concerto, the piece he'd played at the summer concert of his final year of school. He'd smashed it.

His parents had been in the front row, and at the back had stood Jennifer, shining with love and pride. That was the high point. From that moment on, everything had gone wrong.

He started with the second movement, naturally and easily finding the notes as if he'd played it only yesterday. He closed his eyes and let the music transport him.

Emotion swelled inside his body. But rather than Jennifer, it was Valentina, his sister, the pain at ten years of his life lost to Caroline that came to mind. He realised with a jolt that the music was a conduit. It had its innate power, but the real power came from its ability to make meaning out of one's life and experiences.

As he played, joy tingled across his skin. How could he have shut himself off from this for so long? By punishing his parents, all he'd done was hurt himself. Every twatty thing he'd done had not only hurt those he loved the most, but had cut him even deeper.

The music flowed through him, resounding through the piano, dancing off the walls of the library. He smiled, following the melody as if simply along for the ride. As his fingers finally left the keys, the last notes hung in the air like threads of gold.

He heard a sniff and his eyes snapped open.

Valentina was standing just inside the door, staring at him.

She was wearing the black dress she'd worn for their evening in the pub. It clung to her curves as if framing a masterpiece. His body responded immediately, heat and desire expanding past the edges of his skin. She was his agony and his ecstasy. His mouth ran dry. He couldn't speak, even if he knew what to say.

Her eyes were liquid and luminous, her lips parted. She licked them and his cock jerked in his jeans. She walked slowly towards him, stopping a couple of feet away.

'Charlie,' she began, her voice soft. 'I want to apologise.'

What?

'When I came back to the castle,' she continued, 'I rang Rory. He said if I ever needed anything, I could ask. So I did.'

Charlie's brain couldn't compute. She might as well have been speaking Klingon.

'We went to his workshop with Zoe and he told me about Caroline.' She paused and her gaze flicked to his open mouth. He shut it. 'He spoke to your sister this afternoon and shared with me what you said to her.' His cheeks heated. 'Rory was wonderful. It was a very insightful conversation.'

'Rory? Earl of Kinloch, Rory?' he croaked in shock.

She nodded.

'Insightful?'

She smiled.

He couldn't believe it. 'Rory? Half man, half orangutan?'

She giggled and his heart did a backflip.

'I've had more insightful conversations with a haggis than I have with him.'

She snorted a laugh but then her face turned serious.

'So, I want to apologise,' she continued. 'You wouldn't have given me your phone if you had anything to hide. I'm sorry for how I behaved. And I'm sorry for how she treated you. You deserve better, Charlie. You're a good man.'

He shook his head, his jaw clamped shut, emotion strangling him.

'No,' he replied, hoarsely. 'I'm the one who should be sorry. For everything.' He felt the heat from her body as she moved closer, her hand on his shoulder. He was teetering on an emotional knife edge. He didn't dare look at her. 'How is Isabella and her baby?'

'They're going to be fine. Isabella's out of intensive care and the baby is breathing on his own. She lost her phone when she was admitted, but I spoke to her using Matias's. She said they hope to be home next week.'

He nodded, flooded with relief.

Silence filled the room. He heard her swallow. Her hand was burning into his shoulder.

'Charlie?' she asked hesitantly.

He dragged his head up to gaze at her. Her eyes were so big, he felt like he was drowning in them. Her cheeks were flushed. She looked soft, open, needy.

'Yes, love.'

She licked her lips and his dick throbbed so hard it hurt. 'I...' She glanced away and nibbled at her bottom lip.

He couldn't help himself. He turned his body towards her and lightly touched her leg at the point where the dress ended. He watched her breathing hitch, her chest rising a little higher with every inhalation.

'Whatever you want to say, whatever you want to ask, you can,' he said, his voice low. He moved his fingers to the outside of her leg, slowly and lightly.

'Charlie,' she breathed.

Jesus fucking Christ. His free hand gripped the piano stool. He had to keep it together. He couldn't grab her like a maniac.

Her body rocked towards his. 'Charlie, I don't want to use you. I don't want to take advantage of you when it's about to end.'

His heart ached with her truth. But for whatever time they did have left, he wanted to spend it by her side. 'It's okay, sweetheart, just tell me what you need.'

Her expression made his heart stutter. 'I need you inside me, Charlie. I want to feel good again.'

His head was roaring, blood racing around his body, urging him on.

'Okay, er, yes. Christ, Valentina, it's never going to be "no".'

He made a move to stand, but she pressed on his shoulder, keeping him in place.

Her lower lip was trembling. 'I need you now, Charlie. Please.'

'Here? Now?'

She nodded and took his hand from the outside of her leg to the inside. His heart was tripping over itself, his head spinning as she guided him up. He held her gaze until he grazed against her wet curls, her swollen lips. He groaned, his head falling back, his eyes tightly closed. *Fuck!* No underwear. She was fucking killing him.

She rocked onto him, pushing his fingers deeper. She was so wet, so ready. His breathing was heavy and harsh as he fought for control. He was so close to exploding, desire burning at the base of his spine, desperate for release. She rubbed the hard nub of her clit against him, then clenched around his fingers with a cry.

'Valentina,' he gasped. 'I don't have a condom.'

She pulled a foil packet from inside the top of her dress.

'You left some in my room,' she whispered. She kept moving against his hand. 'Please, Charlie. Now.'

He reluctantly pulled away and tugged down the front of his jeans, freeing his cock from his boxers and rolling on the condom. She straddled him and started to work herself down with little gasps of pleasure. He held her hips and watched his cock filling her. He could see how tightly she was stretched around him, feel how wet she was. He was blinded by pleasure, blinded by her.

He slipped the straps of her dress over her shoulders, pulling the top down until her breasts were bare. He sucked a nipple into his mouth, hearing her cry as he tugged at it and rolled the other between his finger and thumb.

She was writhing on him, her body undulating as she rocked herself faster and faster. Her arms wrapped around his neck, holding his head to her breast as her cries became more frantic. His own climax was hurtling towards him with unstoppable force. He circled her clit and gently bit down on her nipple.

She bucked against him and gasped, her body stiffening. Then she shattered around him, crying out, her body clenching and convulsing. He held on for dear life, thrusting into her, roaring her name as his orgasm shot up his spine and exploded every synapse in his brain.

He held her close, his body shaking as the sensations continued rolling through in waves. He'd never experienced pleasure like this, as if his very bones were dissolving, his body merging with hers.

And in this moment of otherworldly pleasure, he knew with absolute certainty that he could never experience anything like this with anyone but her.

27

Valentina slept deeply that night, waking only once to reach for Charlie and make dreamy love in the darkness. She eventually awoke to the smell of food and someone licking her hand. Opening her eyes groggily, she saw Bandit sitting by the side of the bed, tail thumping on the floor in excitement that she was finally awake. Charlie sat on the side of the bed, his green eyes sparkling in the morning light.

'Good morning, beautiful. Sleep well?'

She nodded. 'Did you?'

'Yes. Although the best bit was when someone's wandering hands woke me up.'

'I thought you were awake. Your, er...'

'Cock?'

She nodded, suddenly far too hot under the covers. 'Yes, it was, er, very hard.'

He raised an eyebrow. 'I was in bed lying next to a naked you. Given those circumstances, I could be comatose and still ready to go. Do you want to feel what it's doing now?'

She flapped the bedcovers to release some of the heat. He tried to peek and Bandit barked.

He laughed. 'I see you've got yourself a guard dog.' He gave Bandit a stern look. 'Mate, I'm gutted, and quite frankly, disappointed. You're meant to be my wingman, not a cockblocker.'

Bandit barked again and nuzzled Valentina.

'Traitor!' he cried as she giggled. He shook his head and went to the desk by the window where there was a tray of food. 'You hungry? I've got a full English, as well as porridge, smoked salmon and scrambled eggs, cinnamon Danish, coffee, orange juice, and hot chocolate.'

Her mouth watered. She hadn't eaten properly for days.

'My stomach says it wants everything.' She sat up and pulled the sheets over her chest as he brought the tray over.

'What are we doing today?' she asked, spearing a sausage with her fork.

Charlie looked at the sausage askance and crossed his legs. She giggled, brought it to her mouth and licked the end.

'Oh, come on now!' he cried. 'Play fair.'

'Is this a Scottish or an English sausage?' she asked.

'Is it the best you've ever tasted?'

Taking a bite, she chewed. 'Yes, I think so.'

'Then it's definitely English.' He walked stiffly to the window, giving her and Bandit a baleful look. 'Rory's doing a photoshoot for a magazine today, which I find absolutely hilarious, so I said I'd take Bandit. Although if you try another sex ambush...'

'What?'

'Sex ambush. It's stealthy and one hundred per cent lethal. I think I'm going to tell Tab all about it. It could revolutionise modern warfare.'

She shook her head. 'Charlie...'

He grinned at her from the window. 'Yes? I'm waiting for you to add dickhead to the end.'

She took a bite of the sausage. 'Huevón,' she muttered, her mouth full of food.

'There it is!'

She rolled her eyes.

'Anyway,' he continued, 'It's not raining, so I thought we could take Bandit for a long walk up the mountain after you've eaten, then be back this afternoon for when the Americas wake up?'

'Sounds perfect,' she replied with a smile.

Charlie and Valentina hiked hand-in-hand to the glen, Bandit at their side. The sky was grey but the clouds were high, revealing the expanse of the mountains. It was a sea of heather, the pink and purple flowers a smudge of colour against the green, with bare rock rising vertiginously, like islands reaching for the sky.

Valentina breathed in the clean air, settled, safe and secure with Charlie by her side. She didn't want to think about the future. Whenever her mind went to her next film, she wanted to be sick. And whenever she thought about what to do now that her family wasn't moving to LA, she felt she was staring into an endless black void.

Logically, she knew there was a universe of possibilities waiting for her, but right now she was lost and scared. So she didn't think about anything except for her family, her sister, her new nephew, and the incredible man beside her.

Charlie was so much taller but matched his stride to hers. When he wasn't making her laugh, he would look at her with his emerald eyes in a way that heated her blood to boiling point.

Was it normal to want sex this much? Was it normal for it to feel like she was touching heaven? And after Charlie, how could anyone else ever compare?

She glanced at his torso, knowing that under his T-shirt, her signature was still dark across his chest. She felt guilty about how much she liked the sight of it.

As if he belonged to her, even if only for now.

CHARLIE AND VALENTINA HAD A LATE LUNCH AT THE CASTLE, then went back to her room. Bandit sat to attention even though Valentina was hoping he'd have a nap.

She rang her family for a catch-up as Charlie worked on the embroidery panel for his mother. Her family all wanted to speak to him, which he handled with a smile until she pulled the panel out from under the pillow where he'd hidden it.

His cheeks flushed at their reaction, and he mumbled that Bandit needed taking out before fleeing with him from the room.

After her mother and her grandmothers had reiterated the importance of marrying him, she ended the call, took a deep breath, and opened her email.

Her inbox always filled her with anxiety. She was perpetually late to reply to people, if she even got to them at all. She was stuck on a treadmill that never stopped or slowed—it just kept going, getting fractionally faster every day.

Her phone rang. It was her agent.

'Hey, Cheryl, how's it going?'

'What the hell is going on over there? Did you know? And if you did, why didn't you tell me?'

Valentina's heart sank. *What now?* 'I don't know what you're talking about. What's happened?'

'You filming at the cabin today?'

'No, I don't have any scenes there. Brad and Kirsten are there today, I think. Why?'

Cheryl started laughing. 'Oh, honey, you've just missed the show of the century. The Earl of Kinloch just went cray-cray. He tried to kill Brad, threw him in the loch, then walked off with his arm around Kirsten.'

'Is this a joke?'

Charlie opened the door and entered with Bandit. He glanced at her quizzically. 'Everything okay?'

She pulled a face and shrugged, putting her phone on speaker.

'No, honey, for real,' Cheryl continued. 'It's all over the internet and the entertainment channels. I just called around and the rumour on set is that the earl's lost his mind because Brad's been banging his mom.'

Charlie and Valentina stared at each other.

'Can you get the deets for me, honey? I live for shit like this.'

'Okay, I'll call you back.' Valentina ended the call and turned to Charlie. 'Apparently Rory just went loco, threw Brad in the lake, and went off with Kirsten.'

Charlie laughed. 'The Brad bit I can believe, but Kirsten? He can't stand her.'

'And Brad and Rory's mom?'

He hesitated. 'They've been spending time together. But it's still a bit of a stretch. Fire up your tablet and let's see what's going on.'

Less than a minute later, they were watching footage of Rory running down the hill by the cabin towards the loch, screaming that he was going to kill Brad.

Brad was standing on a wooden pier, having just kissed someone with curly red hair. They knew it was Zoe, but Brad had insisted that Kirsten's character look like her, so anyone who'd seen the press shots of Kirsten dressed as her character would have assumed Rory was with her, not Zoe.

Charlie blew out his cheeks. 'Bloody hell, he's done it now.'

'Rory or Brad?'

'Good question. I think I'd better find Barbara before Rory does.' He kissed the top of her head. 'Back in a bit.'

28

Valentina's phone rang with another call from her agent ten minutes after Charlie left.

'Hey, Cheryl. The Earl of Kinloch is actually with his girlfriend. Brad wanted Kirsten's character to look like her.'

'Ah, okay, honey.' There was a pause. 'Valentina, have you sent any private photos to anyone recently?'

'Private photos?' She was at a loss. 'Like what?'

'Selfies mainly.'

'Only to my sister. Why?' Adrenaline rushed through her.

'Is there any chance she would have sent them to anyone else?'

'No. Absolutely not. Never. Why?'

Cheryl sighed. 'I've just been called by one of the seedier paps. We've got about half an hour before fifty photos of you drop online.'

Her throat constricted. 'What photos?'

'I haven't seen them all, but he sent me some screengrabs. You're mainly pulling faces, which is fine. But in some you look wasted. You're in a toilet stall and look like you've just puked.

There's also a shot of the hottest guy I've ever seen, who's hung like a horse, but you're not in the shot, so we'll deny all knowledge of that one.'

Valentina sat on the rug Charlie had given her, pulling at the tufts of wool. This could not be happening.

'Isabella's phone went missing in the hospital,' she whispered. 'How bad is it?'

Cheryl huffed down the line. 'It's not great.'

'What about the cosmetics contract?'

'I don't know. There's a clause they could invoke to cancel it. And if that happens, it won't just be the money you'll lose, it would be the damage to your reputation.'

Valentina couldn't breathe. Her carefully cultivated career. All those years of work. Her entire image. Destroyed overnight.

'It's the photos of you wasted that are the real issue,' Cheryl continued. 'It could be construed as substance abuse. I can do what I can to spin this, but this is why you need a manager. A team. People around you to deal with this kind of shit.'

'What about the next job? Will they cancel on me?' she asked, hoping the art house film in London would now be shelved.

Cheryl laughed. 'Are you kidding? Pictures of you looking that trashed? They're going to be over the fucking moon.'

Her heart sank.

'Look. I'll draw up a statement now and email it over. I suggest you call your sister and get the police involved. Although I doubt they'll ever find out who did this.'

. . .

WHEN CHARLIE RETURNED WITH BANDIT, VALENTINA WAS looking through all the photos on the cloud that she'd sent Isabella.

'Well, that was entertaining,' he said. 'I had to let Barbara out of her flat because Rory had locked her in. Fuck me. I've seen calmer spitting cobras than the Dowager Countess of Kinloch. Despite her impressive poker face, it appears she is indeed getting jiggy with Brad, and Rory's phone keeps going to voicemail.'

Valentina gazed at him and his smile disappeared.

He crouched in front of her. 'Sweetheart, what's up?'

'Someone stole Isabella's phone and sold all the selfies I sent her to a website. I could lose the cosmetics contract and my career is ruined.'

He sat and pulled her onto his lap. 'Show me.'

She handed him the phone and he scrolled through the photos, his frown turning into a smile.

'Why are you smiling? This isn't funny.'

'You're not naked. You're only pulling faces. You're still the most beautiful woman in the world. These photos show you're so much more than just your phenomenal looks. You're the whole package.'

Had he lost his mind?

'You wanted to do something different with your career, and now you can. You've got the freedom to be you.'

She shook her head. 'You don't understand.'

He shrugged. 'Maybe not, but I think the photos are cute.'

'Charlie, I'm on the floor of a toilet! I look like a junkie!'

'Hmm. I agree that's not your best look. But it shows you're human.'

'They're also using a photo of you I took, on this rug,' she said quietly.

'Valentina Valverde! I can't believe you sent a photo of me in my *underpants* to your *sister*.'

She blushed and hid her face against his chest. 'I'm sorry.'

He kissed the top of her head. 'It's fine. As long as my cock looks huge, I don't give a shit.'

CHARLIE STAYED WITH VALENTINA, BRINGING HER DINNER as she fielded calls with her agent and family. By half ten she was exhausted. The stress bore down on her like layers of sedimentary rock.

The years of relentless work, the knowledge that her dream of moving her family to LA was over, Isabella's early baby, and now this. The thought of losing the cosmetics contract wasn't really about the money, it was about losing the opportunity to elevate her career beyond that of B-movie eye candy.

She blinked to focus as Charlie gently pried the tablet out of her hands.

'There's nothing more you can do,' he said, running his fingers into her hair and massaging her scalp. It felt so good, she couldn't help but let out a moan.

Charlie's phone rang. 'Fuck off,' he grumbled. 'I'm busy.'

'Answer it. At this time of night it must be important.'

He took the call. 'Mate?' There was a pause. 'Er, I'm, er, in my room.' There was another brief pause, then Charlie leapt to his feet. 'Fuck.'

'What is it?'

He was pulling on his boots, not bothering with the laces. 'Rory's about to kill Vlad.' He stopped at the door, his face deadly serious. 'Stay here,' he instructed, then strode out.

She stared at the closed door. How could she miss this? She pulled on her shoes and ran into the corridor. Which way had he gone?

Angry shouts echoed down the stairs to the attic corridor. Valentina started up them as Kirsten thundered down, pushing past her. She was wearing her character's wig, her face pinched with fury.

Valentina ran up the rest of the stairs and got to the top just behind Brad. Every door had at least one head poking out of it, except the one Rory and Charlie were outside.

'Hey, man, what's going on?' Brad asked.

Rory turned. He was covered in blood that ran from a wound above his eye and had dripped onto his clothes.

'Holy crap, son,' Brad exclaimed. 'What happened to your face?'

Charlie grabbed Rory's arm. Behind them, Vlad sidled out of his room, wearing long black robes and a tall hat covered in silver coins. Someone gasped behind Valentina and she turned to see Shauna staring at Rory, her face white.

'Are you okay?' Valentina whispered. Shauna started to shake, tears flooding her eyes. Valentina guided her back down the stairs. 'Come with me.'

By the time they reached the first floor, Shauna was hysterical, repeating 'it's all my fault', over and over. Valentina frog-marched her to the kitchen used by Brad's personal chef and sat her at the table. Shauna's teeth were chattering, so Valentina took off her jumper and put it around her shoulders, then found a bottle of rum and poured a small glass.

'Drink this, chica. We need to calm you down, okay?'

Shauna swallowed it and hugged her arms over her chest.

'You like hot chocolate?'

She nodded.

'Good. Now don't move until I've made it.'

Valentina bustled around the kitchen collecting the cinnamon, milk, and a bar of cooking chocolate. When it was made, she poured it out and topped the mugs up with more rum.

She sat next to Shauna and rubbed her shoulder. 'So then, please tell me how any of that was your fault.'

Fresh tears slid down Shauna's cheeks. 'His Holiness—'

Valentina held up her hand. 'It is against my religion to refer to that man as "His Holiness". You may use the words "Vlad", or "gonorrea", which kind of means "sick bastard" but also describes one of his many sexual diseases.'

Shauna smiled hesitantly. 'Gonorrhoea,' she continued, as Valentina nodded and smiled, 'told me to tell Rory that Zoe was coming back to stay at the castle this evening. So I did, but then Kirsten said it wasn't true, and she dressed up as Zoe and went to his room.'

'Holy shit.' Valentina instinctively crossed herself.

Shauna started crying again. 'So, it *is* my fault.'

'Slow down, chica. You can't add two plus two and get cabbage.'

'But I did what they said and I should have known better.'

'Chica, Kirsten going into his room is not your fault. You didn't dress her up and march her down the corridor, did you?'

Shauna shook her head. 'But—'

'This is *not* your fault.' Valentina heard a ringing in her ears. 'This is not your fault,' she repeated.

Her own voice suddenly sounded very far away.

A blinding pain pierced her chest and she sucked in a breath. A vision flashed through her, so vivid it could have been taking place there and then.

She was in the church for Alejandro's funeral but away from everyone, in a corner by the door with her abuela. It felt so real, but she had no memory of it. It was like she was living it for the first time.

Her abuela was holding onto her arms tightly.

'My baby, listen to me. This is *not* your fault.'

She heard her voice replying. 'It's all my fault, Abuela. If I had stayed home, he wouldn't be dead.'

Her abuela looked so young, but her eyes were creased with pain. 'No, my precious girl. That's not true. Ale made his own choices. There was nothing any of us could have done to stop him—even you, my love.'

'I won't let this happen again, Abuela. I promise.'

Valentina could hear Shauna asking if she was okay, but her voice was distant.

Why had she never remembered this until now? She had absolutely no doubt it had happened. Her family would never have blamed her for her brother's death, but it was only at this moment that one of them had said it out loud, and her mind had shut the memory down.

Until now.

Sadness and relief flooded through her. *Ale's death was not my fault.*

She closed her eyes with a sigh. She would never let her brother go, but she could let go of the belief that it was her fault, and the belief that she had to take her family out of the country they loved so much.

'Valentina? Are you okay?'

She opened her eyes. Everything was the same, but everything was different.

'Yes, I am. I just learned a lesson I should have learned many years ago, and one that I am going to make sure you learn tonight.' She lifted up her mug and indicated for Shauna to do the same. 'But first, I want to ask you something.'

Shauna lifted her mug. 'Yes?'

'Would you like a job working for me?'

 ✢   29   ✢

The next morning Charlie awoke to Valentina kissing him. He flailed a half-asleep arm towards her.

She wriggled away. 'I have to work today. I just didn't want to leave without a kiss.'

He opened his eyes. She was standing by the side of the bed.

'You're wearing clothes,' he grumbled. 'Come closer so I can remove them.'

She shook her head with a smile. 'I have to go and so do you. Rory messaged me to say I had to wake you. He needs you this morning.'

Charlie pushed himself onto his elbows. 'Hang about—you gave *Rory* your number but won't give it to me? How's that fair?'

She looked away, her cheeks pink. 'I'll see you later.'

As the door closed, Charlie flopped back onto the bed. They had three days left.

Valentina had always been upfront about what this was between them—a fling with a clear expiry date—and he'd agreed to her terms. But he couldn't picture a life without her in it.

He'd never been happier than when he was with her. She actually laughed at his shitty jokes, for fuck's sake. She thought he was *funny. And* she was hot for him.

His cock was already rock hard, but she was gone and his hand was no replacement. *Fuck!* He threw back the covers and sent his desire into remission with thoughts of the biggest boner killer there was—Vlad.

Last night in the corridor, Barbara had appeared to defuse the situation. When confronted by his mother, Rory had stormed off to the cabin to find Zoe. Later, when everyone had gone back to bed and the coast was clear, Charlie had returned to Vlad's room, taken the last of the drugs out of his man-bag, and escorted the two women in his bed out of the castle and into a taxi.

This morning he intended to do the same to Vlad.

After a cold shower, he searched the castle, but Vlad was nowhere to be found. Rory had messaged to say the paparazzi had turned up that morning at the cabin and he needed Charlie to help him construct a perimeter in case they returned.

Even though Charlie would have preferred to have been with Valentina, the prospect of making things go bang with his best mate was the kind of fun he missed now he was out of the army.

The two of them drove to Inverness to get supplies, then spent the day making non-lethal surprises and reliving their glory days, whilst Bandit sniffed around happily.

Rory didn't ask him about Valentina, Caroline, Tabitha, or anything current in his life and Charlie was glad. He needed a break from all the deep thinking and soul-searching, and there was no better antidote than running around outside preparing interesting presents for the lowliest members of the gutter press.

That evening, Zoe's mates Sam and Jamie were performing songs they'd written in honour of the film at the pub. Charlie didn't want to go, but Valentina did. So they went and watched them play, her leaning back against his chest, nestled in his protective arms.

During the performance, he stared daggers at anyone who looked like they might approach her, and fantasised they were a real couple on a regular night out. As soon as the duo had finished playing, he took her hand and they slipped back to the castle so he could show her just what she'd be missing when they parted.

THE NEXT MORNING, CHARLIE WOKE TO VALENTINA shaking his shoulder.

'Charlie, I need to ask you something.'

He reached across her body to pin her to the bed, kissing down the side of her neck. 'Whatever it is, the answer's yes,' he replied, disappearing under the covers and finding her nipple with a groan.

She pulled away from him and lifted the duvet. 'It's important. I've had an email from my agent.'

He rolled off her, staring up at the bed canopy. 'Two days, Valentina. We have two days left together. Can't it wait?'

Silence.

Don't be a fucking dickhead! He closed his eyes, willing his emotions to go away. 'I'm sorry.' He sighed. 'Ask away, sweetheart.' He reached over and stroked the soft skin of her thigh. This would have to do for now.

'My agent emailed me last night,' she said quietly. '*Saturday Night Live* got in touch. They want me to be a guest host.'

He rolled to his side. 'Fuck, Valentina, that's amazing!'

She frowned and chewed her lip. 'I don't know, Charlie. They want to make fun of my photos. They want to make fun of *me*. I want everyone to forget about it.'

He took her hand. 'If you can show the world you can laugh at yourself, that's the fastest way for people to lose interest. They won't keep bringing it up if it looks like you don't care.'

She shrugged.

'Has the cosmetics company said anything?'

She shook her head.

He arched an eyebrow. 'Well then, surely no news is good news? You should definitely do it.'

Unease clouded her face. 'Really?'

'Yes. You'll be brilliant.'

She smiled at him, and he squeezed her hand.

'Remind me when you're working today?'

She smirked. 'Charlie, you know my schedule better than I do... I'm working this afternoon, and then this evening...' She rolled her eyes. 'I'm storming the castle with my ninja army. We won't finish till late. Why?'

'I thought we could check another couple of things off your list when you're done.'

'In the middle of the night?'

He raised an eyebrow and she blushed. 'It's a clear night, so I thought we could stay up and watch the sunrise.'

'That sounds lovely.' She smiled, but her eyes looked sad.

'And you'll need to bring your character's dress.'

'Why? Are we going to burn it?'

He grinned. 'We're going to go one better. We're going to blow it up.'

She sucked in a shocked giggle, then the castle fire alarm went off.

· · · ·

CHARLIE THUNDERED DOWN THE MAIN STAIRS, VALENTINA following. He met Rory at the bottom as the fire alarm stopped. 'What's going on?'

Rory looked like a man dragged through the gates of hell. Charlie had seen him calmer in the middle of an ambush in Afghanistan.

'*Vlad*,' he spat.

Rory turned on his heel and they followed him to a room on the ground floor. Lying on the wooden floor in a massive puddle of water was a scorched dummy wearing what looked like Zoe's clothes as well as Kirsten's curly red wig.

'Fucking hell, mate.' Charlie whistled. 'He's properly lost the plot.'

'I'm going after him with Bandit,' said Rory, his face grim. 'Wanna come?'

Charlie glanced at Valentina.

'Go,' she whispered.

He turned back to Rory. 'Yeah, I'm game, but we need something from my room first.'

Rory gave him a quizzical look.

He grinned. 'I've got a pair of his underpants in my wardrobe.'

FOUR HOURS LATER, THE ONLY THING CHARLIE AND RORY had discovered was that either Bandit had lost his touch or Vlad had left his scent everywhere. They'd traipsed through the castle, around Kinloch, and even up into the hills after they discovered a fresh magic mushroom in his room, but Vlad had disappeared.

Giving up their search for the day, they went their separate ways in the early evening as the crew was setting up outside the castle for the night shoot.

Charlie stood to the side when the action started, watching Valentina with so much pride he thought his heart would burst. Despite being clothed in the most dangerously inappropriate battle dress, she was fearsome, leading the charge with Brad, a battalion of stuntmen, and extras behind them.

When Brad eventually called the final 'cut' of the night, there was a round of applause. Valentina looked relieved and ran to his side.

'Give me five minutes,' she said. 'I'll just run and get changed. Meet you back here?'

He nodded. 'Yep, I've got everything we need.'

                      ❅ 30 ❅

Charlie and Valentina strolled hand in hand through
Kinloch, then followed the main road leading out of
the village. A few hundred yards along, Charlie
turned left and led Valentina up a farm track heading into the
hills.

The night was clear and still, the stars shining brightly, the
moon even brighter. They hiked for over an hour until they
reached the peak of the first mountain. The loch was far below,
the surface reflecting the moon, and the black hills behind it
cutting in front of the stars.

He shucked off his rucksack and started unpacking.

'What have you got in there?' she asked.

'Everything,' he replied with a grin. He took out a groundsheet and blanket. 'Take a seat. I've got to finish the device.
I've brought chocolate caliente as well if you want some?'

Her smile was bright in the moonlight. 'You do think of
everything.'

He put on a head torch and took out a bag containing wires
and tools. 'I assembled most of it yesterday when we were

rigging the perimeter around the cabin, so it won't take long to set up.'

'Did it work? Did anyone come back to the cabin last night?'

He grinned at her. 'Yes, and yes.'

She gasped, then giggled. 'Oh my goodness, were they hurt?'

Charlie's face was serious. He slowly shook his head. 'Unfortunately not.'

She slapped the side of his arm. 'You are a bad man.'

'I know.' He smirked. 'I've told you that a million times already.'

She kissed him on the cheek. 'You're not really a bad man, Charlie.'

He stared at her, starlight reflecting off the liquid surface of her eyes. He wanted to bottle this moment, keep it safe in his heart forever, drawing out drops of this memory for the rest of his life. In such a short space of time she'd become the most precious thing in the world to him.

She pulled her costume from a pocket in her coat. 'This thing is ridiculous. I've worn bigger bikinis.' She paused. 'You know I said I wouldn't steal anything?' He nodded. 'Well, I stole this. It's the property of the production. And if they ask me if I know where it is, I'm going to have to lie as well, which is another terrible thing to do.'

He laughed. 'You've nailed being a teenager. I couldn't be prouder, my young Padawan.'

His heart stretched again, a painful yearning as it drew him closer into her orbit. He knew he'd be a distant satellite around her for life—oceans apart, but always feeling that pull.

'So then, want to blow something up?'

'Yes, please.' Her face was alight with excitement.

'Hand me that insult to the art of armour and Native

American culture.' He took the dress and walked down the slope into the heather.

'How far are you going?' she asked.

'Far enough that there's no chance of being hurt by shrapnel. This dress is lethal. If you were hit by one of these beads at max velocity it would not be pretty.'

'Is this a good idea?' She sounded worried.

He grinned as he continued down the side of the mountain. 'It's only a small bang. Think of it as a firework. And anyway, I'm a professional.'

'You told me you were a professional idiot,' she shouted.

'I'm a professional at everything I do,' he called back up the hill. 'The slogan for the British Army is "Be the Best", for the Paras, it's "Ready for Anything", for the SAS, it's "Who Dares Wins", and for Saturday staff at McDonald's, it's "I'm Lovin' It", so I think I've got all bases covered.'

He chuckled as he heard the faint sound of 'huevón' and her laugh. He set the charge and tied the dress around it. He'd included some flares and bangers for effect, otherwise it would have been far too underwhelming.

He strode back up the hill, unwinding a wire from a spool as he went.

'Okay, it's far enough down from us that we won't be hit, even if the shrapnel could carry this far. But just in case I've fucked up spectacularly and can't tell the red wire from the blue, I want you to put this over your face and crouch behind me.' He took a welding mask out of the rucksack.

She stared at it. 'Are you serious?'

He nodded. 'You've got to have several layers of redundancy. So you'll put it on and get behind me.'

'But what is protecting *you*?'

'My thick skin and boundless optimism,' he replied. 'Anyway, a few additional scars will only make me even more rugged and handsome.'

'Are you sure about this, Charlie?'

He kissed her on the forehead. 'Absolutely. I'll film it for you as well if you like? You can look over my shoulder as you set it off—'

'*I'm* setting it off?'

'Of course. Your dress, your bomb, your glory.'

'I can't believe we're doing this.'

'Believe it. The earth is about to move for you, sugar plum.'

'Will you rock my world?' she asked, a mischievous look on her face.

'Sweetheart, I'm going to blow you away.'

She darted forwards and gave him a quick kiss. 'It's always been fireworks with you, Charlie,' she whispered before pulling back.

There it was again. The stabbing pain in his heart.

He forced himself to smile. 'Ready to make sure our relationship goes out with a bang?'

She nodded.

CHARLIE SHOWED VALENTINA THE SMALL BOX WITH THE switch and she gave him her phone so he could video it, telling him to shoot in slow motion. He made sure the mask was on, but she could still see over his shoulder, then handed her the box and began a countdown.

'Five, four, three, two, one, ZERO!' he yelled.

She flicked the switch and the bomb went off. There was a massive bang with a huge flash, then red flares shot into the air and firecrackers competed with Valentina's screams.

As the light from the flares petered out, her screams turned into shrieks of laughter behind him. His heart was full. *Try and beat that, arsehole future boyfriends.* He desperately wanted a kiss, so without thinking, slumped over and played dead.

'Charlie!' she cried.

He heard the welding mask drop to the ground, then her hands were on him.

'No, no, no, no, no! Charlie!'

Oh fuck.

He sat up, holding her. 'Hey, I'm fine, I was just being silly.'

She started hitting him, screaming through her tears. 'Setenta hijueputa, huevón, pendejo!'

'Valentina, I'm so sorry. I'm sorry, love.'

You stupid fucking dickhead! He held still, letting her punches land. She was strong and he deserved the bruises. How could he have been so thoughtless? He hadn't thought for a second about the death of her brother.

As he offered no resistance, she stopped hitting him and sat back on her heels, breathing heavily, her shoulders slumped. 'That was not funny. That was *not funny*, Charlie!'

'I'm sorry. I didn't think.' He reached for her hands and she let him take them. He drew her into his chest and she surrendered with a sigh, holding onto him tightly. He wrapped his arms around her and nuzzled into her hair.

'I'm so fucking sorry, sweetheart.'

He held her as the breeze rustled the heather around them and the stars moved slowly across the sky. When she finally stirred, he let her go and she pulled out a wad of tissues and blew her nose.

'Would you like some hot chocolate?' he asked tentatively.

She nodded and sat back on the groundsheet.

He poured her a cup and one for himself, then sat alongside her, waiting for her to speak. To say anything.

'Charlie, I wanted to thank you,' she began stiffly. 'For everything you have done for me.'

So here it was. The nail in the coffin. The 'so long, and thanks for all the fish' speech.

She glanced at him. 'I've had so much fun.'

Is that all? He swallowed as she continued.

'I've tried things I've never done before. And you've,' she cleared her throat, 'you've been so supportive to me during some very difficult times in my life. I will never forget...' She hesitated, as if choosing her words carefully. 'I will never forget spending this time with you.'

She held her cup out to his and the edges touched.

'Here's to teenage kicks,' she said, her voice artificially light.

They sat in silence, sipping the hot chocolate and staring out into the night. It was at least another half hour before the sun rose, but the sky was starting to brighten.

Charlie needed the drink. He needed the warmth to melt the ice crystallising around his heart. His life had been changed fundamentally by knowing Valentina. Going forward he would always be a happier person. He would strive to be the best possible version of himself. But there would also be the realisation that he wasn't sharing his life with her.

Anger knotted his stomach. Why *couldn't* they be together? He wouldn't let her go without fighting for her.

'Valentina?'

'Hmm?' She sounded distracted.

He'd had his heart broken before. He knew the depths of pain one could go to. But he also knew he was the strongest, the most sanguine he'd ever been. And the loss of Valentina was one set in stone from the outset.

He had nothing to lose by speaking his truth.

'Valentina. I love you.'

The cup in her hand shook. He let the words hang in the

air. It felt good to say them out loud. To stop hiding from what was in his heart.

'I think it happened the first time I saw you. But I was too caught up in my layers of denial and bullshit to recognise it. You're the sweetest, kindest, cutest, funniest, cleverest, most beautiful person I've ever met. You're my ultimate human.'

He paused and smiled.

'I've never been happier than when I've been with you. I've never felt more me.' He took another sip of chocolate, trying to think of the right words.

She was as still as a statue.

'I can live anywhere, Valentina. I can find work anywhere. I can live my life around your schedule—'

'No, Charlie.'

'Why not? I'm not expecting you to love me back. I'm just hoping you'll give me a chance. I know I mean something to you. Give us the time for that something to become more.'

She shook her head. 'It's complicated.'

'Is it? Your family seem to tolerate me. You appear happy most of the time I'm around. The rest of it—the admin, the logistics—is all surmountable. It's just...' He sighed. 'Stuff...' He gazed at her profile. 'Valentina, look at me.'

She shook her head.

He rubbed his face in frustration. 'I'm not asking you to change your life. I'm not asking you to change a fucking thing. I just want to tag along for the ride. I want to be there with you. I want to be there *for* you.'

She blinked and a tear rolled down her cheek.

He didn't know what else to say. He was all out of words. He shifted his body and stared at the hills on the far side of the loch as the stars faded away in the predawn light.

'Charlie,' she began softly. 'Before I came to Scotland, I knew what I was doing with my life and why. Now I don't know what I'm going to do next. I can't think straight. I need time on my own to process what has happened. I need to figure out who I am and what I want. I'm sorry.'

They sat in silence, their eyes locked on the horizon as they watched the sun rise on their last day together.

31

Valentina wasn't needed for the final day of shooting, so she spent the morning sleeping, then the afternoon with Shauna, finding out how a personal assistant could help organise her life.

Charlie was with Rory in the great hall, getting it ready for the wrap party that evening. Brad had paid for a bar and a ceilidh band and the whole village had been invited.

Had Valentina not met Charlie, she would have been looking forward to it, but now she felt empty and flat. That morning, after watching the sun rise, they'd walked in silence down the side of the mountain. At the castle they'd gone their separate ways.

At the time she was too tired to think, too tired to feel. But now, awake, her mind kept churning over his words.

Her two other boyfriends had said they loved her, but it never seemed authentic. It was either said in the throes of passion or when they wanted something from her. Charlie was different. He'd laid his heart out for her and she'd rejected it. Now she was confused and lost.

When Alejandro died, she'd experienced grief, but out of it came a purpose. A way of channelling her pain into something positive for her family. Now that dream was dead and she had no purpose left to guide her.

How could she be in a relationship with anyone when she didn't even know who she was anymore? And how would Charlie cope when she did roles like the one she was starting next week?

She shuddered, a wave of revulsion rolling through her. She'd never broken a contract and she couldn't start now. Charlie didn't understand her world and never would. He'd end up jealous, unhappy, and resentful. She couldn't do that to herself or him.

She wanted their time together to remain perfect—a beautifully boxed memory that she could open when she was alone. She'd lived so long without a boyfriend, without a roommate. If she'd survived so far, then she could easily carry a similar life on into the future.

She was sitting on her bed with Shauna, when there was a knock at the door.

Shauna bounced off the bed and opened it.

'Hey, Charlie,' she said brightly. 'How are you doing?'

Valentina's stomach lurched and her heart thudded as she gazed at him. Every time she saw him, she was blindsided by how much he affected her.

He was frowning at Shauna. 'I'm sorry, I don't think we've been introduced. You look very similar to a friend of mine. But unlike her, you look like you've actually got something to live for.'

Shauna giggled as he stuck out his hand.

'I'm Charlie, by the way.'

She shook it. 'Pleased to meet you, Charlie. I'm Shauna's twin. I'm also called Shauna, but I'm the happy one.'

He smiled. 'Glad to meet you.' He glanced over her shoulder at Valentina, and his smile slipped fractionally. 'I was wondering if I could borrow your rucksack for a few minutes?'

She couldn't speak, so nodded, her heart racing even faster. Shauna gave it to him.

'Cheers,' he said. 'Won't be long.'

Shauna closed the door behind him and came back to the bed.

'He's so nice,' she said hesitantly. 'You and he...' she began.

Valentina tensed.

'...have been so kind to me,' Shauna finished.

Valentina nodded, fighting the tears she was desperate to shed.

'Okay,' said Shauna briskly. 'Let's chat about email management.'

Fifteen minutes later, Charlie knocked again. He had a quiet conversation with Shauna, passed her the rucksack, and left.

Valentina glanced up. She couldn't see what he'd done to it.

'Just put it back on the floor, chica,' she said to Shauna, then checked her watch. 'I can't believe the time. Are you hungry? Do you want to grab some food from the catering truck?'

'Sure. Why don't I go and get us both a plate?'

Valentina smiled with relief.

Shauna squeezed her hand. 'I'll be back in a bit.'

When the door shut behind her, Valentina lay her head on the pillow and stared up at the bed canopy. Shauna was going to revolutionise her day-to-day life and Valentina wished she'd found her a decade ago. Intelligent and empathetic, she already had a handle on her emotional needs, understanding that Valentina couldn't face Charlie or anyone else right now.

She got off the bed and picked up the rucksack. What had Charlie done? She turned the bag over and saw it in an instant. Below the Colombian flag, he'd stitched the Scottish one.

Ale had wanted to travel the world and put the flag of every country he visited on his bag, and now Charlie was showing her she could do it for him.

She held the empty rucksack to her chest, her heart aching for the brother she'd lost and the man she was turning down.

THE CEILIDH HAD ALREADY BEEN GOING FOR AN HOUR WHEN Valentina descended the main stairs with Shauna.

Her new personal assistant was trying to keep her excitement in check, but it kept bubbling out.

'Do you think all the local men will be in kilts? Have you checked out the castle website? The earl is just so...' She sighed. '*Manly.*'

Valentina smiled despite herself. Rory did seem to have quite the effect on the women in the crew—and half the men too. As did Charlie. She bit back a sigh. She'd seen the way people looked at him, even if he appeared oblivious to the attention.

Valentina slowed as they approached the main doors to the great hall. The sound of music and people celebrating was already deafening. Shauna was bouncing on the balls of her feet. Valentina wanted to run away.

Inside, there was a bar at one end, with the band at the other and people standing around the edges. The middle of the room was filled with dancing couples, whirling each other around, and being choreographed by a man barking orders into a microphone.

Rory and Zoe were in the middle, taller than everyone else, with Rory's wild blond hair and Zoe's crazy red curls standing out like torches. Shauna had told her they'd got engaged that morning, and Valentina could see the enormous ring glinting in the light on Zoe's finger.

'Do you want me to get you a drink?' Shauna yelled.

She shook her head. 'Not right now, thank you. You go ahead.'

The music came to an end with a flourish, and the dancers stayed put or dispersed back to the sides. One of the crew's junior electricians approached them. He was wearing a kilt and Shauna's eyes widened.

He bowed. 'Shauna, would you give me the honour of the next dance?'

Shauna glanced at Valentina, her eyes bugging like a child facing a bowl of ice cream larger than their own head.

Valentina pushed her forward. 'Go! Enjoy yourself. I'm not sure I'll stay that long anyway.'

Shauna squeezed her hand and was led off into the middle of the floor.

Valentina shrank back. She'd had years of practice making herself unapproachable and easily slipped back into the role. She scanned the room.

Is he here?

Charlie was so tall—almost as big as Rory. He couldn't hide, even in a crowd this large.

'Earth to Valentina?' a voice said in her ear.

She whipped around to see Peter, the head of hair and make-up. 'Do you fancy a drink, a dance, or a smoking hot Englishman who's licensed to thrill?'

Her face heated. 'Is it that obvious?'

Peter pulled her in for a hug. 'He's not here, sweetie. But that doesn't mean you can't have fun.'

She hugged him back, an overwhelming wave of sadness moving through her. She was so tired. She needed to sleep before she embarrassed herself and cried on his shoulder.

'I think I'm going to go to bed. I've got an early start tomorrow anyway.'

He released her. 'Well, if you change your mind, we'll be here until the early hours.'

She thanked him and darted through the crowds, desperate to get away.

Outside, the corridor was cooler and quieter. Before she could talk herself out of it, she went to Charlie's room and knocked. She couldn't hear anything inside and was about to turn away when the door opened.

The room was lit by a small lamp by the bedside. Charlie was naked, except for a towel tied around his hips. Valentina's body roared to life. Her heart sprinted off the blocks and fire whipped across her cheeks and down into her belly.

His hair was damp from the shower, water still dripping off the muscles of his torso. She stared at her own name still scrawled across his chest.

'Hey,' he said softly.

'Were you about to go to be—*sleep?*' she stuttered.

He nodded. 'I didn't go to bed after we got back this morning, so I've been awake for over forty hours.'

'Oh.'

Now embarrassment was adding to her internal heat. Why had she come? She was so desperate to see him again, but it was unfair. She was taking and not giving.

He stepped back into the room. 'Would you like to come in?'

She followed him and shut the door behind her.

32

Valentina faced Charlie. She wanted him so badly, but was too full of shame to ask.

He reached for her hand. 'You know, Valentina. You can ask me for anything. If this is a booty call, then just say so. I'm not going to turn you down. Ever.'

Her cheeks were on fire.

He gazed at her with compassion. 'You've always been upfront and honest with me. Right from day one. I'm not going to ask you again for what you don't want to give. Just tell me what you want from me.'

She swallowed, her eyes flicking down his body to his feet. God, even his feet were sexy. 'I thought we could cross one more thing off the list,' she said quietly.

'Have you written me a poem?'

Her eyes shot up to his in surprise. He was smiling.

'No. I, er...' She took a breath. 'I thought we could have wild monkey sex.'

He held her gaze. 'No.'

'What? Why not?'

'We don't qualify.'

She frowned.

'You can only have wild monkey sex on a one-night stand or if you're both completely and perfectly in love. We're kind of in the middle, so it's going to have to be something else.'

'Will you have normal sex with me then?'

Shit! How desperate did she sound?

Charlie shook his head. 'No.'

He went into the bathroom, leaving her standing with her mouth open in shock, then returned without his towel, his cock erect and bumping against his navel. He faced her, a wall of hard muscle and sex, then gently ran his fingers down her cheek to cup her chin.

'We're not going to have sex,' he stated. 'We're going to make love. I'm going to take my time, and you're going to let me. I'm going to worship the fuck out of you, Valentina, and you're going to take it.'

She gasped.

'And when you come, you're going to be looking into my eyes and screaming my name.'

Her inner muscles clenched and her body jerked. She was flooding with desire, her nipples hardening under her dress. He lowered his lips to brush against hers and she shivered.

'Do you agree to my terms?' he whispered.

She nodded, a wave of goosebumps dancing across her skin. Her breath was erratic, her head light.

'Say it,' he continued, then ran the tip of his tongue across her bottom lip.

'Yes,' she breathed. 'Oh god, yes.'

Her legs buckled and he caught her with a strong arm around her waist. He pulled her to him, holding her tight against his cock as his lips continued their feather-light passes over hers.

She was trembling against him, struggling to remain upright as her body melted into liquid hot desire. He dipped his tongue into her mouth and she clung to him, pulling his head to hers, wanting him deeper.

His body was a drug and he was upping the dose with every stroke. Stars exploded behind her eyelids as her legs finally gave way.

He lifted her to the bed and removed her shoes. She was breathing in gasps now, already close to coming. His fingers grazed up the outside of her thighs and she twitched involuntarily. He pulled her dress to her waist, then tugged off her panties.

She opened her groggy eyes. He was kneeling between her legs, holding her sodden underwear up to his nose, breathing in her scent. His cock was huge, red, and swollen. She licked her lips.

'These,' he said, indicating her underwear, 'are now mine.'

He dropped them to the bed and knelt, kissing and licking her ankles, holding her legs open as he kneaded the flesh of her calves. Her core was clenching around nothing, willing him higher. Every cell in her body desperate for release. He moved slowly up, pulling the flesh of her inner thighs into his mouth, sucking hard as she started to beg.

'Please, Charlie, please.'

The sensations within were multiplying, colliding with each other. It was a chaotic confusion of unbearable pleasure. She had to come—she couldn't cope anymore.

Her hand crept towards the apex of her thighs and was immediately removed and held to the bed. Charlie licked a little higher and she jerked her hips to try and reach his tongue.

'Do you want to come, Valentina?' he growled.

'Yes! Yes!' she cried. 'Please, Charlie, it's too much.'

Suddenly his hands were at the top of her legs, spreading her and holding her hard to the bed. He licked in fast and furious strokes up the length of her slit. Sharp flashes of pleasure shot from her clit, her hips thrashing against his restraint.

Blood roared through her veins, her cries getting higher and higher with every stroke. He sucked her clit into his mouth, tugging on it as he vibrated the tip of his tongue over the end.

Her climax hit and she screamed, her chest lifting off the bed as if shocked, then thumping back down. Her vision went black as her body shattered into light.

The waves continued through her body, each undulation stopping the breath in her throat. She lost all sense of herself. She was an exploding star, each part of her disintegrating outwards into the universe.

He moved up and removed her dress and bra. Her limbs were sleepy and uncooperative, but she kept her eyes open as she drank him in. He was spectacular. His green eyes glowing with flecks of gold, his gaze intense and reverent. The angled planes of his muscles, covered in tattoos, the dragon snaking down his abdomen to bite at the base of his shaft.

One hand stroked up and down her leg, the other fisted his cock. The end was slick with precum and he rubbed it over the head with a shudder, his gaze never leaving hers.

'What do you want, Valentina?' he asked, his voice rough.

'You. Inside me. Now.'

He reached for the condoms on the bedside table. She put her hand on his.

'I want you inside me bare,' she whispered. 'I want you to come inside me.'

He grabbed his cock at the base and squeezed, dropping his head and letting out a strangled cry. His breathing was harsh, his jaw tight as the air hissed in and out. When he regained control, he stared at her, his gaze questioning.

'I won't get pregnant. And I'm clear.'

His eyes were wild with lust. 'I am too.'

She took his head in her hands and kissed him deeply, pulling his body to cover hers. Their tongues tangled, exploring the hot darkness of each other's mouths in anticipation of what was to come.

She circled her hips onto his cock, her heart skipping with the thought of him inside her without any barrier. She'd never experienced that level of intimacy before but craved it with him.

He broke the kiss with a gasp, kissing and sucking down her neck with agonising intensity until he reached her breasts, lavishing them with attention till she was wriggling under him, filled with the desire to pull him inside her.

Even as another orgasm built, she recognised the primal need, even as a fantasy, to be creating a new life with this incredible man.

She reached between them and grabbed his shaft.

He moved away, panting.

'Charlie, please,' she begged.

'Are you sure?' He looked desperate.

'Yes, yes, I am.'

He settled his cock at her entrance, taking her hands in his as he rested his forearms on either side of her head. She felt secure. Protected. There were only the two of them in the whole of existence. She closed her eyes. She couldn't handle seeing the love in his.

'Look at me, Valentina.'

She shook her head, emotion spiralling up inside her. He nudged his cock against her resistance.

'Look at me,' he growled. 'This is not happening unless you open your eyes.'

She opened them and her heart squeezed. As he pushed in further, she bucked up to meet him. The sensation of him inside her was always breathtaking. But now, bare, it was overwhelming.

He stopped. 'Sweetheart, are you okay? Am I hurting you?'

She shook her head, closing her eyes as tears tracked down into her hair. She felt his soft lips on her skin as he kissed them away.

He nuzzled her. 'We don't have to do this if you don't want to,' he whispered.

She wrapped her legs around his backside, holding him close. She could feel how wet and ready she was, the sweet sensations of his cock and how much she needed him.

She released his hands and gripped the sides of his face.

'Don't stop.' She clenched around him, and he threw his head back with a yell, his eyes closing. 'Look at me,' she demanded.

He stared at her with a desperate, burning intensity, then pushed deeper until he filled her completely. He didn't pause. He just held her gaze, withdrew, then thrust deep into her with a grunt.

A jolt of pleasure shot through her, and she gasped. He did it again, rolling his hips as he thrusted, bumping against her clit. He set up a rhythm, pumping and rolling, pumping and rolling. Pleasure pulsated through her each time he buried himself inside her.

She held on tight, not losing eye contact as her breath picked up, and another climax began to build. Their connection was the still point within the storm. He was inside her mind, body, and soul. He knew when she was reaching the point of no return.

Her eyelids fluttered as she approached the apex of her orgasm at maximum velocity.

'Stay with me, Valentina,' he urged. 'Stay with me, sweetheart.'

She forced her eyes open as the climax crashed through her, a double whammy of blinding sensation and overwhelming emotion. He roared above her with his own release, his cock jerking, his body shuddering. He finally broke her gaze and collapsed on top of her, gasping for breath, his head buried in the pillow.

Her breath was ragged as tears rolled down her cheeks. She felt his heaviness, his tiredness, and pulled out from under him, stroking down his back as he mumbled incoherently.

She soothed him, breathing in and out through her mouth, not wanting him to hear her tears. He was asleep within a minute, but she kept her hand on his back, wanting to remember the feel of him forever.

Eventually she tiptoed into the bathroom to blow her nose. She stared at herself in the mirror. Her eyes were red, her cheeks flushed, her lips puffy. There was a love bite on her neck. She touched it.

Did he think she would forget him tomorrow? That he needed to leave a reminder? She could never forget him.

She crept out of the bathroom, redressed, pulled the covers over him, and turned off the light.

'Goodbye, Charlie Hamilton,' she whispered as she left the room.

❦ 33 ❦

Charlie woke the next morning and knew before opening his eyes that Valentina was gone.

Her scent and the memories from the night clung to him. Wanting to believe she was still lying next to him, he rolled towards the empty side of the bed. On the pillow next to his were her knickers. He pulled them towards him with a smile. It hadn't all been a dream.

He had the familiar urge to box all thoughts of her and stash them at the back of his mind. But he'd changed. That was a coping strategy for the past, not for now.

Thanks to Valentina, he'd unpacked his most painful memories and faced his demons. His time with her was something to be cherished. Something to be kept at the forefront of his mind as a reminder of what kind of person he could be.

He checked the time. He'd promised Rory he would help clear the hall after the party last night, so got out of bed, dressed and left. Passing Valentina's room, he noticed the door was open. He poked his head in, hoping she was still there.

It was empty. The bed was stripped and the rug he'd given her was gone.

Was there any trace of her left? His attention was drawn to a change in texture and colour of the carpet by the side of the bed.

By one of the legs was a tiny pile of fresh wood dust. He moved the bedside table to get a better look. On the side of the leg, hidden unless you were looking for it, the ancient wood was freshly scored. The shape of a heart had been cut. Inside it were the initials CH and VV.

Valentina had done some graffiti.

CHARLIE MET RORY IN THE GREAT HALL A FEW MINUTES later, a smile still on his face. His friend was out of his kilt and back in faded work trousers and a battered tartan shirt. He looked like a lumberjack, not an earl.

Rory hefted a pile of ten chairs into his arms. 'Nice of you to join me. Why do you look so happy? I thought you'd be miserable as sin this morning.'

Charlie shrugged and began stacking chairs. 'There's nothing more I can do. I've told her how I feel. I can't force her to love me back—'

'Hold up,' Rory interrupted. 'You *love* her?'

'Yeah, I do. You don't have the monopoly on that emotion, you know.'

'So why the fuck aren't you following her? She's awesome.'

'Why didn't you follow Zoe to London after she left your sorry arse?'

'Fair point but different. I was a total dick to Zoe. If I'd pushed her any more, she would never have come back. But you and Valentina? Much as it pains me to say it, you haven't done anything wrong. Once she's got her head straight, she needs to know you're still there.'

'But she lives on the other side of the world and never gave me her number.'

Rory gave him a look. 'Fuck me. When did you become such a wuss? Seriously, mate, grow a pair and throw in a new spine while you're at it.'

'Thanks for the advice. Have you ever considered volunteering for the Samaritans?'

'You know, I've got her number if you want it.'

Charlie shook his head. 'I need to give her space. That would be a temptation too far.'

Rory shrugged and they continued moving chairs out of the hall, then turned their attention to dismantling the temporary bar.

'So, what's next?' Rory asked. 'Back to wiping rich people's arses?'

'Fuck off,' he replied good-naturedly. 'I'm going straight from here to my folks for their wedding anniversary shindig. After that...' He puffed out his cheeks. 'Who the fuck knows? I'll figure it out. I've rung Mack. I'm sure he can find me something.' He paused. 'By the way. Do you know what happened to Vlad? Did he ever turn up?'

Rory had a strange look on his face. 'He was, er, taken care of.'

Charlie glanced around. They were alone. 'When did that happen? And how come I missed all the fun?'

Rory looked sheepish. 'It wasn't me.'

'Then who was it? Bandit?'

'Mum,' his friend replied quietly.

'What the fuck? Your *mum*?'

Rory lowered his voice further. 'She shot him with a tranquiliser dart and Zoe helped load him in the boot of the Rolls.

They handed him off to one of Mum's friends a few miles out of town and he drove Vlad down south and dumped him in a hedge near Heathrow.'

Charlie started laughing. 'Holy shit, Rory, that's fucking epic. Did you know?'

He shook his head.

Charlie bent over, holding his stomach. 'That makes it even funnier. Jesus Christ, the women in your life. Fuck me. You'd better never piss Zoe off again now she's been schooled by your mother.'

Rory shook his head slowly as he smiled. 'Mate, that thought has already crossed my mind.'

CHUMLEIGH UNDERBOTTOM WAS PREDOMINANTLY THE HOME of the well-to-do. It was the kind of place Americans like Brad Bauer envisioned when they thought of Jane Austen and Shakespeare.

The buildings were all at least two hundred years old, their upper-middle-class inhabitants appearing to be only a few years behind. Wisteria grew up the sides of the cottages, the yew trees in the churchyard predated Christianity, and the only nod to modernity was that the old red phone box now contained a defibrillator rather than a telephone.

Charlie stared at his parents' house, nerves stabbing at his stomach. They lived in the old rectory, a beautiful Georgian building, built to last out of Bath stone. It was set back from the road down a sweeping gravel drive, but Charlie had parked out on the street for a quick escape in case everything went south.

It was a beautiful summer's day, and the grounds were perfect—not a faded bloom or dandelion in sight. He'd arrived early, and the caterers were setting up tables and chairs around the garden and inside an open-sided marquee. It was a scene of bucolic perfection.

He opened the heavy front door and stepped quietly into the hallway. The tiles were ancient and worn from years of footfall. Fresh flowers ran up the banister in front of him, and to his right, next to an umbrella stand, stood an ancient grand-father clock.

Come on, mate, you've got this.

He squared his shoulders. Down the long hall from the front entrance was a wooden door, the top half paned with glass, which led straight onto a large open-plan kitchen. He could see his parents through it: his dad, tall and lean with thick white hair, his mother, shorter with shoulder-length white-blonde hair. They looked like models from a cruise liner advert.

He watched his father pull his mother in for a kiss, gently cradling the back of her head. *Holy shit!* Charlie had never seen them kiss like that before. Had he even seen them kiss at all? His mother had her arms around his father and he saw one of his dad's hands move down the curve of his mother's spine, down to cup her—

Charlie dashed left into the drawing room, completely confused. His parents *loved* each other? They were *physical* with each other?

He let out a shocked laugh, then wanted to punch himself for his blind naivety. *You're such a twat.*

Who was he to decide what his parents were like? How could he pass judgement on their relationship with each other, their thoughts and feelings, when such judgements were based on the myopic view of a self-absorbed teenage boy, then that of a surly, angry adult?

Was it taking him this long to finally grow up and remove his head from his arse?

He glanced around at the room that was most familiar to him. The drawing room had a fireplace, antique upholstered chairs, oil paintings passed down through generations, shelves of leather-bound books, and a baby grand piano.

The room smelt exactly the same as it always had—a mix of coal dust, musty books, wood polish, and flowers. Opposite the fireplace was a sash window looking out on the garden. It was so big that on hot days it could be opened and you could easily step through it. It was currently closed, but he could see people moving around the garden outside preparing for the party.

He sat at the piano and lifted the fallboard. In front of him, resting on the top, was a collection of silver photo frames.

His parents on their wedding day, his sister on hers, both sets of grandparents on theirs. Then one of his sister at her passing out ceremony and one of him at his. Finally, there was a more informal photo of him and his sister as children, their arms around each other, smiling in the garden. He remembered being happy.

He settled his hands over the keys and played some arpeggios. It felt like rediscovering an old friend, the two of them immediately slipping back into their original intimacy. He stilled. What should he play? The answer came immediately. The eighteenth variation from Rachmaninoff's *Rhapsody on a Theme of Paganini*, his mother's favourite.

Charlie smiled and let his fingers glide over the keys. The variation started simply, the melody building slowly before opening out and soaring like a bird. He closed his eyes, letting the piano sing.

The door opened and he glanced up. His parents were in the doorway. His father was standing behind his mother, holding onto her shoulders, staring at him as if for the first time. His mother's eyes were full of tears.

He stopped playing, his own eyes blurry.

'Hi, Mum, hi, Dad,' he said thickly. 'Happy anniversary.'

THE AFTERNOON PASSED IN A DREAMY HAZE OF CUCUMBER sandwiches, strawberries and cream, champagne, and good feelings.

Charlie threw open the windows to the drawing room and played Mendelssohn's 'Wedding March' as his parents came out to greet their guests. His parents' old friends seemed genuinely pleased to see him and thrilled he was playing the piano again.

One by one they came to ask for requests until Tabitha climbed in through the window with a glass of champagne and shut it behind her.

'They could at least tip you,' she grumbled.

He indicated the glass. 'Is that for you or me?'

She pulled a face. 'You, unfortunately.'

Handing it to him, she sat on the nearest chair with a thump.

'Honestly, I've got such a rep on the base as a booze hound, everyone knew I was pregnant ten minutes after I took the test. I hadn't even told Miles. I was presiding over a formal dinner and had to dash out to ring him after my bastard second-in-command held up a bread roll and asked if I had one in the oven.'

Charlie grinned and took a large glug. He grimaced. 'Tab, you're not missing anything. It tastes like shit.'

'Nice try, little brother—I know how good it is. I had a sip of yours before I climbed in the window.'

He got off the piano stool and sat next to her.

She smiled. 'It's incredible to hear you play again. Thank you. I know today couldn't have been easy, but you've knocked it out the park. And that tapestry thing you made for Mum.

Honestly, one more kind and thoughtful gesture from you, and she'll have an embolism.'

They sat in a companionable silence, Charlie's heart full.

'What are you doing for your birthday?' she asked.

Charlie thought about Valentina. What would she be doing to celebrate hers?

'I don't know. I'm not sure where I'll be. I hadn't really thought about it.'

'Well, if you're in the UK and don't have anything better to do, let me know.'

'Thanks, Tab. You're the best,' he replied, meaning every word.

His sister looked away, blinking rapidly.

'Are you okay?' he asked.

She sniffed loudly and wiped her eyes. 'Yes, fine,' she replied crossly. 'It's just these bloody hormones. Can you please start acting like a dick again? Right now, I can't cope with this version of you.'

❃ 34 ❃

Mack had come through with another job, so Charlie packed a bag and headed into Belgravia to meet his latest client, a Nigerian oil baron.

The man wanted someone to make sure his palatial London home was never left unoccupied, and to look after Charles, his five-thousand-quid pedigree Cavalier King Charles spaniel.

When Mack had told him about the job, he indicated Charlie would be guarding a king, but then cracked up when he explained the details.

'So,' Charlie had said, his teeth gritted. 'I'm a house sitter, and the only king I'm protecting is a spaniel. Called Charles.'

'Yes!' Mack finally wheezed. 'You only got the job because of your name and Judy from the shelter gave you a reference.'

In fairness, the dog was the easiest client Charlie had ever had, but his owner spent most of the day out, so he was trapped inside with nothing to do except watch all of Valentina's films, then do callisthenics to burn off the energy created by watching her.

The worst thing was knowing she was also in London, naked in front of a room full of men who weren't him. Every time he thought of it, he felt sick.

Three days in with Charles, he'd watched every movie of Valentina's he could find and was even more in love with her than he'd thought possible. Any equanimity he'd had about letting her go was torched, and every five minutes he considered calling Rory or her abuelas to ask for her number.

Then, after five days of going stir-crazy, his boss brought his new girlfriend home for the day. He handed Charlie the small dog in a bag and told him to take him out to see the sights.

As soon as the front door closed behind him, Charlie sprinted off, Charles's head poking out the top of the bag, barking with excitement.

For any chance with Valentina, he needed to see her, not ring her and hope she answered. If they met face to face, he could get a better read on her feelings for him.

He went straight to the offices in Soho of the production company behind her latest film. He'd memorised the address from the front of the script he'd read with the intention of writing them a strongly worded letter about misogyny and gender equality, or simply putting a brick through their window. Now he just wanted to find out where they were filming, blag his way in, and talk to Valentina in person.

Their offices were on Lexington Street and the reception desk was staffed by a young man with oversized black-rimmed glasses, hair scraped into a man-bun, and a moustache with waxed ends.

He glanced up as Charlie set the dog carrier on the desk. 'Can I help you?'

'Yeah, hi, I'm looking for Valentina Valverde. Can you let me know where she's filming today?'

'I'm afraid that's confidential information.'

The dog growled.

Charlie slowly shook his head. 'I'm afraid I can't accept that. This dog is a gift from a mutual friend, Brad Bauer, and I have to deliver him personally.'

The man fiddled with one end of his moustache and stared at Charlie with disdain. 'You know Brad Bauer?'

'Yes,' he replied, putting his hands on the desk and flexing his muscles. 'I'm his personal trainer.'

'And I'm the King of England,' the man replied, rolling his eyes.

Charlie pulled out his phone and opened his new Instagram account. He was only following two people: Valentina and Brad Bauer, after Tab had called him in fits of laughter to say there were photos of Charlie on his feed.

He handed the phone over and watched the man gazing at photos Crystal had taken of the two of them working out, plus some that Brad had taken of him.

'Oh.'

Charlie's foot tapped impatiently on the floor. 'So, can you tell me where she is today, please?'

The man looked embarrassed and glanced around. 'Er, the film isn't currently shooting. The start date has been pushed back.'

'For how long? Is she still in town?'

He shrugged. 'I don't know. She didn't show up, so we're delayed until we can recast the main role.'

Charlie grabbed Charles and strode outside. If he couldn't see Valentina in person, he had to get her number and call her.

By the time he reached the street, his phone was already ringing. It was her abuelas. He couldn't help but smile as their faces filled the screen.

'Is that Dave?' asked Abuelita.

'It can't be,' replied Abuela. 'He's got two eyes.'

The dog barked and they waved at him. 'This is Charles,' he said.

'You named your dog after you?' Abuela sounded confused.

Abuelita looked worried. 'What happened to Dave? Is he okay?'

'Dave's great. This dog is my latest client.'

'You're a doggyguard?' asked Abuela. 'I thought you looked after people.'

'Well, normally, yes. But this is a special situation.'

'Can you get someone else to look after him?' she demanded.

'Er, probably. Why?' He'd only had a few conversations with Valentina's grandmothers, and all of them seemed to veer into the surreal.

'Do you love Valentina?' Abuelita asked.

'Yes, of course he does. We know that,' Abuela said crossly to her before turning back to him. 'You do, don't you?'

He nodded. 'Yes, I love her completely.'

'See,' Abuela said pointedly to Abuelita.

'But...' Charlie began.

'But what?' they replied as one.

'She doesn't love me back.'

They both started talking at once. Abuelita said that Valentina wasn't used to putting herself first and being happy, and Abuela said, of course she loved Charlie, she was just a stubborn-headed mule and didn't want to admit she did.

Charles the dog wasn't sure who he agreed with, so he barked at everything they said.

He calmed Charles down and looked back at the abuelas. 'I can't force Valentina to be with me.'

'But you can *fight for her*, Charlie,' Abuela insisted.

'How? She wouldn't even give me her number.'

'Come to Colombia and surprise her,' said Abuelita.

'We've got it all worked out,' added Abuela. 'It's your mutual birthday in a few days, and she's coming home for it. You can be here and play Happy Birthday on the piano. It will be perfect.'

'But—'

'We've already bought your ticket,' said Abuelita excitedly. 'You're flying tomorrow. And you're going first class.'

What the fuck was going on? 'You can't buy me a ticket,' he spluttered.

'Why not?' asked Abuela, eyeballing him, her nose pressed up against the screen. 'She gives us too much money. We don't know what to do with it all, so we're giving it back to her in a roundabout way.'

'But you can't buy a ticket without my details, my passport number—'

Abuela waved dismissively. 'We have all of that already.'

'How?'

Abuelita clapped. 'We were spies!'

Charlie slumped against the nearest shop window. None of this made any sense.

'We were thinking ahead,' said Abuela. 'We know your date of birth and your name, so we rang up the castle and spoke to a lovely girl called Zoe who's marrying the King of Kinloch.'

His jaw dropped.

Abuelita chipped in. 'And he got your passport and sent us a copy. He also said he was going to give you some of his special shortbread to bring to us.' She paused and stared at him. 'You haven't eaten it already, have you?'

He shook his head. Rory had made him take several boxes

and promise to hold onto them until after the anniversary party.

'Good,' continued Abuela. 'So you need to take Charles back home, then go and pack. Your flight leaves London tomorrow morning. We're emailing your tickets and instructions on how to catch a bus to our house. Take a book to read. It's a three-hour ride.'

'But how do you know my...' Charlie sighed and gave up. They probably knew more about him than he did. 'Anything else?'

'Yes,' replied Abuelita. 'Don't forget the shortbread.'

WHEN CHARLIE EVENTUALLY GOT OFF THE CALL, HE glanced around to check he hadn't slipped into an alternate dimension, then rang Mack who seemed unsurprised that Charlie wanted to quit his latest job. 'Mate, I'm gobsmacked you lasted this long. Do you want me to look for something else?'

'Not right now. I'm going to take some time off.'

'No problem. Let me know if you come back.' Mack cut the call before Charlie could ask how he knew he was going anywhere.

He ran his hands over his face, feeling the grin that spread from ear to ear. He was going to see Valentina. He just had to think of what he could do to impress her. The one thing in his favour was that he would be in Colombia for a couple of days before she arrived. He'd have time to meet her family and get their help.

Could he surprise her at the airport? Find out what her favourite song was and play it? Buy her a gallon of chocolate ice cream?

A pang of self-doubt hit him in the chest. What was he

doing? What if her family hated him? What if they thought an oversized, tattooed Brit wasn't good enough for her? And what if Valentina agreed?

He held the dog bag up to his face and stared at Charles.

'Should I do it?' Charles barked. 'Should I go and fight for her?' Charles licked the end of Charlie's nose. 'Okay, buddy, you've convinced me. I'm going to Colombia to win her back.'

35

It was the first time Charlie had ever turned left getting on an airplane. Once he stepped into the rarefied air of first class, part of him wished he hadn't. The rest of the passengers were still boarding and fighting over baggage space whilst he was drinking champagne and stretching out his long legs. He'd made sure he scrubbed up well before arriving at the airport, however, glancing at the other first-class passengers in their leisure wear, he felt overdressed.

His phone rang. He put his glass down and pulled it out. He didn't recognise the number, but they were calling from the States.

Valentina?

'Hello, Charlie speaking.' His voice sounded tense.

'Hi, Charlie, this is Lorraine Olson.' *Who?* 'We got your number from Brad.' *Huh?* 'I'm calling from International Asset Management. We'd like to speak to you about working with us. Have you got a few minutes?'

Close protection work in LA? Yes, please. He gazed out the window at the line of people still shuffling down the walkway to board the plane.

'Yeah, sure. Go for it.'

THE FLIGHT WAS NEARLY THIRTEEN HOURS, SO CHARLIE ATE, dozed, and dreamt of Valentina. What could he say to convince her to take a chance on him? She was, quite literally, a star. Whereas he was one of the millions of lumps of rock in the asteroid belt, lucky to have even spent time in her orbit.

He was so proud of her for walking away from that shitty job in London. So pleased she'd taken Shauna on to help. Even if Valentina still turned him down, at least he knew her life would be better now than it was before they'd met.

When he couldn't eat or sleep any more, he flicked through the entertainment channels, looking for something to watch. He stopped when he saw Valentina's face. It was the latest episode of *Saturday Night Live*.

No fucking way. She'd done it.

He started to watch, his heart filling as he saw the Valentina he loved shining out of the screen. She was vibrant, alive, glowing, and laugh-out-loud funny. The producers must have realised they'd stumbled on someone with a gloriously expressive face and impeccable comic timing, as she was in almost every sketch.

The highlight was devoted to her selfies. It was set in a government office and she'd come to get her passport photo taken. The joke being, of course, that she was incapable of pulling a straight face. Charlie watched it over and over, remembering every incredible moment they'd spent together, his heart beating double time at the thought of seeing her again.

It was already night-time when the plane touched down in

Bogota. Charlie glanced at his watch. He didn't have long to get his bags, get to the bus station and find the right one for the next leg of his journey.

The abuelas had given him detailed instructions, but he was worried he was cutting it fine. He was also concerned about turning up on their doorstep in the early hours of the morning. However, Abuela had insisted that a handsome stranger turning up in the middle of the night would finally give the neighbours something to talk about.

Charlie may have been first off the plane, but his bags were not. His eyes flicked from his watch to the carousel as bags came and went and the hall emptied.

Fuck! Any later and he was going to miss the bus.

Was there another he could catch? He searched on his phone and found one with a connection at 3.00 a.m. in another city. That would have to do.

He glanced up. *Finally.* He grabbed his bag and stalked out of the hall, through a deserted customs area, and out into arrivals.

Behind the barrier was a long line of middle-aged men holding signs. He stopped abruptly as he read the first one. In big, bold letters were the words 'Charlie Hamilton'.

Huh?

He went over. 'I'm Charlie Hamilton.'

The man stared at him with a look that made Charlie wonder if he should now claim to be someone else.

'Do you have a tattoo of a dragon?' the man asked.

He nodded. Had the abuelas arranged a car in case he missed the bus?

The man looked unimpressed. 'Show me.'

Fuck's sake! Charlie dropped his bags to the floor and pulled up his shirt.

The man's expression changed. 'Where does it end?'

'Where do you think?' he replied testily, tucking his shirt back in. He picked up his bags. 'Happy now?'

The man shrugged in response.

'Are you here for me?'

The man shook his head and pointed to the man standing next to him, also carrying a sign. This one read 'I thought I was fine, with my plan and my life.'

What the fuck?

He glanced to the right, at a third man holding another sign, this one reading, 'But then you came along, to cut my lies with a knife.'

Charlie stepped back to see that the line of over twenty men were all carrying signs the same size and shape. His heart stuttered.

Valentina? Was she here?

He couldn't see her.

An ostentatious cough drew his attention back to the first man, who pointed at the signs. 'Read please, Mr Hamilton.'

Charlie's throat was tight, his head buzzing. Was this some kind of crazy joke by the abuelas? He returned to the start of the line and started reading.

Charlie Hamilton.
I thought I was fine, with my plan and my life,
but then you came along, to cut my lies with a knife.
I was actually lost, adrift out at sea,
but then you swam out, and rescued me.
You showed me new places, out there, and in me,
and I dared to believe there was more I could be.

Charlie stopped and looked around again. This was from her. It had to be. Emotion rushed through him, an urgent anxiety to get to the end and find her.

He carried on reading.

You showed me the stars, the moon and the loch,

then showed me the way to the head of your… Croc.

He let out a laugh. Valentina was amazing. She was fucking amazing.

You taught me to question, you taught me to dream.

You made me laugh, and you made me scream.

Your eyes are like globes of golden green,

your lips are soft pillows on which I dream.

Your body is ripped, as hard as a rock.

I love all of you, but mostly your—ability to make me laugh.

Charlie snorted with laughter and the man holding the sign stepped back.

Then I left you alone, I walked out that cold day,

and felt like my heart had been taken away.

It's true when they say you don't know what you've had,

till it's gone and you're left, empty and sad.

You've made my life better, in each little way.

And I want you beside me, for every day.

There were only three men left, but he still couldn't see her. Where was she? Was she even here? His heart was being pushed past tolerance, beating erratically, pounding against his ribs.

So, Charlie, I'm yours.

Please know that it's true,

There was only one man left, the height of a house and as wide as a whale. This was the end of the line.

I give you my heart, my life…

Was that the end? A small figure stepped out from behind the man, holding her own sign.

I love you.

Valentina. She was here. She loved him. The rest of the world stopped moving. Nothing else mattered. His life, his purpose, his joy, had crystallised into this moment and this woman.

She was smiling, her face lit up, her eyes bright with happiness. He tried to speak but his heart caught in his throat. His bags hit the floor. The sign slipped from her fingers.

They fell into each other's arms, their lips meeting with a rush of love. He ran one hand into her hair, the other grabbed her bottom as he groaned into her mouth. She clung to him, her hot tongue dancing with his.

Around them were whoops and hollers, cheers and claps. He dragged his head from hers, his breathing heavy. Her eyes were dark with desire.

'Valentina. We need to find a hotel.'

She blushed, as if only just aware of the commotion they were causing. 'I have it sorted.'

'You've got a room?'

She shook her head and smiled. 'I have a bus.'

 ❧ 36 ❧

For the first time since he'd set eyes on Valentina, Charlie was distracted by something other than her.

'That's not a bus. It's a penthouse on wheels.'

He held her hand as he stared at the sleek black vehicle. It seemed the height of a two-storey house and the length of a street.

A sudden worry stabbed him in the nuts. 'Is your entire family inside?'

She shook her head.

Halle-fucking-lujah.

'Are we driving this to their house?' How could he drive *and* have sex? He'd take out half the car park within seconds.

'No, and not yet,' she replied with a grin. 'We have a driver, Miguel, who is sleeping in the cab. I'm going to take you on a little holiday before you meet everyone. This is our home for the next few days.'

She pressed a button on a key fob, and a small section of the bus slid up with a quiet hiss, revealing an entrance hall with marble tiles and glossy wood panelling. Warm LED lights were embedded in the floor, and lanterns on the wall flickered as if they contained real candles.

'Holy shit.'

Valentina giggled. 'I know. Wait till you see the rest. It's at least twice as big as my apartment in LA.' She squeezed his hand. 'Come on, I'll give you the tour.'

He gazed at her. 'Valentina, the only thing I want to see in there is you.'

THE DOOR WAS STILL CLOSING BEHIND THEM WHEN Charlie's shirt hit the floor, buttons pinging off in all directions. Valentina was on the intercom to Miguel telling him they were ready to leave, so he figured the fastest way to get them both undressed was to start on himself. His hands were too shaky to undo the buttons, so he'd ripped his shirt apart to get it off.

'Get naked,' he growled as she said goodbye to Miguel. 'Now.'

Her cheeks were flushed and she was giggling. She shucked off her jacket and hung it over the back of a chair. He was only vaguely aware they were in some kind of open-plan living area and that the bus was moving.

'Just chuck them on the floor, Valentina,' he said desperately.

He removed the last of his clothes as she turned back to face him. He stood before her, hot, naked, and hard, his cock jerking against his belly. She gasped.

He spread his hands wide. 'All my clothes, versus,' he pointed to the chair, '*one* jacket. Come on, Valentina, is that all you've got?'

She stared at him, a dangerous glint in her eye, and a bolt of electricity shot through him. She took off her shoes. Charlie tried to calculate how many items of clothing now lay between them. *Dress, pants, bra?*

She sauntered slowly towards him, licking her lips. What was she doing? Before his brain could catch up, she dropped to the floor and had his cock in her mouth.

'Holy fuck!'

One hand cupped his balls, the other grasped his shaft as she sucked him. He couldn't breathe. His body was stabbed with sensation, his cock the centre of an inferno. He flailed his arms out, connecting with a cupboard. He gripped the handle, his body strained with tension.

Her hot tongue swirled around the head, rubbing on the sensitive underside, her hands pulling out more pleasure. His jaw was clenched to the point of pain, his teeth grinding. As his lungs laboured to get enough air, he fought to hold onto his sanity. Was this really happening? He glanced down, then threw his head back with a cry.

'Fuuuck!' he yelled, his voice hoarse.

The image of her lips stretched around his cock, her small hand pumping him up and down, was burned into his brain. His body was pulsing, flying apart in waves, then violently contracting back into a white-hot nucleus at the base of his spine. It was too much. He couldn't keep it together.

'Please, Valentina,' he gasped. 'Wait.'

She stopped moving and he held his breath, all the muscles of his body fighting back the onrushing climax. He felt the tide turn and let his breath go, his chest heaving. He glanced down and she gave him a devilish grin, darting her tongue out to lick up his slit. He jerked back with a cry, bashing into the cabinet behind him.

'Valentina,' he growled.

'Yes, Charlie?' she purred.

Fuck! He reached down, grabbed her around the waist and

tossed her over his shoulder. She giggled. He slapped her bottom and she shrieked with laughter. He slapped it again and she moaned.

Holy shit.

He pulled the bottom of her dress up and the silk of her underwear down. He ran his hand over the smooth plumpness of her backside, feeling her squirm against him, her thighs squeezing. He brought his hand away and she started to pant. He waited a few tantalising seconds, then slapped her lightly again. She moaned deeper.

Holy fucking fuck.

He rubbed her cheek in wider and wider circles, then suddenly slapped her again.

'Oh, god,' she gasped. 'Charlie.'

He caressed her cheek and stroked between her legs to her sopping core. She bucked against him, trying to reach his fingers. He pushed slowly into her tightness. She cried out, clawing at his back. He pumped in and out. She was so fucking hot and so fucking wet. He had to taste her.

He slid his fingers out and she whimpered. He pulled her underwear off and lay her down on a polished wood dining table, then sank to his knees, spread her legs, and plunged his tongue deep into her sweetness.

'Charlie!'

She clenched around him, shuddering and shaking. Growling, he licked her clit, feeling her pleasure scorching down through him. Each time she cried out he was struck by another lightning bolt. Getting her off was the ultimate high.

Her breathing was changing, shortening into urgent gasps, whipping his own desire into a frenzy. He worked two fingers inside her, curling them up to rub against her top wall.

He increased the pressure with his fingers, pressing hard as she went off with a scream. Her thighs clamped around his head like a vice, her body stiffening, then convulsing. Her inner muscles tightened, then hot fluid gushed over his hand.

She tried to push him away, but he held her to him, a stupid grin of satisfaction on his face.

'Oh my god, Charlie. What just happened? I'm so sorry!' She pushed onto her elbows, still breathing heavily.

He lifted his head and smiled. 'You ejaculated. It was fucking awesome.'

Her eyes widened. She placed her hands on his chest. He let her push him backwards to a wide sofa.

'Lie down,' she said, her voice low and breathy.

He lay back and watched as she shimmied her dress and bra off. *Finally.* She stroked over her full breasts, sucking in a breath as she rolled her nipples and rubbed the tips. His cock twitched. He sat up and she pushed him back down.

'Stay.'

She straddled him, one hand on her nipple, the other grasping his shaft and guiding it to her entrance. He could see her arousal glistening on the inside of her thighs, coating the head of his cock as she moved it back and forth against her. She settled herself and began to work her way down.

The sensations were too much. He was overflowing with pleasure and overwhelmed with love. He watched as she eased him all the way in. She paused and they breathed together, their eyes locked. This was it.

'I love you, Valentina,' he said tightly.

Her face was flushed and dreamy.

'I love you too, Charlie,' she whispered. 'You're my everything.'

He held his breath, his throat choked with emotion. She raised herself up till only the head of his cock was inside, then sat down with a soft cry. He circled her clit with his fingers and she did it again.

His breathing returned in fitful gasps as she moved, finding her sweet spot. He held on for the ride, pushing back against his climax as it surged inside him.

She moved faster and faster, tugging at her nipples. Her chest flushed red. He knew she was close. He needed her to come again before he fell apart.

'Come for me, sweetheart,' he panted. 'Let go.'

She fell forward to his chest with a cry, her tongue diving into his mouth. He grabbed her bottom and squeezed, holding her tight as she fucked herself on him. The pressure built at the base of his spine. He couldn't hold back. She tore her mouth from his with a scream and bit down on his shoulder.

Her body shook, shuddering as her orgasm wracked her body. As her muscles milked his cock, he let the wave of his own climax break, thrusting up fast inside her. Pleasure crashed through him, every particle in his body exploding into a billion photons of light. She continued shaking in his arms and he felt the side of his neck wet.

'Sweetheart, don't cry.'

She sniffed. 'I love you so much, Charlie.'

He kissed her. 'I love you too. Everything's fine. Everything's perfect.'

'But I did a pee pee on your face and bit you,' she wailed.

He laughed. Relief, joy and happiness bubbled out. He gazed at her anxious face and smiled.

'Valentina, my love, congratulations. You've just had wild monkey sex.'

37

Valentina led Charlie to the bathroom. In the shower she leaned back against him, her body tingling and humming with delight as his hands soaped and massaged her breasts. She felt his cock pushing into the crease of her buttocks and smiled.

He nipped at her earlobe. 'When were you going to tell me about the tattoo?'

She smiled. 'I was waiting for you to notice.'

He turned off the shower and dried her, getting distracted along the way until she dragged him to the bedroom. Snuggling in his arms, she revelled in the feel of his skin against hers. His lips were hot and insistent, coaxing out kisses until she rolled on top of him and lifted her head from his.

'It's about five in the morning UK time. Aren't you exhausted?'

He shrugged. 'The last time I passed out in a bed next to you, I woke up and you were gone. I'm not letting that happen again.'

'I'm so sorry.'

He smiled. 'Don't be. You had your life to sort out. And I'm here now.' He kissed the inside of her wrist where the tattoo was located. 'Our date of birth, surrounded by hearts that look like birds taking flight, and all done in the colours of the Colombian flag.'

She nodded, an overwhelming rush of love filling her heart. 'Yes,' she said shyly. 'It's about my roots, my truth, my freedom and my love.'

His eyes glowed as he held her gaze. He swallowed.

'I'm so proud of you,' he said, his voice tight. 'Valentina, I'm in fucking awe of you.' Her cheeks heated. 'You walked off that job in London. You smashed it on *Saturday Night Live*. And you nailed the best love poem I've ever heard. I love you so much.'

'It was all because of you.'

He shook his head and opened his mouth to speak.

'No, Charlie, it was. I would never have done any of that if I hadn't met you. I was on autopilot, living this crazy, relentless non-life. I had no idea how worried my family was about me. You woke me up. You showed me who I could be. You were always there for me.'

He shook his head again and she punched him on the arm.

'You listen, Charlie. You *will* take this. You're the most incredible man I've ever met, and I owe you my life. Have you any idea what it would have done to me, had I done that film?' she demanded.

He nodded.

'I was sleepwalking myself into an early grave. Now, thanks to you, I'm going to have an actual life.' She paused. 'With you.'

She could see the emotion on his face, and the struggle to

accept the difference he'd made to her. He pulled her close and held her tightly.

'Valentina,' he whispered hoarsely. 'I've got my family back and let my past go, thanks to you. I'm even marginally less of a dickhead now.'

She kissed his neck. 'You'll always be a huevón. But you're *my* huevón.'

He let out a huff of laughter.

She propped herself up to look at him, suddenly unsure. 'Charlie,' she began.

'What?'

She could see the panic in his eyes. 'Nothing, it's fine,' she said hurriedly. 'I just wanted to check.' Her stomach cramped with anxiety.

'What is it? You know you can ask me anything.'

She nodded. 'I know some men might get a bit strange about money. I don't want you to be like that. I have so much. I have more than enough. I know it's selfish, but I just want you with me. I don't want you to feel you have to go off somewhere and get a job. Can you give me a few months? At least?'

'Valentina, I can pay my way, but I'm confident enough in my own skin not to feel emasculated by you earning me under the table. Fuck, sweetheart, I'll do anything I can to support you. There are many more ways to be there for you than earning a wage.'

He smiled at her.

'My career was in the army and now it's over. Yours is in full bloom. But if you want to retire now, I'll support you. I can always do close protection work. And...' He looked away, his cheeks flushing.

'What?'

'I might have a weird job in LA,' he muttered.

'Huh?' He wouldn't meet her gaze. 'Charlie, what's happened?'

She'd never seen him look so embarrassed.

'I got a call before I left London. It was from a woman who knows Brad. I thought it was for close protection work, but I was wrong,' he mumbled. 'I don't know what to do and could really use your advice.'

When he'd given her the details, she howled with laughter. She only stopped laughing when he pinned her down and kissed her into submission, moving down to worship her breasts when her laughs turned into moans. She lay back and gazed at their reflection in the polished ceiling above.

Everything was perfect.

Charlie and Valentina spent three days touring Colombia in the bus, although most of the time was spent in bed. On the morning of their birthday, they made love, ate breakfast, and arrived with perfect timing mid-morning to celebrate with her family.

Valentina could tell Charlie was nervous, but she knew he had nothing to fear. In their own way, her family was just as in love with him as she was. They were so grateful for the support he'd given her, and overjoyed she'd found someone they approved of with whom to share her life.

Charlie was pulled from group to group. The men wanted to see the dragon tattoo and arm-wrestle him, and the women wanted to see the dragon tattoo and get his opinion on their sewing projects.

It may have been their joint birthday, but her abuelas held centre stage, telling everyone who would listen how it was all thanks to them that Charlie was there.

Valentina had bought a piano for her parent's house, and

after everyone was full and sleepy, Charlie played. Valentina sat on a sofa next to Isabella, cradling her new nephew.

'That's your new gringo uncle, Alejandro. Isn't he amazing?' she said to him.

He stared up at her with huge, serious eyes and her heart melted.

Isabella smiled and rested her head on Valentina's shoulder. 'I'm so happy for you, Tina. You deserve this. He's amazing.'

Valentina kissed the top of her head. 'I know, little sister, I know.'

THE PARTY WENT ON LATE INTO THE NIGHT. KINLOCH'S spiced shortbread was passed around, alcohol continued to flow, and people started to dance. After a pleading look from Charlie, Valentina announced that the human jukebox was taking a break and pulled him away from the piano. They turned on the radio and everyone carried on dancing.

Valentina tugged on his hand and they slipped outside.

The air was warm and the stars were bright. They walked away from the house into the darkness, the sound of cicadas all around them.

Charlie stopped and pulled her to him, his hot lips finding hers. She clung to him, moulding her body to his as waves of pleasure rolled through her with every flick of his tongue. His cock was already hard and pushing into her stomach.

He broke the kiss, breathing heavily. 'God, I've been wanting to do that all day.'

She giggled. She never knew it was possible to be this happy.

'I love your family, Valentina—they're incredible.' He kissed her again and her knees went weak. He lifted his head. 'But I love you more. Can we go back to the bus now? Please?'

She stared at him. He was so beautiful. And he was hers. Her heart raced as she stroked down the side of his face. 'Yes.'

He reached down and swept her into his arms. She held onto him, laughing and kissing his neck.

'Happy birthday to us,' she whispered, knowing she would never spend another birthday apart from him again.

EPILOGUE

Valentina always took the long way home when coming back from meetings in LA. It was worth it. Driving past the billboards with her image from the cosmetics advert was affirming.

The company had changed their approach after her selfies had been leaked. Rather than the original plan to have a campaign with her looking sultry and vampy, they'd changed tack. Now it was about honesty and being true to yourself. Make-up was there to enhance your natural beauty, not to transform you into someone else.

However, that was not why Valentina took this route. Her eyes were drawn to something else. For once she loved the heavy traffic. She was quite content to slow to a crawl, the window down as she gazed at the image that covered the side of an entire skyscraper.

It was advertising a famous cologne for men, and apart from one small detail, the photo was in black and white. The model was sex on legs. Naked, apart from a pair of tight, white briefs that did nothing to hide how well-endowed he was, he stared out from the poster, his lush lips slightly parted, his expression saying he was seconds away from tearing your clothes off with his teeth.

The only colour in the image came from his startling green eyes, flecked with accents of gold that reflected the bright LA sunshine. The way he'd been lit emphasised his ripped physique and the scars on his shoulder and arm. His body was decorated with tattoos, but the one across the left of his chest was the one Valentina was most interested in.

It was her signature in black, written big and bold, with the imprint of lips above it, as if she'd finished signing her name with a kiss.

The image and the model had become infamous. He was now referred to as 'The Package', or 'Charlentina' when linked to his girlfriend. Even though he was a reluctant model, more endorsements had followed the perfume campaign, much to his embarrassment and Valentina's amusement.

She'd moved with Charlie out to Topanga Canyon a few months before, preferring the laid-back style and local community. Here, they could hang out in peace and quiet without women's underwear flying over the walls at regular intervals.

Parking outside their house, she let herself in.

'Hey, honey, I'm home,' she called in a faux-American accent.

There was a noise: half bark, half wheeze, all crazy, as a scruffy ball of insanity bounded towards her in a vaguely straight line.

'Dave!' she cried. 'Mommy's home.'

Dave launched himself at her, missed, and skidded into the front door with a yelp. She scooped him up and he wriggled with excitement in her arms.

Charlie ambled around the corner, his only clothes a pair of faded jeans hanging low off his hips. Valentina raked her eyes over him, cocked her finger and beckoned him forwards. When he was close enough, she grabbed the front of his jeans to pull him closer.

She planted her lips over the tattoo on his chest, then trailed kisses up to his neck as Dave went mental between them, not sure which of his favourite humans he needed to lick most.

Charlie pulled Dave out of her arms and looked into his one good eye.

'Mate, there's a time and a place. And this is neither of them. Do you want to watch radio-controlled cars instead?' Dave barked his approval and Charlie carried him off.

Valentina followed them into the large open-plan living area. Charlie was talking to Dave as he set him up in front of his favourite YouTube clips. She sat on one of the cream sofas, her head resting on the sheepskin rug draped over the back, and watched them.

When Dave was sorted, Charlie turned to her.

'How did your meeting go?' he asked, gently pushing her onto her back and laying his body over hers.

'Interesting,' she sighed, running her fingers down the muscles of his back. 'I missed you.'

'I missed you too,' he murmured, nuzzling her neck. 'Every beautiful inch.'

He nipped at her skin and the heady throb of desire that had been building during the commute home exploded into a pounding, urgent need.

'Charlie,' she gasped.

He ran his hand over the front of her dress, cupping her breast with a groan.

'I, I can't concentrate when you're doing thaaa—' she broke off as he rubbed her hardened nipple. 'Charlie, I...'

He yanked the top down with a growl and sucked the aching tip into his mouth.

'I'm trying to tell you—'

He looked up, his green eyes smouldering. 'Actually, sweetheart, I've temporarily lost interest in your meeting. Right now, I only care about getting you off. Everything else can wait.'

He lowered his head to her breast and ran his hand down her leg to pull up the bottom of her skirt. Pleasure blocked out all other thoughts and she reached between them to tug his jeans open.

He was right. Everything else could wait.

THE END

Thank you so much for reading Kissing Games! I hope you enjoyed reading it as much as I loved writing it. If you have a moment, please write me a review!

If you want to know what Valentina's meeting was all about and what secret surprise Charlie has planned for her that evening, then join my newsletter list to read their super-swoony extended epilogue from Kissing Games!

Sign up now at
www.eviealexanderauthor.com/subscribe/

***

Sam and Jamie's story is coming up next in Musical Games. Here's a sneak peek at the first chapter...

MUSICAL GAMES

'Oi!'

Sam stopped dead, her heart pounding. The shout was aimed at her.

'You slag!'

Striding towards her, heels click-clacking and fury crackling, was Lorraine.

Sam's feet stayed glued to the pavement. She clutched her handbag to her chest as if for protection. *She knew.*

Lorraine was a storm of anger and pain. 'You could've had anyone,' she screamed. 'But you had to steal my Wayne! How could you?'

Sam swallowed her panic. She tossed her hair and cocked her hip. 'Well, who would blame him when you won't give him what he needs?'

There was a beat, then Lorraine launched herself forward like a heat-seeking missile carrying a payload of rabid cats.

'You cow!' she screeched, her manicured nails locking onto Sam's face.

Sam dropped her bag and caught Lorraine's wrists just before impact. The women tumbled to the ground.

Lorraine straddled her on the dirty pavement, yanking a hand free and grabbing a fistful of hair. Sam tugged at her fingers, trying to break the grip. Lorraine was snarling, her bared teeth an inch away, spittle raining onto her cheeks.

Why isn't anyone helping?

One of Lorraine's dangly earrings caught in Sam's hair and a sharp pain tore across her scalp.

'Agh! Loz, stop!'

Lorraine went still. 'You okay?'

'Your bloody earring's just ripped half my hair out.'

'Fuck, love. Sorry, hang on.'

'Cut!' a voice rang out. 'Shelley, can you give them a hand?'

In Sam's peripheral vision another pair of hands reached into the bird's nest of her hair where Lorraine's earring was snagged.

'Hold still, ladies, while I sort out this wardrobe malfunction.'

'Cheers, Shelley,' said Sam. 'At least my boob didn't pop out.'

Lorraine giggled. 'If this show went out after the kiddies had gone to bed, I bet they'd write that scene in.'

Sam jiggled her breasts towards her friend. 'Too right. These puppies have power. You've seen them, haven't you, Shelley? They're mag-nif-i-cent.'

Shelley shook her head. 'Yes, darling, your boobs could awaken the dead. Now, hold still. Don't make me get my scissors out.'

An hour later, Sam had been surgically removed from Lorraine without lasting damage and was in a taxi heading into central London. The driver was a regular for the production and Sam was grateful. She wouldn't have to answer endless questions about Bethany—the character she played on the long-running soap—or deflect questions about future storylines.

Kicking off her vertiginous heels, she stuck in her earbuds and scrolled through the video library on her phone.

Three months ago, her best friend, Zoe, had moved from London to the wilds of Scotland. Sam missed her terribly and had hoped she'd come back. However, once Zoe fell in love with Rory, the Earl of Kinloch, it was clear her heart and soul were now in the Highlands.

Zoe had sent her a video of Jamie, her childhood friend from Kinloch, playing guitar and singing a love song he'd written. Sam refused to mark the videos, or any of the pictures of Jamie she'd saved, as favourites. That would be an admission of interest.

There was no way she was interested in someone three years younger than herself, who still lived with his mum, hundreds of miles away in the arse end of nowhere.

It was unfortunate, however, that Jamie possessed a certain level of physical attractiveness. He had deep brown eyes framed by long, dark lashes; thick, dark brown hair that looked as if it had just been ruffled out of place by an affectionate aunt, and a shy smile that pierced through the phone screen straight to her heart.

Even hunched over his guitar, she could tell he was tall. She stared at his thick, corded forearms, his long fingers plucking the strings. His big, gentle, *clever* hands...

Heat rose in her cheeks. *Forget about his hands!*

She'd watched the video hundreds of times, but each time her viewing followed the same script: stare at him as he chatted to Zoe and imagine he was talking to her. Look at his fingers as he started to play. Feel too hot. Close her eyes. Jump as he started to sing. Feel unwarranted emotions swirling inside her. Open her eyes and keep staring. Sing along with him in her mind.

'That's nice, love. What is it?'

Sam met the cab driver's gaze in the rear-view mirror with a start and fumbled to shut off her phone.

'What?'

'That song you were singing.'

She sucked in a breath. It was like he'd caught her watching porn. 'It's nothing.' This was ridiculous. Fuck, she'd be less embarrassed if it *had* been porn. 'Just a friend of a friend messing about.'

'Well, it gave me goosebumps.' He raised a tattooed arm from the steering wheel. 'See? And you've got a lovely voice, too. Beautiful.'

Sam huffed a laugh as she looked out the window, then checked her watch. She was early. 'Actually, Stan, can you drop me here?'

'No problem, darling.' He signalled and pulled over. Sam rammed her feet back into her heels and manoeuvred with practiced grace out of the car.

'Thanks, Stan. See you soon.'

He gave her a wave over his shoulder as he drove away.

Sam gazed at the huge red-brick Victorian facade of the Royal Marsden Hospital. Standing at the bottom of the stone steps leading up to the main doors, she felt small and inadequate. A familiar knot of tension coiled tighter in her stomach. She deliberately let out a long, slow breath, flexed her fingers, and took out her phone.

She couldn't remember the last time she'd reached out to her oldest sister or spoken to her outside of family get-togethers.

The call connected.

'Esther Adamson.'

'It's me. Sam.'

She could hear her sister speaking hurriedly to other people in the background, then her attention was back. 'Is everything okay?'

'Yeah, yeah,' Sam replied. 'I had a minor head wound earlier from some cheap earrings, but—'

'Head wound? You've been checked over? Vision okay? Slurred speech? What happened?'

'Shit, no, I'm fine. I just got my hair caught in Loz's earring, that's all.'

'Jesus, Sam.' Her sister let out a loud breath. 'Don't do that to me.'

Fuck.

'So, you're okay?'

'Yep, all A-okay,' Sam replied brightly, squatting on the step and resting her forehead on her free hand. She chewed her bottom lip as she listened to her sister talking to others, the noises of feet running and doors slamming.

'Look,' Esther continued, 'I was meant to be finishing a twelve-hour shift, but there's been a serious traffic accident so I'm going back into surgery. Can I call you later? Where are you?'

'I'm still on set. You know, busy, busy.' Sam rolled her eyes at herself. 'Sure, call me—' The noises from her sister's end of the line stopped. Sam stared at her phone, then dropped it into her bag. *Way to go, Smulan...*

'Oi, oi, Bethany!'

Sam stood, the smile already fixed on her face. She saluted two men as they ambled past carrying takeout coffees.

'Fancy a quickie?'

Her smile froze. 'Not today, gentlemen. It's my day off.'

She strode briskly in the opposite direction, her arm raised to hail a taxi. Just because her character put out to half the street didn't mean she did.

· · ·

HALF AN HOUR LATER, SAM WAS IN SOHO BEING SHOWN INTO her agent's office. Sandra Billings was in her sixties. She'd been there, done it, and had the photos and the gravelly voice to prove it. The walls were covered in black-and-white headshots of her clients and press shots of them holding awards. Each was signed with a gushing message thanking Sandra for their success.

Sam looked at her own, remembering how excited she'd been to land the part of Bethany on *Elm Tree Lane*. Yet now, less than a year after starting on the soap, she wanted more.

Sandra pulled Sam in for a kiss, then gestured for her to sit on the other side of her desk as she reached for a chrome and diamanté e-cigarette. She sucked deeply on it, accentuating the lines around her mouth, then exhaled a plume of sickly-sweet vapour.

Sam hated the smell of cigarettes, but this was worse. It was as if someone high on ecstasy and unicorns had staggered into a lab and instructed a minion to mix as many E numbers as they could until they came up with the smell of pink.

The stench from the real cigarettes Sandra used to smoke had seeped into every piece of furniture. It was now in a three-way fight for supremacy with the cloying vape and heavy punch of Cacharel's Lou Lou that Sandra had been marinating in since the eighties. No matter how many painkillers Sam popped in preparation before a meeting, she always left with a headache.

As they exchanged pleasantries, Sam tried to stay calm. Sandra's secretary had called her in for the meeting with the promise of 'something big', and her imagination had been running wild with possibilities.

Eventually Sandra put her vape to one side and leaned forward.

'Right, love, I've got you the biggie.'

'*Strictly?*'

Sandra shook her head. 'Not this year—it's Lorraine's turn. You're too new.' She paused for effect. 'I've got you another commercial.'

A few months ago, Sam had done an advert for a brand of instant coffee. The money and exposure had been good, but it wasn't as high-end as she wanted.

Doubt pricked at her stomach. 'It isn't the thrush medication again? I told you, there's no way I'm doing that.'

'No, love, I've got you the one every hot young thing wants.' Sandra sat back looking satisfied.

Sam's brain went into overdrive. *The Christmas advert for the John Lewis store? One for Coca Cola?*

'What is it?'

Sandra smiled enough to reveal yellowing teeth. '*Mopeoke.* I've gone and got you Mopeoke, love.'

What the fuck is that?

'Er, Mopeoke?'

'Yeah. Didn't you see the pitch on *The Bear Pit*? They literally got into a fight over who was going to invest. Come on. You must have seen it?'

Sam struggled to think. She was so exhausted with the long days on set she rarely watched TV. Sandra spun her laptop around and Sam stared at the screen.

'It's a mop.'

'And...'

She looked closer. 'Is that a microphone at the end of the handle?'

Sandra nodded. 'Syncs via Bluetooth to any device. Mop one end, karaoke microphone the other. Mopeoke. Fastest start-up since Trunkis and Loom bands.'

Fuck right off. She fought to buy time. 'Er, why me?'

'You're the target demographic: lower middle-class, in your

thirties, young family, house to keep clean, dreaming of stardom. Plus, you're a household name now and I told them you could sing.'

'I only turned thirty last month,' Sam spluttered. 'I'm single, childless, and my entire family are doctors.'

Sandra sat back, her smile gone. 'Yeah, but *you're* not a doctor, are you? And millions of people every week don't hear your Home Counties accent. They hear Bethany, who's rough as a badger's arse.'

Sam stared at the edge of the desk and rubbed her forehead. The headache had arrived and was dancing the cancan inside her skull.

'Look, are you interested or not?'

No, no, no, no, no. 'Can I think about it?'

'You've till the end of the day.'

Sam nodded, and Sandra sighed.

'What do you want, Sam?'

She glanced up. 'You know what I want. I want bigger. I want films. I want *more*.'

Sandra dragged on her vape and engulfed Sam in a fog of overripe fruit.

'You need a stronger platform before we make that move. You've got to start small. Your contract with *Elm Tree Lane* is up for renewal in a couple of months. Don't rock the boat. Take the Mopeoke gig. Trust me, it's the best thing in your life right now.'

SAM PUSHED OPEN THE DOOR TO THE BASEMENT STUDIO WITH her backside, holding coffees for her co-stars, Lorraine and Ian. They were filming a love triangle storyline on *Elm Tree Lane* and were doing a photoshoot for the cover of *Soap First* magazine that would go out when the plot aired the following month.

The shoot wasn't complicated—just portraits of the three of them looking sufficiently angry or aroused, so they only needed a green screen backdrop and a few lights. The studio was small, old, and damp. Sam repressed a shudder as the soles of her shoes stuck to the tacky floor.

A door at the end of the corridor opened and Lorraine rushed out.

'How's your hair? I'm so sorry about earlier. How did it go with Sandra? What's the big job she's got for you?'

Sam pushed the coffees towards her friend. 'I'm fine, sweetie. Can you take these?'

'Are they for us? You're a diamond.' Lorraine read the sides of the cups. 'Bethany.' She rolled her eyes. 'Loz, yep, like it. And... *Dickhead?*' She giggled. 'He's not here yet, so we can drink these while we wait.'

They entered a small room and perched on a cheap and uncomfortable sofa that had once been red but was now a muddy brown.

'So tell me,' asked Lorraine, 'what was the job?'

Sam tapped the side of her nose. 'It might not happen, so I've got to keep schtum about this one. But I did hear a rumour that a certain someone is going to be on *Strictly* this year?'

Lorraine squealed and tapped her feet on the floor. 'I'm so excited! I've been watching that show since I was a baby. I can't believe I'm going to be on it!'

Sam squeezed her arm. 'You deserve it, Loz. You're going to be amazing. I'll be glued to my telly every Saturday night and have your voting number on speed dial.'

Lorraine teared up. 'You're the best, Sam. The older sister I never had.'

Sam smiled back, her throat tightening.

The door opened and Shelley bustled in, followed by a photographer, an assistant, and two of the wardrobe and make-up team from *Elm Tree Lane*.

'Sorry we're late, ladies. There was a snarl-up on the drive in.'

'No worries, Shelley,' replied Sam. 'Can we give you a hand?'

Shelley dismissed her with a wave. 'You two stay put. I'm going to sort your outfits, then you can get changed. Ian here yet?'

They shook their heads.

Shelley glanced at the word 'Dickhead' written on the third coffee cup and grinned. 'Any later and that'll be cold.' She gave them both a wink and turned away.

'Sam,' Lorraine whispered. 'Can I tell you something else?'

She leaned in. 'Of course, sweetie. I presume it's something good?'

Lorraine was jiggling again, her eyes darting about to make sure they weren't overheard. 'Yes! It's almost as exciting as *Strictly* and I want you to be the first to know.'

Sam hadn't seen such excitement outside of a child on Christmas morning. 'Come on then, out with it, or you might have an accident and improve the colour of this sofa.'

Lorraine snorted and moved closer. 'I'm second on the shortlist to do the ad for Mopeoke!' She held her finger and thumb a millimetre apart. 'I'm *this* close to promoting the product of my dreams!'

Sam swallowed. 'That's amazing, Loz.'

Lorraine sighed. 'I love cleaning. I know it sounds sad, but I do. I get so excited when the Lakeland catalogue arrives in the post. Do you know what I mean?'

Sam grinned. 'I'm afraid the only way I'd get excited about a mop would be if it had a ten-speed vibrator attached.'

Lorraine laughed as the door to the studio was flung open with a bang.

'Speaking of giant dildos,' Sam murmured.

Lorraine's laugh turned into a snort as a man strode in. The last point of their love triangle had arrived.

Ian Berresford had gone from stage school to a moderately successful boy band to being cast as the 'bad boy' on *Elm Tree Lane*. It was a role he was born to play and the only difference between his onscreen and offscreen persona was that 'market trader Wayne' wasn't sponsored by a condom company.

'Ladies!' he announced to the room. He shucked his leather jacket, ran his hands through his slicked-back hair, and stood in front of Sam and Lorraine with his legs too far apart. 'The king has arrived.'

'Have you disinterred Elvis?' Sam asked.

'The king is dead; long live the king,' he replied with a wink at Lorraine.

Sam passed him his coffee cup.

He screwed up his nose as he read 'Dickhead' on the side. 'Have you spat in this?'

'No, but if you put your tongue in my mouth again during a scene, I will. If you're that desperate to taste my saliva I can spit in all your drinks for you.' She stood. 'I'm just going to make a quick call.'

Pushing past Ian, she left the studio.

When she returned a couple of minutes later, Ian was next to Lorraine on the sofa, showing her his phone. He glanced at Sam.

'I've got one hundred and sixty-four thousand Instagram followers. You'll never catch up now, Adams.'

'I wasn't aware we were in a race, Berresford.'

He grinned. 'Yeah, yeah, keep telling yourself that when you're watching me accept "best bad boy" at the soap awards for the third year in a row. Remind me, you've yet to be nominated for anything, right?'

Sam willed her hands not to clench into fists.

Lorraine slapped Ian on the arm. 'Don't be such a twat.'

He flexed his muscles in response. 'Do that again, Loz... you almost gave me a semi.'

Lorraine rolled her eyes and moved to Sam's side.

Ian leapt up, fiddling with his phone. 'This is your best mate, right?' he asked, shoving the screen under Sam's nose.

She glanced down and adrenaline drenched her like an icy bucket of water.

Ian had Brad Bauer's account open, showing a photo of him sitting next to Zoe on wooden thrones in Kinloch castle.

Brad was the biggest star in Hollywood, a polymath who'd put his foot down on the accelerator of life and never once raised it. He was an actor, writer, producer, director, and serial shagger. Whatever he touched usually turned to gold, including the careers of his exes.

He'd recently discovered Zoe's Instagram account and Kinloch castle. Now he was preparing to shoot *Braveheart 2* there and had decided Zoe was his muse.

'If we weren't shooting so much, I'd be up there like a shot,' said Ian. 'Look. He's following me. Game recognises game. Has he followed you back yet?'

Sam gritted her teeth. 'I don't follow him,' she lied.

Ian laughed. 'Yeah, right. You're too small to register on his radar.'

'Ian, can we have you first?' Shelley called over.

He ripped off his T-shirt and flexed his pecs. 'Sure, Shelley, you can have me anytime.' He winked at Lorraine and strode off across the studio.

Sam felt her friend's hand on hers, squeezing. 'Ignore him.

He's being a royal prick today. Come sit down. Don't let him get to you.'

Sam sat with a thump and let out a breath. 'It's like he knows every single fucking button to push.'

Lorraine curled up next to her and rubbed her arm. 'I should warn you. He told me yesterday he's also been offered *Strictly*.'

Her head dropped. 'Fuck's sake.'

'Shh... you can't trust what comes out of his mouth, but I wanted you to have the heads-up. In case it's true.'

Sam gazed at her friend. 'Loz. I need to get up to Scotland. Brad's single, I'm single, and Zoe can get me in front of him.'

'But we're filming without a break until the summer. There's no time.'

'What if my grandmother suddenly got ill? And wanted me at her deathbed?'

Lorraine gasped. 'But that's not true! You can't lie.'

'Loz, I'll never have a chance like this again. I can't miss it.'

'Sam, you can't take that risk. We're so lucky to be on this show. Promise me you won't do anything stupid. Please?'

Enjoyed the first chapter of Musical Games?
Get your copy now at
www.eviealexanderbooks.com

REVIEW KISSING GAMES
WRITE A REVIEW & MAKE MY DAY!

Thank you so much for reading Kissing Games! I hope you enjoyed reading it as much as I enjoyed writing it!

Even if just a couple of lines (or star rating), writing a review is the most amazing thing you can do! It helps people find my books, and lets them know what you loved about them.

You can review Kissing Games at:
Apple
Amazon
Kobo
Barnes & Noble
Google Play
Goodreads
Bookbub
And any other storefront or platform you use!

And, if you want to share more about Kissing Games on social media or your blog, please **help yourself to our library of graphics, elements and more by going here!**

www.eviealexanderauthor.com/kissing-games/

Thank you!

Evie ♡

READ MUSICAL GAMES

Enjoyed Kissing Games? Next in the Kinloch series is **Musical Games**!

MUSICAL GAMES
He's never been kissed, and she's about to rock his world...

Bubbly actress Sam Adamson is *this* close to making it big – all she needs is one lucky break. But when she lands a meeting with Hollywood's biggest star, she blows it by blurting out a lie.

Now, she's got ten days to write an album with a man who wants absolutely nothing to do with her.

Unwillingly swept up in her grand plan is shy virgin Jamie MacDougall. He has the voice of an angel and the body of a god, but he's never set foot outside Scotland – or his comfort zone – and fame is the last thing on his mind.

As the music flows, sparks fly. But when the limelight beckons, Sam's about to discover that getting what she thinks she wants might mean losing what she really needs.

Musical Games *is a steamy, standalone romantic comedy packed with small-town shenanigans and all the feels. No cheating or cliffhanger – just a hot and hilarious ride to a guaranteed happily-ever-after!*

Get Musical Games in eBook, print or audiobook format now at www.eviealexanderbooks.com

NEWSLETTER SIGN-UP

Want to know what Valentina's meeting was all about and what secret surprise Charlie has planned for her that evening? Join my newsletter list to read their super-swoony extended epilogue!

In my newsletter you get Evie news before anyone else, as well as exclusive content and goodies.

Newsletter subscribers are my extra special friends, and get everything from bonus epilogues, 19,000 words of deleted sex scenes, free stories, free audiobooks, extracts from my current work-in-progress, and exclusive offers and giveaways.

Sign up now!

www.eviealexanderauthor.com/subscribe

SEX INDEX
(AKA THE GOOD BITS)

There have been many great contributions to the world of literature. Gutenberg invented the printing press, Shakespeare invented romantic comedy, and J K Rowling invented Harry Potter. However, all of these achievements pale into insignificance compared to my contribution – the sex index.

Using this sex index, you can easily find the steamier moments from Kissing Games. Enjoy...

And if that wasn't enough, don't forget I've got nineteen thousand words of super-hot deleted sex scenes from Highland and Hollywood Games as well as Charlie and Valentina's extended epilogue available exclusively for newsletter subscribers.

If you want some extra action, then sign up to my newsletter today!

www.eviealexanderauthor.com/subscribe/

ACKNOWLEDGMENTS

Kissing Games is dedicated to Aimee Walker who was one of the first people ever to read this book and fall in love with Charlie!

Thank you to my Colombian friend, Annie, who inspired me to write Valentina and for looking over my manuscript even though romance novels really aren't her thing...

Thank you to my editing team: Aimee Walker, Mike Thomas, Margaret Amatt, Mike AF and Chris Wheary, all of whom helped get this book to where it needed to be. And thank you to my sensitivity readers; Pixie, Julia, and Sarah for your invaluable insights.

Thank you to my outstandingly supportive friends, in particular my alpha reader, Pash, my Scottish sister, Margaret, my work wife, Kelly, and Linden, Lyndsey and Satz. Thank you for reading my early drafts and always believing in me, even when I didn't believe in myself.

Thank you to Bailey McGinn for designing this wonderful cover and Mark Karasick for taking such fabulous photos of me.

A very special thank you goes to someone who will never read this book, and probably doesn't even know what a book is. Yes,

I want to thank Dave the dog, who is actually one of the most beautiful pooches in existence. Thank you for letting me use your name and your joie de vivre!

My team at Emlin Press: Victoria, Mandy, Taryn and Liezl. Thank you for doing everything I can't, won't, or don't have time for. Thank you for tolerating my foul mouth, laughing at my unfunny jokes and sticking around.

My family of course gets a special mention, in particular the two people who suffer the Evie Experience on a daily basis. Husband, you are the best decision I have ever made. Elway, you are the best luck I have ever had. I love you to the end of the universe and back.

And last, but by no means least, I want to thank my fabulous ARC team, the incredible online community of book lovers and YOU, the reader! Thank you for your continued support and for reading Charlie and Valentina's story. Each time you read my books, write me a review and recommend me in countless different ways, my heart gets a little fuller. Thank you!

Ps - I love love LOVE hearing from my readers so please get in touch via email or social media to ask me anything or just tell me about your day!

hard truths. Can they find a future together, or will their love remain
a Highland fling?

Tropes

Small Town, Dark Secrets, Bodyguard/Actress, Forced Proximity,
Alpha-roll hero, Dating Game

MUSICAL GAMES

After lying to a Hollywood megastar, Sam needs Jamie to write an
album with her in just ten days He's got the voice of an angel and the
body of a god, but fame is the last thing on his mind. Will he help
make her dreams come true?

Tropes

Small Town, Grumpy/Sunshine, Male Virgin, Cinnamon Roll Hero,
Opposites Attract, Fish-out-of-Water, Forced Proximity

WEDDING GAMES

Rory and Zoe want to get married. Not easy when their mothers are
mortal enemies and Rory's step-father is a Hollywood star with a
death wish. Can they unravel the tangles in time to tie the knot, or is
eloping the only answer? Get ready for Scotland's wedding of the year!

Tropes

Small Town, Grumpy/Sunshine, Opposites Attract, Soulmates, Fish-
out-of-Water

CHRISTMAS GAMES

Having a baby's easy, right? Until wayward in-laws, an out-of-control
cow and mad Santa get in the way. All Rory and Zoe want is a relaxing
Christmas before their baby arrives, but straightforward is not their
style...

Tropes

Small Town, Grumpy/Sunshine, Opposites Attract, Soulmates, Fish-

❦

THE FOXBROOKE SERIES

ONE NIGHT IN FOXBROOKE

When chef Ben 'Kenobi' Walker gets the call to help save a VIP dinner at Foxbrooke Manor, he doesn't expect to run into old flame Leia Perry. She's all grown up and even more attractive than when they were teenagers – but she hasn't forgotten what happened ten years ago, and she *definitely* hasn't forgiven him. Will one night give Ben the second chance he needs to prove himself and win back Leia's heart?

Tropes

Small Town, Second Chance, Return to Hometown, Enemies-to-Lovers, Bet, Brother's Best Friend, Work Colleagues, Forced Proximity, First Love, Reverse Grumpy-Sunshine, Opposites Attract

LOVE AD LIB

Shy and reserved Lord Henry Foxbrooke needs a fake girlfriend. Free-spirited actress Libby Fletcher needs a job. But when they arrive in Somerset for Henry's birthday celebrations, neither are prepared for their reception. As friendship blurs and faking it starts to feel a little too real, disaster strikes. Can Libby and Henry stick to the script, or has their entire act just bombed?

Tropes

Small Town, Fake Dating, Grumpy/Sunshine, Opposites Attract, One Bed, Different Worlds, Fish-out-of-Water

AN UNHOLY AFFAIR

Gorgeous Jack Newton has fallen in love with Eveline Shaw. But she's a female vicar dreaming of marriage and kids, and he's a male escort heading out of town. Can Jack show Eveline heaven and keep his secret safe, or are they both headed straight for hell?

Tropes

Small Town, Forbidden Love, Love at First Sight, Sworn off a Relationship, Priest, Different Worlds, Opposites Attract, Dark Secret

THE UPPER CRUSH

James Hunter-Savage is a cocky city boy who isn't used to anyone else taking the reins. Lady Estelle Foxbrooke is a fiery country girl who's about to show him who's boss. Can they learn to fight for love rather than with each other, or will their love hate relationship destroy everything they're working for?

Tropes

Small Town, Enemies-to-Lovers, Alpha Hero, Love/Hate, Playboy in Love, Different Worlds, Workplace Romance, Fake Dating

THE LOVE POSITION

Beautiful academic, Sophia Hunter-Savage, has run away to an ashram to reinvent herself. Hot yoga teacher, Isaac Hayward, has left town to avoid the only woman able to tempt him off the spiritual path.

But karma sucks.

Now Isaac's teaching Sophia and they're finding themselves in all kinds of unexpected positions. Will their forbidden love bring inner peace and happiness, or end in a tangled mess?

Tropes

Forbidden Love, Opposites Attract, Teacher/Student, Sworn off a Relationship, Forced Proximity, Love at First Sight, Different Worlds, Fish-out-of-Water

CHRISTMAS OFF SCRIPT

Best friends, Leo Foxbrooke and Ella Chamberlain, have never been single at the same time. Until now... Playing Cinderella and Prince Charming in the Christmas pantomime, their on-stage chemistry kindles an unexpected spark behind the scenes. Can they rewrite their friendship this festive season and finally unwrap true love?

Tropes

Small Town, Friends-to-Lovers, Best Friend's Ex, Oblivious to Love, Unrequited Love, Fake Relationship

ONE NIGHT ONLY

Pop star Avery Taylor craves a break from her public life, and a one-night stand with a stranger feels like the perfect escape. A year later, while recovering from an injury, she's stunned to find her nurse is Connor Foxbrooke, the man who touched her soul that night. Avery is ready to break the rules for love, but Connor, who values his quiet life, fears heartbreak. With Avery set to return to the spotlight as soon as she's recovered, can they bridge their worlds and turn their one night into forever?

Tropes

Second-Chance, Mistaken Identity, One Night Stand, Different Worlds, Opposites Attract, Injury, Forced Proximity, Fish-out-of-Water, Celebrity, Pop Star, Small Town

RIGHTING MR WRONG

Mooning a party of nuns is bad for anyone, but for TV star Aiden Wilder, it's catastrophic. Enter Willow Foxbrooke, a quiet PR worker who's tasked with saving his reputation through a fake relationship. As Willow teaches him how to recover his image, they start to fall for each other. But how can true love grow from something that was never real to begin with?

Tropes

Small Town, Fake Dating, Grumpy/Sunshine, Celebrity, Opposites Attract, Different Worlds, Fish-out-of-Water

UNDER THE INFLUENCER

Sunny Summer Foxbrooke's career as an Influencer is over. Now she's forced to work with grumpy Finn Oakley, the man who's avoided her for years. Will Finn finally return her love, or will she always just be his best friend's little sister?

Tropes

Brother's best friend, Grumpy/Sunshine, Beauty and the Beast, Age Gap, Unrequited Love, Rivals, Different Worlds, All Grown Up, Small Town

❧

By Evie Alexander and Kelly Kay

EVIE & KELLY'S HOLIDAY DISASTERS SERIES

Evie and Kelly's Holiday Disasters are a series of hot and hilarious romantic comedies with interconnected characters, focusing on one holiday and one trope at a time.

CUPID CALAMITY

Featuring **Animal Attraction** & **Stupid Cupid**

Patrick and Sabina have ditched their blind dates for each other. Ben's fighting a crazed chimp for Laurie's love. Insta-love meets insta-disaster in these laugh-out-loud Valentine's day novellas.

COOKOUT CARNAGE

Featuring **Off With a Bang** & **Up in Smoke**

Cute farm boy Jonathan clings to a love ideal, blissfully ignoring what the universe has planned, while keeping track of his pet pig. Posh Brit follows his heart into the American Midwest in search of Sherilyn, his digital dream love.

CHRISTMAS CHAOS

Featuring **No way in a Manger** & **No Crib and No Bed**

In Scotland, Zoe and Rory attempt to have a civilised and respectable rite of passage, but straightforward is not their style. In Sonoma, Bax and Tabi attempt to throw a meaningful Christmas celebration. But there are too many people involved and it's nothing like they expect.

Get Evie's books in all formats as well as special offers, early releases, and exclusive deals direct from her website:

www.eviealexanderbooks.com

EMLIN
PRESS

ABOUT THE AUTHOR

Evie Alexander is a multi-award-winning author of sexy romantic comedies, blending snort-laugh humour and panty-melting chemistry into unputdownable stories that will steal your heart.

When she's not dreaming up swoony heroes and relatable heroines, Evie can be found in the beautiful West Country of the UK, where she lives with her ridiculously patient husband, miracle daughter, and two dogs who think they run the show.

eviealexanderbooks.com

www.eviealexanderauthor.com

instagram.com/eviealexanderauthor

facebook.com/eviealexanderauthor

x.com/Evie_author

bookbub.com/authors/evie-alexander

amazon.com/Evie-Alexander/e/B08ZJGLP29?ref=sr_ntt_s-rch_lnk_1&qid=1630667484&sr=8-1

pinterest.com/eviealexanderauthor